Early's Winter

A James Early Mystery

Jerry Peterson

EARLY'S WINTER

A family murdered for no apparent reason. The worst of the deaths in that isolated ranch house for James Early are those of the children, two of them twin boys less than a year old.

No, not the worst.

Before his investigation is over, a friend will be killed while helping Early, and Early will see it as his fault, that he was responsible.

Peace, if there is to be any for James Early, must come from a new acquaintance no one believes exists.

ALSO BY JERRY PETERSON

Early's Fall

Iced

DEDICATION

To Marge, my wife and chief copy editor.

To my mother who died last year. I read her portions of the manuscript during her final months of life.

To a friend and one-time colleague who prefers to remain unnamed.

ACKNOWLEDGEMENTS

We writers–most of us–work alone, beating out our stories on our keyboards one letter at a time, one word, one sentence, one paragraph, yet a lot of people have a hand in bringing our books to publication.

Chief for me are the members of my writers group, *Tuesdays with Story*. They get the first read. Their comments and questions are direct and their suggestions on target, particularly those of John Schneller who is writing his own book series, an edge-of-reality trilogy for young adults. We have been working together for a long time now.

Certainly Marshall Cook deserves a mention. He's now retired, but for years he shepherded a lot of us Wisconsin writers through the University of Wisconsin Extension Service's literary arts outreach program.

The Coach, as Marshall prefers to be called, read my first manuscript more than a decade ago. It was a mega-sized saga that I had set in the Great Smoky Mountains. Although I now know the story was not well written–I was learning the novelist's craft–the Coach said you can do this.

I've been a teacher at the middle school, high school, and college level. I know how important it is to a student to hear someone tell them you can do this, that I believe in you.

With the Coach, I was now the student.

I came along as a new novelist at a time when the best way to get your book out there for people to buy and read was to have your manuscript picked up by a good publishing company. Two years ago, Five Star, a Gale/Cengage imprint, published *Early's Fall*.

Changes in our business were a foot. Amazon brought out its Kindle e-reader and captured the sales business for electronic books. Last year, half of all Amazon's book sales were ebooks.

Barnes & Noble answered with its Nook.

Amazon went further. The company made it easy for any writer to upload her/his manuscript. Consequently, we could publish our stories as ebooks at very little cost. For a bit more money, we could convert our manuscripts into print books through Amazon's CreateSpace affiliate.

No longer did those of us who are good storytellers and good writers need a traditional publishing house. We could become indies–independents.

And I am now one of them with the publication of *Early's Winter* as an ebook and a trade paperback.

We indies, if we want to put the very best books in the hands of our readers, do not work alone.

I needed a cover designer. I found an excellent one through Facebook. Melissa Alvarez, whose company is Book Covers Galore, asked to be my Facebook friend. I scanned the covers she'd posted on her website–really fine work–and sent off a proposal.

Melissa responded that afternoon. We talked by phone the next morning, and, by the end of the day, she sent me six draft covers.

She works fast.

After several refinements to the cover Marge liked best, we had a winner.

Cheryl Perez, of You're Published, then came on to design the book spine and the back cover, and format the manuscript for printing by CreateSpace.

Sue Trowbridge, of Interbridge–friend and webmaster for my website–came on, too, to format the manuscript for ebook publication.

We writers also need some good words about our book on the cover from somebody who has street cred. I went to Larry Sweazy. He writes Old West crime stories featuring Texas Ranger Josiah Wolfe as his detective.

Larry said yes.

So did John Galligan. He writes mysteries that fishermen love.

And there are more people who deserve a tip of the hat, lots more, but most particularly the librarians around the country and you and your fellow readers who enjoyed *Early's Fall* and asked what's going to happen to James Early's baby. Will the baby be in the next book?

Barbie Sue is here. Daddy James calls her Toot.

CHAPTER 1

December 12–Tuesday short of midnight
U.S. 24

Headlights dead-on blasted James Early back into the real world.

He shot his free hand to the steering wheel and spun it, whipping his Jeep away from the lights and toward the side of the highway. Early's vehicle swung into a crosswise skid, its tires scraping grooves into the hard-packed snow that blanketed the highway, grooves that became circles as the Jeep's rear end chased its front around. Early braced himself as the right tires raked into the gravel and snow of the shoulder, sending out a shower of white and rock. The Jeep stopped hard, once more facing north, the direction in which Early had been going.

His hands shook while he sat there. He willed his left away from the steering wheel, to the switch for his spotlight. Early rattled the light on. He turned its beam into the headlights. By squinting, he made out a four-door halfway in the ditch at the far side of the highway, the ditch drifted full. How long had the car been there and why? The car–a Buick, Early was certain of that, and there was something about the car, something familiar. He thought he recognized it, but whose? He let out the clutch and his Jeep rolled on. Early swept the side of the Buick with his spotlight as he idled by–someone inside on the driver's side–but he couldn't make out the face through the half-open window. And why didn't the man respond to the light? Why didn't he try to shade his eyes?

When past, Early eased his Jeep around. He brought it up behind the Buick–stuck in the snow? Possibly. He flicked off his spotlight and turned on his bubble light, the red light revolving, a warning to any other fool out so late who might be nearing this troubled spot. Early stepped out onto the hard snow, flashlight in hand, his boots soundless for the snow had no give in it. He flicked on his Everready as he approached the driver's door. He aimed the beam inside, splaying it over the profile of the driver–and he recognized him. Al Garret, a rancher from up near May Day. Garret's head nodded forward. His chin rested on his ample chest. And Early could hear it, the car's engine idling.

"Al, 'scuse me," he said. When Garret didn't answer, Early reached in. He shook the man's shoulder. "You all right, buddy?"

Garret woke with a start. His eyes triple blinked at the revolving red light and Early's badge. Garret dropped the transmission into first. He stomped the accelerator to the floor.

Early yanked his arm out of the car and, as he stepped back, watched the howling rear tires throw up snow, the car going nowhere. Garret rammed the transmission into second and again tromped down on the gas pedal.

That gave Early an idea. He came up beside the car and jogged in place, running harder as the Buick's speedometer rose. When the needle touched fifty, Early hollered at the driver's window, "Hey! Pull over. Now!"

Garret, startled again, glanced toward Early running all out and took his foot off the gas. He turned his steering wheel to the side as his speedometer's needle fell back toward zero, Early slowing as the needle dropped.

"Better turn the engine off," Early said, huffing, faking hard breathing. He leaned against the driver's window glass.

After Garret did as he had been told, he peered over, glassy-eyed. "You the sheriff?" he asked, his voice salt-cracker dry.

"Right."

"Sure run fast for an old guy. Musta been doin' fifty-five."

"Al, are you drunk?"

"No. You know where I am?"

"Headed for Manhattan."

"Naw, can't be. I'm goin' home."

"Home's the other direction, buddy. Better step out here."

Garret fumbled at the door handle. It didn't yield, so he wrestled with it. Still the handle did not give. "Some yahoo locked me in my car, sheriff," he said.

Early wanted badly to laugh, but forced himself to keep a straight face as he pulled up on the outside handle. The door swung open, and Garret tumbled out. Early helped him up with car driver clawing against Early's arm for support.

"My feet don't wanna work," he said, leaning against Early.

"Well, see if you can make them work well enough to walk a straight line."

"Huh?"

"Walk a straight line."

"Why?"

"It's a test. Can you do that?"

"Any day of the week, by damn."

"Well, this is your day, Al."

Garret, puffy, with the heavy shadow of not having shaved for some time, pushed off, his overcoat wrongly buttoned and his hat askew. He teetered a moment and collapsed against the side of his car, sliding down to rest on his butt in the snow.

Early gazed at him, then went to his Jeep. There he took down his microphone from its hanging place, over the mirror. He pressed the transmit button. "Big John, you out there?"

Static answered, followed by an easy baritone. "Coming out of Manhattan on Twenty-Four. Need something?"

"I'm five miles ahead of you. I got Al Garret here, skunked out of his mind. How about you drive him home?"

"Wouldn't you prefer jail for him?"

"No, Marlene will punish him a whole lot more than we can."

"She's a hellfire. Be there in a couple minutes."

"Roger that." Early hung his microphone back over the mirror. He went back to where Garret, father of three young children, snored, unaware of the snow and cold.

Early hunkered down beside him. "Al, what trouble have you got yourself into? Bet drinking's only a part of it. One thing's certain from the smell, you've got enough alkie in you, if I lit a match, you'd go up in flames."

Early blew on his gloved hands. He rubbed them, working up friction to warm them. "Your daddy, rest his soul, he'd be ashamed to see you like this."

Headlights coming from the south poked over the far side of a rise.

"Bet this is your ride," Early said. He pushed himself up and waved at the approaching headlights. The vehicle slowed, and Early could tell from the descending whine of the engine that it was a Jeep–a four-cylinder Ford motor, not a V-Eight rumbler like he had in his.

The vehicle stopped short, with its headlights bathing Early, the Buick, and Garret–Garret still asleep. A big man stepped out, silhouetted as he strolled forward, cowboy hat on and a fur collar turned up around his ears–John Silver Fox, a Potawatomi Indian and once an MP with the occupation army in post-war Japan.

"Hey, John," Early said.

"Hey, sheriff. You don't want to take him?"

"I was supposed to be home hours ago, but that darn county commission meeting just kept dragging on."

"Can be a pain, can't they?"

"He's all dead weight. Think it's going to take both of us to get him up."

"Might if I was as little a fella as you." Silver Fox stepped over to Garret. He grabbed the drunk by the front of his coat and jerked him up. Silver Fox tossed Garret across his shoulder with the same ease a man would a sack of grain. "Get the door for me?"

Early hustled ahead, to the passenger side of his night deputy's Jeep. He wrenched the door open, and Silver Fox dumped Garret inside, the canvas roof raking Garret's hat off. Early recovered the fedora. He handed it to Silver Fox as the two rambled back to the Buick. There Early's nose wrinkled when he turned off the car's headlights–the interior reeked of Jack Daniels. He rolled shut the driver's window and pulled the ignition key.

"Give this to Marlene," he said and passed the key to Silver Fox. "Tell her, after she blisters old Al's ears, I want her to have him in Judge Crooke's courtroom first thing in the morning."

"The hangin' judge? You got it in for young Mister Garret?"

"Fool broke the law. I figure the county's got a right to a chunk of his money. You'd like a raise, wouldn't you?"

"Wouldn't object," Silver Fox said. He went back to his Jeep and drove off, waving to Early.

Early, slouch shouldered, sheepskin-lined denim jacket, a cattleman's hat, and a shaggy mustache that made him look every bit the cowboy that he was, tramped to his Jeep. There he leaned against the door and wondered what the heck Al Garret had been doing out there drunk, kids at home, well to do–a man who, by all appearances, had everything anyone could want.

CHAPTER 2

December 13–Wednesday morning
Courtroom

Early slurped his coffee as he strolled into Judge Hanover Crooke's courtroom. He made his way down to the never-occupied first row, dusted an oak chair with his hand, and sat. As he did, he glanced up at the clock–a Regulator–over the door to the jury room . . . Eight fifty-seven.

A voice came from behind. "Mind if I join you?"

Early twisted around, and his eyebrows rose. "John, you oughtta be home in bed."

"Figured you might need a second witness," John Silver Fox said. He slid onto the hard chair next to Early and, after he threw one leg over the other, he parked his hat–a black windcutter–on his knee.

Early raised his coffee mug. "My word and Al's hangover ought to be evidence enough."

"Uh-huh."

"Don't think so?"

"You've lost a couple recent traffic stops where you were the only witness."

"The passengers lied and the offenders had better lawyers than they had a right to." Early nudged Silver Fox. "How'd Marlene take it when you poured Al into a kitchen chair?"

"Not good."

"Oh glory."

"She gets in a real bad mood when you wake her late. I had to pound on the door a good ten minutes."

"I do believe you exaggerate, John."

"All right, maybe five. Bruised my knuckles for my trouble."

"So?"

"I gave her your message, and I left abruptly when she started up. Such language."

"Well, most times Marlene's got a good heart."

"One could not prove it by last night."

Early again glanced up at the clock. "You smell popcorn?"

"No."

"I do. Was the Four-H club showing movies here last night?"

"Wouldn't know."

Judge Crooke, a tall man with an Abe Lincoln beard, entered the courtroom while Early and Silver Fox conversed. He came in by way of the door behind his bench and settled in his high-backed leather chair. Crooke nodded to his bailiff who hustled to the corner and hauled down on a rope that ran up through the ceiling to the bell in the courthouse's tower. A heavy clapper clanged against the massive brass bell, sounding the first stroke of what would become nine.

Silver Fox clamped a hand over his ear. "Does he have to do that?"

"It's custom," Early said.

"It's a head-banger. No other judge does that."

"Well, old Han's a stickler for tradition. Ringing the bell was once the way you announced court. Townspeople with nothing better to do would drop their business and run in to see who was being tried."

"It's still loud."

"That it is."

Crooke peered up from a paper when the bailiff, Harlow Swanson, took his place to the side of the bench. Swanson swelled like a bullfrog and bellowed, "Oh yea, oh yea, the district court of the County of Riley, State of Kansas, the union of the United States of America, is now in session, the honorable Judge Hanover R. Crooke presiding. Everybody on your feet, dammit."

A squeaking of chairs and benches followed as people pushed themselves up. Crooke waved for all to sit. He looked again at his paper. "The county against Alvin Garret, Junior, a charge of driving while intoxicated. Mister Garret, are you here?"

No one answered.

Early and Silver Fox craned around, and Crooke gazed over the heads of those in his courtroom. "Mister Garret?"

Again no one answered.

"I haven't time for this," the judge muttered. He scribbled on another paper, signed it with a flourish, and held the paper out to Early. "Bench warrant for the sonuvabitch. Cactus, you get Mister Garret by the bee-hind and drag him in here. I want him before noon."

Early, sucking on his coffee, reached for the warrant. The judge shot him a harsh look. "Next time, sheriff, leave your blasted coffee in your blasted office. I'll have proper decorum in my courtroom."

"Yessir," Early whispered. He took the paper and turned away.

"Before noon," Crooke said one more time, "you understand me?"

Early mouthed the word "absolutely" and humped off, more droop in his shoulders than usual, Silver Fox a pace behind him.

"What'd you do to get him so mad?" the night deputy asked.

"Took his money at poker the other day."

"You going to need help on this arrest?"

"Shouldn't think so, but Hutch is out of the county, so if you want to tag along–"

*

Early slumped in the passenger seat of his Jeep while Silver Fox drove, the sunlight blistering off the snowfields.

"You gonna be able to keep awake?" Early asked, fingering the warrant. "You come back on at eight."

"I'll ask the spirits for a slow night. Maybe I can pull off and sleep somewhere."

"Can't say as I heard that."

"You never slept during a slow time, Chief?"

"Once or twice."

"Nice to know you're like the rest of us mortals. You like this job?"

"For the most part. Paperwork can be a beast, and I have to fight with the commission for a budget."

Silver Fox slowed. He turned the Jeep off State Sixteen and onto a county road that went on up to May Day, a long drive north and west of the county seat of Manhattan. The Garret ranch–the

Circle G–laid south of May Day, paid for and owned by Alvin Senior until a bull gored him to death.

"Strange, isn't it," Early said as Silver Fox stepped down on the gas pedal. "Nobody thought Al could run that ranch he inherited, and he's not half bad."

"He drinks."

"Sure would like to know why."

"Going to ask?"

"Suppose I should, but he's not gonna tell me. Would you tell me why you were drinking?"

"That issue is not ever going to come up."

"Why's that?"

"I'm an Orange Crush man, nothing harder."

The Jeep rumbled on, the ride becoming a bone shaker as the tires bounced over the gravel beneath the snow.

"I ever thank for hiring me?" Silver Fox asked.

"Big John, I didn't do you a favor. You have what the job needs."

"Maybe, but no other sheriff around would touch me."

"Why's that?"

"I'm an Indian."

"Can't say I ever noticed."

"My skin color didn't give you a hint?"

"Look, you could be green with purple poka dots and it wouldn't make any difference. You're one fine lawman."

"I appreciate that."

"It's the truth. Tell you what, next time we sheriffs barbecue a steer, I'll brag you up."

Silver Fox pointed through the windshield. "Circle G there."

Early studied the place–a corral and windmill, its vanes not moving, old barns but a new house, a low-slung, one-story affair built to replace a dilapidated two-story that had been the original house. "Quiet," he said as he gazed around. "Cows must be out on a back pasture, by a haystack."

"Could be." Silver Fox herded the Jeep onto a lane that led to the ranch buildings. "They've got a boy, haven't they, about five?"

"And twins not yet one."

"Nice morning like this, one would think the boy would be romping in the snow."

"Maybe he's helping his hungover daddy get up, you suppose?"

"It's possible." Silver Fox guided the Jeep around the corral and up to the house. He stopped short of the steps to the kitchen door. "Somebody's been here," he said as he stepped out, gesturing at a set of tire tracks. "Somebody with snow chains."

"Yup, well, lots of people around here run on chains." Early made his way from the Jeep up the steps to the door and knocked. "Al? Marlene? Anybody home?"

No answer came.

"Maybe the owner of the tire tracks picked them up and took them to court," Silver Fox said.

"If so, we sure missed them. You know, something just doesn't feel right." Early twisted the door knob. It gave and he pushed the door open. One step inside and the smell of parched coffee washed over him. "Aw, jees."

"What is it?"

"Al. Someone shot him."

Silver Fox hustled in, pistol drawn, but Early waved at the gun. "Put that away. Can't imagine whoever did this would hang around waiting on us."

Before the lawmen sat Al Garret in his ill-buttoned overcoat, slumped forward at a Formica-topped table, a darkening blood pool to his side. Early turned the flame off under the coffeepot before he stripped off a glove. When he had his fingers free, he pressed them against the carotid artery in the rancher's neck. "Didn't expect a pulse. He's cold. . . . Bullet to the head. One round."

Silver Fox crouched to the side. He studied the exit wound, part of the skull and brain blown away. "A heavy caliber," he said.

"Damage sure shows that. Find the kids."

Silver Fox rose and ducked out into the hallway. "Chief?" he called back.

"Yeah."

"You're not going to like this."

"Like what?"

"Marlene. She's out here, dead."

Early moved into the hallway. There, he pushed up a switch with his elbow, and a flood of light showed his deputy kneeling next to a body in a nightgown.

"Two bullets to the chest," Silver Fox said. He closed the woman's eyes. "Kill a man, that I can see, but not a woman."

"The kids?"

The deputy got up and went on. He turned in at the first bedroom. "Nothing," he said and went across the hall to the second. "Babies here."

"Alive?"

"I wish."

Early squeezed his hands against his face. He drew down, stretching the skin of his cheeks and jaw. "Shot?"

"Appears so."

"The boy?"

"Don't see him."

"The closet?"

"I'll look. . . . Not here."

"What would I do if I were the boy?" Early asked. "Hell, I'd run."

He turned up a side hallway that led to the front room, an airy place with a hardwood floor and rag rugs. On one of them–the one in front of the door that opened to the outside–laid a boy in Hopalong Cassidy pajamas, face down, his body twisted. A scent from a rose potpourri infused the air, Early hardly aware of it.

Silver Fox hustled in. "Oh, Jesus."

"Yeah," Early said. "Make a preacher want to put his fist through the wall."

The deputy, his tanned face going pale, knelt beside the child. He fingered the back of the pajama shirt. "Two shots," he said, exhaustion filling his voice. "Chief, I've walked in on a couple murders as an MP, but never five."

"What the hell happened here?" Early asked as he leaned back against the wall.

"Want me to call it in?"

"Better. Get Doc Grafton out here and Dan Plemmons. Need the State Police in on this."

Silver Fox left. Early, alone, squeezed shut his eyes against what he'd seen, yet a tear trickled down. He snuffled and wiped at the tear. "Son, you deserved a full life, not this."

He pried his mind away from the body, to bullets. A large-caliber slug had passed through Garret's head. If the others had been shot with the same gun, those slugs, too, should have passed through. Early gazed at the door before him–expensive, teak with beveled glass. Three feet up he saw a spray of blood and tissue, and the wood of the door splintered. He went to it, jacked out his pocketknife, and cut away the splinters. Early dug into the wood. He pressed and probed until his blade struck something hard. Early dug more, dug until the dull silvery end of a lead bullet showed itself. He grubbed at it, and the bullet rolled out into his hand and to the floor. He scooped the bullet up, felt the weight of it, knew it well, recognized it. Early patted his pockets as he tried to decide in which he should put the bullet. He selected his jacket's left outside, then went after the other bullet.

Silver Fox returned, toting a wooden box. "Everybody's coming. I've got the kit. What you want me to do?"

"Take the pictures. I've got two bullets here. I'm gonna look for the others. The ones that killed the boy came from a forty-five."

Silver Fox brought out a camera–a news photographer's Speed Graphic–and a flash bulb from the box. While he pressed the bulb into the camera's flash gun, Early went on to the bedroom where the two babies laid side by side in a crib, pictures of lambs and colts on the wall beyond. Could the babies have been asleep? No way to know. If they had been awake and standing, the bullets would have burrowed into the floor a short distance from the crib. Early looked down, just ahead of the toes of his boots as he circled the crib. Nothing other than a Panda bear one of them must have dropped over the side. The place smelled of a baby's room–dirty diapers and talcum, a Gold Bond shaker can of the powder next to a stack of clean diapers on a changing table.

And if they had been asleep? With his knee, Early pushed against the crib. He shoved it from its place in the center of the room, and there he saw them–two holes in the floor. Early got down and dug with his knife. A flash from the doorway told him Silver Fox was taking pictures in the hallway, of Marlene Garret, pictures that wouldn't in the slightest resemble the portrait he had seen hanging on the wall in the front room. The cutting and slicing in the pine floor went with modest speed, producing first one bullet, then the second. He held them up, squinted at them, compared them–neither significantly deformed. He liked that in bullets. The one that had killed Baby Left went into his shirt breast pocket left, the one that had killed Baby Right into his shirt breast pocket right.

Silver Fox leaned through the doorway. "Ready for me in here?"

"I moved the crib."

"The babies?"

"'Course not," Early said as he came up. "Help me set the crib back."

Silver Fox put the camera on the changing table, then grabbed one side of the crib. With Early on the other side, they slid the baby keeper back where it had been, Early kneeing in one last adjustment.

"I can't help but wonder," Silver Fox said as he slipped a new film holder into the back of his camera, but a howl of voices cut him off, voices coming from the direction of the kitchen, one of them shouting, "You come in here and I'll have Cactus goddamn shoot you."

"Coroner's here," Early said and ran from the room. In the hallway he hopped across Marlene Garret's body and charged into the kitchen where he found two men faced off in the doorway, the one outside dodging, trying to get around the other.

"What part of 'get out of here' don't you understand?" the inside man bellowed.

"I got a right. I'm a reporter."

"You're a goddamn nuisance."

Early pulled his Army-issue forty-five, the gun he'd brought home from the war. He reached over the shoulder of the inside man and stuck the pistol in the face of the outside man. "Do you want me to shoot him in any particular place?"

"Crotch'd be fine," the inside man said.

Early lowered the muzzle. He took aim at the man's testicles.

The outside man, in winter garb, blanched. "Cactus, you can't do this."

"Red, it's been one awful bad day, worse if my gun were to go off by itself. I'd back my way down those damn steps."

"A family's murdered in there. Not a chance."

Early racked the hammer back.

"Cactus—"

"How do you know what we've got in here?"

"Got a police radio."

"You steal it?"

"I built it."

The inside man, surgeon and coroner Paul Grafton—almost as wide as the door—twisted around to Early. "I had to race the bastard out here."

"Slip on inside. I'll take care of Red."

Grafton ducked around Early, and Early went out, snow on the steps crunching under his boots. He holstered his gun and pulled a pair of handcuffs from his back pocket. "Here's your choice," Early said as he put his arm around the shoulders of Red Vullmer, newsman for KMAN radio and the newspaper that owned it, "you get in your truck and leave or I shackle you to my Jeep and charge you with interfering. You know Judge Crooke hates the sight of you."

"I'll broadcast everything I know."

"And just what's that?"

"That Al and Marlene Garret and their three kids have been murdered, shot by a party or parties unknown, and that you, Cactus, you threatened me."

"Oh, please."

"Cactus, this is the biggest news story in the history of the county."

"Not true, and you'd know if you'd studied your county's history." Early kicked at the snow. "You're intent on blabbing the story, aren't you?"

"Count on it."

"All right, what's it going to take to keep your mouth shut short of me throwing you in the stock tank in the hope you'll freeze to death?"

"Tell me everything you know."

"Do I get a blood oath you won't talk about it until I tell you you can?"

"As long as I get a blood oath you won't tell any other reporter first."

"Red, you drive a hard bargain." Early took out his pocketknife, a Barlow his father had given him. He opened it and held it out to Vullmer. "Let's see the color of your blood."

"You're hot-damn serious."

"You got that right." Early turned the knife back. He sliced his right thumb, and the blood oozed. Again he held out his knife to Vullmer.

The newsman took it. He put the blade to his thumb, but hesitated, then, scrunching his face, nicked the skin enough that a drop of blood showed. Vullmer pressed his thumb against Early's.

"Have I got your oath?" Early asked.

"Where the hell do you get this blood-oath business?"

"The Saturday movies."

"You're putting me on."

"Could be."

"Jesus, Cactus, you're strange."

"Aw, I'm just your friendly neighborhood sheriff." Early wrapped his thumb in a handkerchief. "Wait in your truck."

A four-door Ford, with a bullet grill, lurched onto the ranch lane, the car's bubble light turning. Early watched the State Police cruiser bounce through the ruts as it came around the windmill to slew to a stop in front of him.

The officer at the wheel, eyes hidden behind silvered aviator glasses, rolled down his window. "Cactus, couldn't you call me out just once when you have good news?"

"Like what?"

"Like maybe you caught somebody's stray dog?"

"I'll try to remember that."

"Here I am, just about to stop in Clay Center for the world's best apple pie when John squawks on the horn. He right, the whole family dead?"

Early grimaced.

"Guess you want me to look in, huh?" Trooper Plemmons asked.

Early pulled the door of the cruiser open, and Daniel Plemmons stepped out. The trooper, in tans, riding boots, and a fur-collared leather jacket, squared his campaign hat as he strolled beside Early toward the house, Plemmons moving with the ease of an old-time gunslinger, the long-barreled Colt revolver in the holster tied to his leg adding to the effect. "Could you at least satisfy my curiosity about your thumb?" he asked.

Early held up his wrapped digit, a splotch of red showing through the white cotton of the handkerchief. "A little blood-oath business."

"Pardon?"

"It's nothing."

"If you say so. Any idea what happened?"

"I'd rather show you."

The two lawmen stepped up onto the kitchen porch and went inside, Early kicking his boots against the doorjamb, knocking the snow from them. Grafton, the coroner, sat scribbling on a report form at the table, the dead rancher next to him.

"Doc," Plemmons said.

"Trooper," Grafton responded without looking up.

"Kinda creepy there, you by a dead body."

"Dan'l, that dead body's right well-mannered. He doesn't interrupt me like some people."

Early knelt to the side of Garret. With a stub of a pencil from his shirt pocket, he pointed to the entry wound in the right temple. "See that? Powder burns."

Plemmons stripped off his aviator glasses as he leaned down.

"The gun had to be right at his temple," Early said. "Classic suicide, wouldn't you say, Doc?"

"I'd call it that," Grafton said, again without looking up.

"Only there's no gun."

Plemmons rubbed the base of his thumb against his chin. "You're thinking execution?"

"Had to be." Early rolled back on his haunches. "Somebody was here before us. Drove in, drove out. The tracks were there, tires with snow chains."

"So this somebody shoots your guy, shoots the others so there are no witnesses, and drives away. I can buy that."

"But answer me this, who kills little babies? They can't tell anyone what happened."

"Some sick bastard," Grafton said. He stabbed his pen at his report. "Cactus, you catch him, I'll perform an operation on him that'll leave him scuttling about with his knees pressed together for the rest of his life."

"I'm tempted to let you. How you going to call it, Doc?"

The coroner took off his wire-rimmed spectacles. He squeezed his eyes shut as he pinched the bridge of his nose. "Five deaths by gunshot. Based on what I've seen, murder all around."

Silver Fox stepped in from the hallway. "Chief," he said, "do you want me to dust for fingerprints?"

"Day like today, everybody's going to be like us, wearing gloves. It's a waste of time."

"Maybe the stove controls? The coffeepot?"

"You're thinking the killer made the coffee?"

"Somebody did."

"I can't picture that, but go ahead."

Plemmons interrupted. "So, sheriff with the wounded thumb, who do you think did it?"

"Danny, if I knew I wouldn't have asked you out here. How about you take the county road west, stop in on all the ranchers, talk to them and their families. Someone had to see something."

"And east?" Plemmons asked.

"John can do that. Old Doc and me, we'll track down the school bus driver and Virgie the mail carrier. They had to be out."

"Want me to walk through the house before I go?"

"I welcome your eyes. You might see something we missed."

Plemmons touched an index finger to the brim of his hat, then ambled off toward the hallway, but he turned back. "This isn't related to this, but there was a car theft last night, at that lot out on Eighteen by Fort Riley."

"Fat Willy's?"

"That's the one. Somebody stole a 'Thirty-eight Hudson two-door, worth probably all of forty bucks. I told Fat Willy I don't handle small stuff, that I'd pass it on to you."

"Dan'l, you make me so happy."

Again Plemmons touched the brim of his hat. The rumble of a diesel engine came from the yard as the trooper went on out into the hall. Silver Fox, working by the stove, glanced out the window. "Chief," he said, "we've got a road grader out in the yard."

Early came over. He watched a man climb down from the canvas cabin on the long machine the color of butter. "My God, it's Garret's grandpap."

He bolted from the kitchen, hauling on his gloves as he ran across the porch and down the walk toward Red Vullmer and the grader operator talking by Vullmer's truck.

"Red, you stay outta this," Early bellowed. He barged between the two, got his arm around the shoulders of the wisp of a man–the grader operator rancid from cigarette smoke–and guided him off toward his Jeep.

"What's goin' on here?" the man asked, the stub of a cigarette in the corner of his mouth jiggling with each word, his watery eyes overflowing with worry.

"Hoolie, there's no nice way to put it, I'm sorry. You're grandson, he's dead."

Hoolie Garret's knees buckled. Early caught him and muscled him into the passenger seat of his Jeep.

"Marlene? The children?" the graderman asked after some time, his lips quivering.

Early could not bring himself to answer. He instead chewed on the inside of his cheek.

"Oh, not my great grandbabies, please. . . . What was it, a gas leak?"

"No."

"Well, what?"

"Hoolie, it appears somebody murdered them."

"You can't mean that, not little Martin and Ronnie." Garret, the wattles beneath his chin shaking, stared at Early. "Charlie, too?"

"Uh-huh."

"Oh Lordy. Oh Lordy, how'm I gonna tell Mazie? Took her to the hospital yesterday, that bad heart of hers. This'll kill her."

"It's gonna be hard. Maybe not so hard if it were to come from me."

"Cain't ask you to do that," Garret said. He took the cigarette from his mouth as he struggled up from the Jeep's seat. "Kin I see 'em?"

"Hoolie, this isn't the way you want to remember them. I got Brownie coming out. You see them at the funeral home when they're ready. You got any idea who could have done this?"

CHAPTER 3

Early slapped the back door of the grocery truck Sherm Brown had borrowed to transport the bodies to his funeral home, and the vehicle started away, leaving Early, Red Vullmer, and Doc Grafton in a swirl of powdery snow.

"You gonna let me use the story?" Vullmer asked.

Early scratched at his brow with his wounded thumb as he considered the request. "I guess."

"All of it?"

"That isn't much."

"Well, I've got the who, the where, and the when. You know the why or who might have done it?"

"Nope, and I don't want you saying a word about the how." Early kicked at the snow with the toe of his boot.

"But it was gunshots that killed them," Vullmer said.

"I don't want you saying that."

"Why not?"

"I just don't."

"Not even after I get a copy of Doc's report?"

"He's not going to give you a copy. It's not public 'til there's a trial and it's submitted as part of the evidence."

"But I could get it from Brownie."

"You run that part of the story, and I don't care where you got it, I'll jail you."

"You're serious."

"Red, you finally got something right."

Vullmer stared at Early, stared hard.

"That staring thing doesn't work on me," Early said.

"Works on the police chief."

"I'm not Andrew, so stop it."

The newsman shrugged. He slumped away toward his pickup.

Grafton joined Early in kicking at the snow as they watched Vullmer depart. "S'pose you want a ride."

"I'm without my Jeep," Early said. He waved at the radio reporter heading his truck out the ranch lane. "No hurry, though."

"I got patients waiting."

"You've always got patients waiting. You're more popular than Santa Claus."

"And just as jolly." Grafton went to his Cadillac, a post-war job he intended to replace the next fall, when the Nineteen Fifty models came out. "So why can't we hurry?"

"I want Red to be a looong way away before you and I take a peek in Al's car," Early said as he hoofed it for the passenger door of the Cadillac.

"I didn't see it around."

"It isn't here."

The two settled inside, and Grafton fired the engine. He backed the car around. "You gonna tell me where it is?"

"Toward town, on the side of Twenty-Four. You see it there when you were coming out?"

Grafton stopped. With effort he pulled the shift lever down into first and aimed his behemoth toward the county road. "I did see a car. Didn't pay attention because I was working too hard to stay ahead of Vullmer. Think we might find something interesting?"

"Never can tell."

"You got a look last night, didn't you?"

"Darn little. My concern then was poor drunk Al."

Grafton waved at his windshield. "You wanted to talk to the mail carrier? There he be."

"She–Virgie Brand."

"Well hell, I thought the postmaster canned her after the war and gave her job to a man."

"Her daddy called in a fistful of political IOU's to block it."

Ahead, at the county highway end of the ranch lane, a sun-faded black Chevrolet stove-bolt-six coupe stopped at the Garrets' mailbox. A side window rolled down, and out reached a gloved hand with mail.

Early motioned at the car. "Pull in front of her." With that, Grafton kicked up his speed and sounded his horn.

The Chevrolet did not move, but the side window rolled up.

Grafton slurried his car to a stop, and Early and he bailed out. They came to the passenger door of the Chevrolet. Early rapped on the window. He pointed down.

The glass rolled down, revealing the face of a woman of indeterminate age, her hair hidden by a fur-lined earlapper cap, the lapper strings tied beneath her chin.

"Kinda cold in there, huh, Virgie?" Early asked.

"Heater in this thing never was worth a nickel. Is there a problem?"

"'Fraid so."

"What's that?"

"You may want to take the Garrets' mail back to the post office. Somebody killed the family."

Brand's cheek and jaw muscles fell. Color drained from her face. "When?"

"Last night or this morning."

"Even the children?"

Early glanced away rather than answer the question.

"Charlie was such a good kid, and those babies," Brand said. "Who'd do such a thing?"

"We don't know."

"Something I can do?"

"Uh-huh. Tell your dad Hoolie's gonna need help, would you? The ranch falls back to him now, and there are the funerals."

"Jimmy, we got people up here can do all that. Mazie's in the hospital, you know."

"Hoolie told me. Got to ask, have you seen any strange vehicles around while you've been out?"

Brand drummed her gloved fingers on the steering wheel. "Murdered, huh?"

"Yeah."

"Unbelievable."

"Strange vehicles, Virgie?"

"I'm thinking. . . . No, not really."

"By chance you didn't come past here earlier?"

"Kinda, yes." Brand pointed ahead. "Around eight I came up the side road. I can see the Circle C from there."

"You look this way?"

"Sure."

"Any vehicles here?"

"Come to think of it a pickup truck. Black, maybe brown or blue–can't be sure of the color."

"Do you know whose?"

Brand shook her head.

"The make? A Chev, Dodge, Ford?"

"Jimmy, I wasn't paying that much attention, and it was pretty far."

"But you're sure it was a pickup."

"Pretty sure. Yes, I'd say so. Hay bales piled in the back. At least it looked like it."

"Well, that's something."

"But that's half the pickups in this end of the county and Clay County next door."

"I know. Virgie, you hear anything, you give me a call, all right?"

She answered with a nod, then reached past Early for the mail she had put in the Garrets' box.

Early and Grafton went back to the Cadillac, warm from the engine having been left running. They drove on, Early quiet with thought.

"Well?" Grafton asked.

"Well, what?"

"Talk to me. When you shut up, I know you've got something."

Early turned quarter to Grafton who glanced at him and back to the road.

"We're assuming it was murder," Early said. "Most murders are committed by family or someone else the victim knows. Garret didn't put up a fight. Nothing in that kitchen suggests he did."

"I'll agree with that."

"So this wasn't a stranger. I'm guessing Garret let the person in, the person in the pickup truck Virgie saw. Maybe Garret was even making coffee for him. They were sitting there talking, waiting for the coffee to boil, and bang."

"Okay."

"The pickup truck, hay bales in the back? That's someone local."

Grafton slowed for the turn onto State Twenty-Four. When he had the Cadillac back up to speed, he nudged Early gazing absently out the side window. "Who had grudge enough or hate enough to do that?"

"Huh?"

"Who do you think could have been mad enough to kill Garret?"

"No idea. Al and I didn't move in the same circles. Slow up. That's his car up ahead."

Grafton moved his foot from the accelerator to the brake pedal and pressed down. He drifted his car across the centerline to the far side of the highway and onto the shoulder, the tires, as they slowed, crunching through the snow.

"Car locked?" Grafton asked after he got out.

"Trunk only," Early said. "But I can pull the seat back out and get in that way. You want the front?"

Grafton opened the driver's door without answering, and Early a back door.

"Ripe in here," Grafton said. "Real stink of booze. Oh my, I found a dead soldier." He held up an empty fifth.

Early studied the bottle but only for a moment, then gazed around the back seat and the floor. He found nothing of interest, so climbed in. There he took hold of the sides of the seatback and gave it a wrench, but it didn't come.

"Isn't easy, is it?" Grafton said.

Early ignored him. He worked the fingers of his left hand in along the side of the seat and yanked. That side of the seatback popped loose. Early wrestled the other side free and pushed the affair out the door. After he aimed his flashlight into the exposed interior of the trunk, he reached in and pulled out a wrapped package. "Someone's been Christmas shopping."

"'Tis the season."

Early examined the package but didn't break the paper. Instead, he pushed the package aside and pulled a shopping bag from the trunk. "Emery Bird Thayer," he said as he read the label.

Grafton pawed through the glove box, his back to Early. "That's Kansas City and high class, my friend."

"So our boy's been traveling."

"By train." Grafton held a packet of railroad tickets over his shoulder. "Round trip. Been going to Kansas City."

Early took the tickets. He thumbed through them. "Goes in Mondays and comes back the next day. By these, he's been doing it for the last ten weeks. I'd say Al was doing something more than Christmas shopping in old KC."

"Hotel receipts here, from the Muehlebach."

"Very nice."

Early stuffed the tickets and the receipts Grafton passed back into a side pocket. Then he hunkered down. He pushed his head and shoulders inside the trunk where he shoved and sorted through the contents. "No valise, no suitcase. Musta traveled only with the clothes he wore. Not even a shoe brush."

"Maybe the Muehlebach keeps his things for him."

"Possible, Doc, if he was a regular."

"I've got lots of chewing gum wrappers–Blackjack and Teaberry."

"That's Al, a reformed smoker."

"Then why all these matchbooks?" Grafton held up a handful. He fanned them out.

Early gave up on the trunk. He twisted around and took a matchbook. He studied it. "Names on the back in pencil and look here," he said, pushing open the cover, "numbers. What have they got to do with anything?"

Grafton also opened a matchbook cover. "I got numbers here, too. Telephone numbers? License plates? Code?"

Early chortled. "Are you thinking our Al was a spy, maybe? For what, the Riley County Cattlemen's Association?"

"I don't have to figure that out, you do," Grafton said. He stuffed the matchbooks into Early's hand.

Early, after a cursory look, pressed them into his jacket pocket. He hauled the rear seatback inside and jammed it back in place. As the two were about to walk away from the Buick, Early had a thought. He opened the driver's door. "You look under Al's seat?"

"Felt with my hand," Grafton said. "That's where I found all the gum wrappers."

Early knelt in the snow. He leaned inside the car, pressed his hat and his ear to the floor, and peered beneath the seat. A smile creased his face. Early reached up into the springs and pulled out a leather holster–empty.

Grafton gazed at the find. "I'll be jiggered."

"All right, Al, what did you do with your gun?"

CHAPTER 4

December 13–Wednesday afternoon, late
The office

Early sat at his desk, scratching down notes that were less than legible, the matchbooks, hotel receipts, and train tickets bunched in separate piles in front of his paper. Gladys Morton, the secretary he'd inherited from his predecessor–her hair color changing by the day–stared from beside him.

"I can't read that," she said.

Early glanced up. He peered at her hair. "Chartreuse?"

"Emerald," she said, primping.

"Well, what I'm writing, you don't have to read." He scooped the matchbooks into a brown sack, stapled the top shut, and taped one of three notes to the sack.

"You can't read it either."

"Can too."

"All right, read it to me."

Early squinted at the note. "Ten matchbooks recovered from Al Garret's car on Twelve-Thirteen-Forty Nine, each book containing names and numbers thought to be secret, a code we deciphered with the department's Captain Midnight Decoder Ring."

"You're making that up."

"Am not."

"That last part you are."

"How'd you know I lost the decoder ring?"

"Jimmy, you could dictate your notes to me. I could type them up."

"Wouldn't want to make work for you." He shoved the tickets and receipts into separate sacks and taped notes to them, all of it evidence of what Early didn't know. He placed the sacks in a shoe box and pushed it toward Morton.

"I'm supposed to do something with this?" she asked.

"How about you sit on the box and hatch a new pair of shoes?"

Morton gave Early the cold eye.

He nudged the box closer to her. "State Police say we have to be a bit more organized with the evidence we collect, say we need an evidence lockup."

"So?"

"So take one of the deputies and find a room we can lock so we can keep our stuff there."

"Where?"

"I don't know. I think I'd start in the courthouse."

Morton stared at the box, then Early. "You going somewhere?"

"Out."

"Where's out?"

"Fat Willy's, if you have to know."

"Why?"

"Says someone rustled one of his cars."

"I can't for the life of me think who would. They're all wrecks."

Early went for his fleece-lined denim jacket. "I got to ask," he said as he pushed his arms into the sleeves, "do you ever say a kind word about anything or anybody?"

"I've made it my life's mission not to, although I'll tell you this, James Early, I thought the world of your wife." She picked up the box as he planted his work-worn cattleman's hat on his head. "Thelma was the best thing that ever happened to you, you know that? You doing all right?"

"Most days. It's hard to drive by the cemetery, though."

"You still got your little girl."

"Almost three months old now." A doughy smile lifted the corners of Early's mouth.

"You ought to bring her in so we can see her."

"Yeah. Yeah, sometime. . . . I gotta go."

Early swung about and strode out of the department's basement offices and down the hall that led to a side exit and freedom–the outdoors. Reports that had to be filled out and desks and walls closed him in. Give him a Jeep or, better, a horse, and he was a happy man. Gladys Morton had touched a sorrow. Thelma, Early's wife of two years, had died in an accident in October, driving his Jeep too fast. Or maybe she had killed herself to escape the pain of that plagued her mind. Early didn't know. He was following her–chasing her–a couple minutes behind, and found her thrown from his Jeep, the Jeep on its side, she dead in the gravel.

In the days that followed, he went into his own funk. The Jeep haunted him. The thought that it may have killed his wife nagged, so Early ordered John Silver Fox to haul the Jeep off and junk it someplace far removed from Manhattan, then get him a replacement from Army surplus.

He shook his head and shoulders in a semi-conscious effort to free himself of the memories. He had work to do–always his salvation–and the work at hand, talk to a hustler of used-cars about a stolen beast.

Early slid onto the butt-freezing seat of his Jeep. He closed the canvas and plexiglass door, and turned the ignition switch. The needle on the gas gauge swung up to the top. That brought a smile. Silver Fox had filled the gas tank.

A step on the starter button and the V-Eight Early and Silver Fox had dropped under the hood rumbled to life. Early rolled his Jeep out of the courthouse parking lot, not all that eager to see Fat Willy Johnson. On Poyntz Street heading west he waved to three students bundled against the cold, hustling out of the high school. A couple blocks more and he turned south on Fifteenth Street, one of several cut-overs to U.S. Eighteen that ran out to Fort Riley. With no leaves on the trees and only their skeleton fingers to shatter the sun, Early puckered his eyes when he turned onto the Super-Two highway. The sun, fading toward the horizon, appeared to be little more than an overly large hood ornament but hot on the eyes. Early thought it odd that he had the highway to himself. If only Fat Willy didn't ramble on, he might get away and home in time to put his baby daughter to bed. Nadine Estes would have supper waiting for him. She and her husband had taken Early and Thelma into their home when Thelma's mind got progressively worse. And they insisted he and the baby stay on after Thelma died. It turned into a good deal for all. Early had healed there on the Estes ranch, wrangling cattle and fixing fence for Walter Estes who, because of his age, needed help. And Nadine and Walter looked after the baby when Early had to be away, doing his sheriff's work.

A vehicle—a box truck—came out of the sun. The driver tapped his horn and waved, and Early waved back. As the truck passed, he saw the Dependable Hardware sign on the side and realized who the driver was—Judge Crooke's son, Albert, who ran hardware stores in Junction City, on the far side of Fort Riley, and in Manhattan.

Ahead in the growing twilight a neon sign came on proclaiming FAT WILLY'S BEST BUY USED CARS. Early fought against a laugh, thinking the sign should read FAT WILLY'S WORST BUY USED CARS. He slowed his Jeep and turned off the highway onto Fat Willy's snow-covered lot. There he stopped beside the door of the humpback trailer that served as the car dealer's office. Early stepped out of his Jeep and, in a short three paces, went on inside the trailer where the feathers of a dart whipping past his face grazed his nose. He jerked back.

"You trying to ruin my game?" Johnson bellowed from the swivel chair where he sat, a dumpy man of three-hundred pounds holding a second dart cocked behind his ear, about to let it fly. "Get in here and close the damn door. I can't afford to heat the whole world."

Early, with caution, leaned in. He glanced at the far wall. "You don't have a board up there, Fat Willy."

"Hell, I don't need one. I got that pitcher of that damn Democrat Truman. Give myself a dime ever time I pierce him in the snout."

"Well?"

"I'm up two bucks and twenty for the day."

Early stepped inside. He eased the door closed behind him, shutting out the winter air. "Hear you lost a car, huh?"

Johnson did not rise. "You gonna find it for me?" he asked as he set his dart aside for a silver flask on his desk. Johnson held the flask out in an offer to share.

"No, I'm a Baptist gin man," Early said.

The car dealer took a long draught from his flask. "Good stuff. Takes the chill off the pumpkins." Johnson belched. He gestured at an overstuffed chair, the cushion torn and one arm patched, the patch a yellow-and-black plaid on a solid but faded green fabric. "Sit a spell?"

"I'll stand," Early said. "Tell me about the car."

"Hudson Custom, Nineteen-and-Thirty-Eight. So few miles on it you'd think your grandmaw drove it and only to church." Johnson took a box of raisins from a desk drawer. "Want some?" he asked as he poured himself a handful.

Early waved off the offer.

The car dealer tossed the raisins into his mouth and chewed, like a cow content with her world. "Sweet, sweet car," he said, ruminating. "Then last night some bastard hot-wires her and drives her off."

"Hot-wires, you're sure of that?"

"What else could it be? I keep the gawddamn keys locked in my desk."

"Mind if I look?"

"You won't know 'em if you saw 'em." Johnson hauled a drawer open and hefted two keys on a chain into the air. "These are them."

"So what's this car worth, all of forty dollars, maybe forty-three?"

"You and that damn trooper. Jimmy, put a C-note on that and you're right in there."

Early turned the cold eye on Johnson, and the car dealer threw up his hands. "If I'm lyin', I'm dyin'."

"You just want to jack up the insurance company. Come on, be truthful."

Johnson's hands came back down to rest on the detritus of a week's worth of mail. He stared at his box of raisins. "Don't have insurance, haven't for a couple of months. I want my car back, Jimmy."

Early took a notepad and a stub of a pencil from his inside pocket. He placed the pad on Johnson's desk and leaned down to write. "Give me the particulars."

"Better." The used-car dealer held out a paper folded over. "Everything you need–color, VIN number, plate number, even the bit that there's a cigar burn in the center of the front seat."

"You said this was a grandma's car."

"Well, I dropped my cigar when I was drivin' it in."

Early read down the list. "You still selling to soldiers?"

"They're my market. Good cars for patriotic men with a little cash in their pockets."

"Junk cars, Fat Willy."

"Nothing of the sort. You still driving that antique war machine?"

"Uh-huh."

"I've got the perfect replacement car for you, Jimmy, a Packard with the biggest damn engine in it you ever saw. Out-run anything on the road."

"No thanks."

"Make you a steal of a deal."

"Nope."

"Don't say I never gave you a chance at a bargain. But back to my car, what're you gonna do?"

Early stuffed his notepad and Johnson's list in his pocket. "I'll ask my deputies and the constables to keep an eye out. But I'll tell you straight, that car's not worth our time to look for."

Johnson picked up a dart and, from somewhere among the litter on his desk, a swatch of emory paper. He worked the dart's steel point against the grit. "You disappoint me, Jimmy."

"How's that?"

"That damn cavalier attitude you take toward crime. I just might run against you in the next election."

"Fat Willy, you'd have to get out of your chair, and I'd pay a two-dollar bill to see that."

CHAPTER 5

December 13–Wednesday night
Home at last

Full dark had long replaced twilight by the time Early backed his Jeep under the lean-to that sheltered Walter Estes' International flatbed and piles of hay bales. He threw a tarp over the Jeep's windshield. Early had no desire to scrape frost in the morning. Bad enough he had to do that at the courthouse parking lot–frost, snow, ice, whatever winter gifts Mother Nature left behind when she moved on to torment the landscape and people to the east.

Arch, the Esteses' Newfoundland that had befriended Early and Thelma, particularly, when they moved to the ranch, wriggled out of his nest beneath the International. He shambled over, lazing his tail as he moved. He lifted his lips in a dog grin.

Early rubbed the Newfoundland behind his ears. "Pooch, hope your day's been better than mine. Musta been because I think you got a smile there. How about you get back to bed and I head to the house?"

The dog peered up at Early for a moment, then, as if he understood the greeting was over, wandered back under the International.

Early detoured on his hike to the ranch house. He slipped instead into the barn, the place windowless and coal-mine dark, smelling richly of hay and horses. Early inhaled the aromas. He savored them. He didn't need light because he knew exactly how many paces it was to the stall where his horse resided. It was with reluctance that he had sold the roan, a top cutting horse he'd trained, when he lost his own ranch to the bank a couple years back. After he and Thelma had settled in with the Esteses, he and Walter went down to Morris County. There Early bought the roan back, rode her the thirty-five miles home rather than trailer her, rode at a pace that took the day because he loved the gentle creature's company.

He heard a whiffling–the fluttering of a horse's lips, his horse blowing out air, signaling she knew he was there. Early stepped up to the stall's Dutch door and, sensing her warmth, her nearness, he reached up into the dark for the animal's face. It was there, and he stoked the broad muzzle.

"Molly, you have a good day?"

She whiffled again.

"Think I got a treat here," Early said. He rustled in his jacket pocket for the two sugar cubes he'd filched from Fat Willy's. He had hardly opened his hand and the lips of the horse nuzzled in, vacuuming up the cubes and the loose granules of sugar that had rubbed free. She crunched the cubes down, head-butting Early's shoulder, her way of asking for more.

"Sorry, girl, that's all I got." Early stroked the roan's face once more, then left. He retraced his steps to the door and on outside where the snow reflected back the pale light from the thin smattering of stars visible in the heavens. That light made the walk to the ranch house an easy one.

When he got near, he saw a car–a Kaiser Traveler by its outline. Curious for so far into the night. Company sure, the mellow light streaming from the house's windows confirmed it, but who? On the porch Early tramped the snow from his boots and went inside where domestic smells greeted him, coffee and pipe smoke–applewood-flavored tobacco, a sweet scent.

Walter Estes waved from his chair in the great front room. He pointed to the visitors seated on a sofa. "Jimmy, you gotta hear what these fellas are selling."

The two men rose, one in the rough clothes and work shoes of a farmer, the other in a blue serge suit, the coat double-breasted.

"Hey-dee, Dink," Early said as he shook the big-knuckled hand of the farmer, Dink Frazier, from west of Leonardville, a briarwood pipe clamped in his teeth. "Gotcha a new car out there?"

Frazier gave an awkward shake of his head. He thumbed to his colleague. "Belongs to this'n, Wade Stuwoldski. He's with the Rural Electric people out of Kansas City."

Estes ooched as he tried to rise from his chair. "Arth-a-ritis," he said to his guests and settled back. "Jimmy, you're late. This got something to do with those murders up at May Day? Heard about it on the battery radio."

The gazes of the guests, fixed on Estes, at the mention of murder swivelled to Early.

"Don't want to talk about it," he said.

"Red Vullmer said it was a bad'un."

"It was, and let's leave it at that."

"All right," Estes said. "Jimmy, reason Dink's here, he and some of the others around want to start a co-op. They want to bring juice for lights out here."

Frazier took his pipe from his mouth. He pointed the stem at Early. "The city companies aren't a-never gonna do it. Too expensive, they say. So, if we want 'lectricity, we gotta do it ourselves. Personally, I'm gettin' darn tired of toting a kerosene lantern whenever I want to work around the barn after dark."

"And you're looking to sign up subscribers, I hear," Early said.

"We get enough, Mister Stuwoldski says he'll run the paperwork through to get us a federal loan cheap to make it happen."

Early stripped off his hat and coat as he glanced at Estes. "What do you think?"

Before the old rancher could answer, a baby squalled. Early bolted from the room without so much as an 'excuse me.' He ran to the back of the house, to his bedroom where, at the end of a bed stood a crib. Inside writhed a child hammering at the air as she bellowed.

Early scooped the baby up. He rocked her or, the way he did it, jostled her around as if she were a jug of milk replacer in need of mixing. And then his nose wrinkled. Early plopped the child down on the bureau top–his changing table. He stripped off her acrid diaper, dropped it in a bucket at the side of the bureau, and grabbled for a wash cloth in a water basin he kept on the bureau top. He squeezed the cloth out and wiped his child's bottom clean, the baby howling at the frigid touch of the wet cloth.

"Aw now, Toot, this is not gona kill you," Early said as he finished the job. He opened the top drawer and . . . no diapers.

He tried the next and the next, and from the bottom drawer Early whipped out a clean pair of his khaki boxers. He slipped his daughter's legs through the legs holes and, fumbling with pins, pinned up the excess fabric.

"That all right for you?" he asked.

The yowling evaporated. The hammering fists became waving hands, and the child grinned.

Early lifted her to his shoulder and thrummed his fingers against her back. "You can be a good kid when you want to be, can'tcha?" he said as he made his way back to the front room.

Nadine Estes bustled in from the kitchen, a cake pan in one hand and saucers in the other. At the sight of Early and the baby, she came close to dropping the saucers. "Jimmy, is that any way to dress your child?"

"It's all I could find."

"I've got clean diapers on the drying rack in the kitchen."

"I didn't know that."

"You want me to take her and change her proper?"

"No, Barbie Sue seems happy enough," Early said, still thrumming the baby's back.

"Nadine, we were talking about those murders," Estes said.

She touched Early's hand. "Are we safe? May Day's not all that far away."

"We didn't see anything that suggests the killer's after anybody else."

"But are we safe?"

"Don't see why not."

"I'm thinkin' of keeping a shotgun by the front door," Frazier said.

Early turned on him. "Now, Dink, don't go doing something wild."

"Bein' ready for you-know-what, I don't think that's wild."

Nadine handed a saucer to Frazier and one to Stuwoldski. "This talk about murders and electricity, I don't want you boys making any world-shaking decisions without a little something to eat." She gave a saucer to her husband and set the extra aside. Nadine followed that with forking a generous square of cake onto Stuwoldski's saucer, then Frazier's.

"Looks mighty good," he said.

"It's my famous apple dump cake."

"Wish my Bessie could make something like this. 'Fraid she's got but one kitchen skill–burning things."

"Come on, Dink."

"No, she's real good at it, and after thirty years I've come to appreciate charred food."

Nadine snickered and went on to her husband and, after him, she placed a large square on the extra saucer–for Early. "I got forks for you all."

"Fingers is fine," Frazier said as he wrapped a hand around his cake.

Nadine patted Early's arm. "Make you a sandwich–meatloaf. You didn't get no supper, did you?"

Early, rocking his child, mumftt around a mouthful of cake. When he could speak, Nadine was gone. He pointed at Estes. "This electric, what do you think?"

"Jimmy, I'm an old duffer. Lanterns are all I've ever had, don't really need to change as I see it. On top of that, what Dink wants for an enrollment fee, that would press me some. Now if you were to buy me out."

Early turned back to the visitors. "I gotta say I'm with Walter."

Frazier licked the frosting from his fingers. "I'm sorry for that," he said.

"Now hear me out. What we really need out here–what I really need–is a telephone."

Stuwoldski, finished with his cake, made a business of wiping his fingers on his handkerchief. "If it's telephone you want, this cooperative could provide it, telephone and electric. In fact, we could get a telephone to you a year earlier than electric because we would only have to build a few trunk lines."

Early inched an eyebrow up.

"Leonardville's got a little exchange and Manhattan's got a big exchange, but neither are going to run lines out here. We could form a rural exchange that hooks into theirs for long distance, run our lines down the state highway with a drop line to the top wire of a fence bordering a county road. We can push voice down that wire to every rancher on that road."

"But my telephone–"

"Simple. You take a line off that fence to your phone, and you can receive and you can talk."

"We don't need insulated wires?" Early asked.

"You'll get a better signal with an insulated wire, but you don't really need it. When we do finally build lines to bring you electricity, we can string telephone wires on the same poles and bring you better telephone service then."

"How soon?"

"If enough of your neighbors want telephone, I'd say sixty days after you organize a cooperative, ninety at the most."

"By summer?"

"I can get to the manufacturers and contractors to make it happen. The federal government wants universal electric and telephone. No reason you shouldn't have both like the people in town do. The money's in place."

"Walter?" Early asked.

"Your call, Jimmy."

"And the subscription fee?"

"Fifty dollars," Frazier said. "Makes you an owner in the co-op."

Early backed over to Estes. "Get my wallet out of my pocket and see what I got."

Estes took out Early's billfold polished smooth from wear. He studied the contents, counted the bills. "You got twenty-one, no, twenty-two dollars here."

"Dink," Early said, "you can have that and the rest on payday end of the month."

Frazier accepted the money held out by Estes. "This makes you number seventeen," Frazier said. "Eighty-three more and we got us a co-op. Jimmy, if you'd be willing to serve on the board, we can get the rest signed up lickity-split on the strength of your name."

"Not my name. No, you need a salesman. Put Walter on the board. He can charm a raccoon out of a tree."

"Walter?" Frazier asked the old rancher.

"Well, I guess it'd give me something to do in my declining years."

"Then it's a done deal." Frazier shook Estes's big mitt and attempted to shake hands with Early holding a child with one hand and stuffing cake into his mouth with the other. "That's all right, Jimmy. We'll be on our way."

With that, he helped himself to a barn jacket and cap hanging on a peg near the front door, and Stuwoldski to an overcoat. They bundled themselves against the cold and stepped out onto the porch, Early holding the door for them.

"This is gonna be a good thing, Jimmy," Frazier said.

"Yeah, it's needed."

"You take care of that baby."

"I'll do that. My best to your wife."

Frazier waved a last time and walked away into the night, trailing Stuwoldski.

After Early closed the door, he turned back to the warmth of the room.

"That family," Estes said from his chair.

"Never seen worse. You knew them?"

"Not really. Now the Garret boy's granddaddy, Hoolie, him and me were pretty tight as young coyotes."

"How's that?" Early asked as he came over to the sofa. He settled his sleeping child against a pillow and took a seat for himself next to her.

"You were in the big war, Jimmy. Hoolie and me, we were in the little war–Spanish-American. Joined up with Teddy Roosevelt's volunteer cavalry."

"You get to Cuba?"

"Uh-huh, and both of us made it home without so much as a scratch from a sand burr. Got any idea who could have done this?"

"Don't I wish I knew."

"Hoolie, he was a wild man, and so was I until I married Nadine. Hoolie's boy I know inherited the wild streak. I expect the grandson did, too. You make enemies when you're wild, because you're stupid, because you don't think." Estes sucked on his teeth. "Jimmy, when you get to poking around, you're likely to find a lot of people didn't care for that boy."

"But bad enough to kill him and his family?"

"Now that's got to be somebody's who's bug-house crazy."

CHAPTER 6

December 16–Saturday
May Day

Early and Walter Estes stamped snow from their boots as they entered the barbershop in May Day, the town little more than a dot on County Road Seventeen–five houses, a blacksmith shop/gas station, grocery store/post office, Methodist church, and Buck Fleming's open-Saturdays-only barbershop.

The place smelled of talc.

"Cold out there, boys?" Fleming asked, glancing up for the barest moment from his scraping at a customer's well-lathered beard–the customer bald.

Early took off his ear muffs. "A tad if you go by the icicles in my mustache."

"Yup. Me, I couldn't get my old jalopy started this morning. Had to wait out by the road, thumb a ride in with the mail carrier."

"Virgie Brand?" Early asked as he and Estes hung their coats and hats on hooks by the door. An elk's head, with an expansive rack of horns, gazed down at them, impassive.

"You know her?" Fleming asked.

"Doesn't everybody?"

"Yep, she's quite a gal. Been driving that mail route for, omigosh, about eight years now." The barber waved his straight razor with its load of soap bubbles and whiskers at a couple folding chairs set against the wall. "Have a seat there. I'll get to you in a few minutes." Fleming tipped up the chin of the man in his barber chair– sturdier than the folding ones, a chair that might have come from somebody's kitchen. He put his blade at the base of the man's neck. "Charlie, sneeze now and it's your blood all over my fine floor."

Early glanced down at the pine boards and clumps of hair clippings that covered them, and wondered what was so fine about the floor.

Fleming drew up on his razor. "Gawddamn shame about the murder of that young Garret and his family, isn't it?"

"Murder?" Early asked as he picked up a four-year-old Collier's magazine from another chair.

"Didn't hear about that, huh?" The barber wiped his blade clean and again drew up on it. "Big talk around our town. You'd think the sheriff or the state police would be all over us on this, but I haven't seen a soul with a badge. Lazy slugs."

Estes mouthed the words 'tell him' to Early, but Early only shook his head.

"So you fellas aren't from around here," Fleming said.

"Down by Leonardville. Walter and I are going up to Washington County to look at a bull. Saw your shop and thought we'd stop in for a trim."

"Good thing you come today, only day I'm open. . . . I'm a rancher myself. Learned this barber trade in the Army and found having a side income is kinda nice. Now, boys, if it's a bull you're looking for, I've got a mighty fine one coming on two years old I'd be willing to sell."

"No, we're committed to seeing this one up the road, but we'll keep yours in mind. So who's this Garret?"

"Rancher like me, east of town. Circle C–must have been about thirty. Three little kids. It's just awful. Who'd want to do that?" Again Fleming wiped his blade clean on the towel that laid on his customer's shoulder.

"I suppose somebody who didn't like him, wouldn't you say?" Early, paging into the magazine, stopped at a story by Ernest Hemingway. He read down.

"That could be a lot of people, including me," Fleming said as he tossed the dirty towel aside. He brought a clean, hot towel out of a pot on the stove that radiated heat in the center of the shop. Fleming wiped down his customer's face. "Al beat me bad in a trade last year, stuck me with a wild hair of a horse that threw me through the side of my barn first time I got in the saddle. Knothead wouldn't trade me back, so, yep, I was ready to kill him."

"But you didn't."

"Aw, you get over things." Done with the towel, Fleming shook aftershave into his hands. He warmed the liquid, then rubbed it into the raw skin of his customer's face and neck. The man cringed. "Stings a bit, huh, Charlie? But you're gonna smell of sweet heat, so good your wife'll rip the clothes off you when you get home and take you to bed. Be six bits for the shave."

The man stood. He nodded to Early and Estes as he went to a side table where he put a dollar down and took a quarter from the assortment of change there. He then helped himself to a coat and hat and moved toward the door.

"Next week?" Fleming asked and got a wave as the man went out.

"He doesn't talk much, does he?" Early said.

"Kicked in the throat by a horse. Busted his jaw and damaged his voice box. Charlie's lucky to be alive." Fleming helped himself to a half-sheet hanging from a hook by the table. He snapped the sheet open and stood at the ready beside his chair. "So which of you fellas is next?"

Early nudged Estes.

"Guess it's me," the old rancher said as he pushed up. He went over and parked himself on the barber's hard chair.

Fleming whipped the sheet across Estes' chest, draped the covering over the old man's shoulders, and drew the ends together. The barber leaned back. He studied Estes' hair. "When's the last time you seen the inside of a barbershop?"

"Three, maybe four months ago."

"Looks it. Well then, it's a shearing today, huh? I'll get you looking so handsome your woman won't recognize you." Fleming took scissors from his back pocket and snipped away at a sideburn.

"This Garret," Estes said, "he Hoolie Garret's grandson?"

"You know the old man?"

"Yeah, long time ago."

"You got the family connection right."

"Everybody disliked this young fella, you say?"

"I didn't say everybody," Fleming said. He moved around to work on the other sideburn. "I'm sure his momma loved him when she was alive, God rest her soul."

"Most mothers do like their babies."

"But I'll tell yah, there was serious bad blood between Garret and Gilly Dammeridge. Gilly's got the next ranch south, and they've been fighting for years on where the line fence is supposed to be. To hear Gilly tell it, a good twenty-five acres of prime grassland was at stake–his grassland."

Early tossed his magazine aside. "Walter," he said as he got up, "think I'll go down to the store, maybe get a pack of Teaberry gum."

Fleming didn't miss a snip as he worked above an ear. "Ten minutes and I can get you in the chair."

"I expect Walter'll want a shave."

"Twenty, twenty-five minutes then." Fleming moved behind Estes and cut away at the hair hanging over his collar.

Early donned his coat. He buttoned up, clamped muffs over his ears and reached for his hat. After he secured it to the top of his head, he gave a wave and went on outside. On the board sidewalk, he turned toward the store–Warden's General, by the sign that hung from the front of the clapboard building–but stepped out in the street when he heard organ music coming from across the way, from a building that had a slight lean away from the wind, a building long in need of paint. Early went on over and inside, the smell of must and abandonment discouraging his nose.

He hauled off his hat when he saw an altar and a cross up front, both plain affairs. To the side sat someone hunched forward, pumping at the bellows of an ancient, wheezing reed organ, the person's fingers changing the stops, moving over the instrument's keys.

Early slipped onto a chair. He pulled off his ear muffs and listened. The hymn, he recognized it even without the words–'Shall

We Gather by the River,' a standard in the Worrisome Creek Baptist Church he attended.

"Like it?" the person at the organ asked as he played on.

"Didn't mean to interrupt."

"You didn't. The church is so small I don't have an organist, so I play and preach both. I like to get in a little practice before Sunday."

"You're the preacher then?"

"That's right. Reverend L.H.T. Smith."

"That's a lot of initials."

"Legzeligs Halcyon Thanatos Smith. A mouthful, wouldn't you agree?"

"How'd you come by those unusual names, if you don't mind me asking?"

"My father. He was a scholar of Hebrew and Greek."

"Mine was a scholar of ranching."

"Far more practical." Smith turned away from his keyboard, toward Early.

"Reverend, I get around the county a bit. Shouldn't I know you?"

"Not necessarily. I've only been here a short time. I serve two congregations, this one and the one over the county line in Kimeo. But I know you."

"How's that?"

"Let's say in my business I've got a pipeline to the ultimate source of all information." Smith came away from the organ bench and down the aisle, the hem of his long winter coat sweeping the floor. He held his hand out, his hand in a fingerless knit glove. "James McBride Early. I've been expecting you."

The two shook, Early without rising. He peered up at this man who claimed to know him, a rotund fellow with flowing hair like all the religious artists pictured Jesus as having. But no beard. No mustache. And no eyebrows either, and skin that looked to be stiff, that had a pearl sheen to it.

"My face bother you?" Smith asked.

Early sensed that whatever he might say would be wrong.

"Burned in the war," Smith went on. "I was gassing my Jeep, and, wouldn't you know, some GI flicks a cigarette my way. All those fumes around, and whoosh. I can't blame the Germans for what happened to me. You were in the war, weren't you?"

"Big Red One. Just a lowly corporal with a carbine."

"And you got a leg full of shrapnel for your trouble."

Before Early could ask Smith how he knew that, Smith said, "I saw you in the field hospital. I was a chaplain. You were one of my calls. Baptist as I remember. And now you're the sheriff of Riley County, and you want to know what I know about young Mister Garret."

One of Early's eyebrows arched up. "You know something?"

"It's possible."

"It was a bad murder–grisly–the worst I've seen."

"So you've seen others."

"Comes with the job."

"Wears on you, doesn't it?" Smith, with his boot, hooked a chair and swung it around. He sat down, facing Early. "A murder of a friend took the life of your wife, didn't it?"

Early sucked in a breath.

Smith raised a hand. "I'm sorry. I didn't mean to bring that up, but stories make the rounds."

"I s'pose. Death's got to be pretty hard on you, too, Preacher. Everybody you baptize or marry you eventually bury."

"I've not let it bother me. The Great God Above wrote it in my job description that I'm to be there when somebody dies, and, like I suppose you are, I'm pretty good at my job."

Early reached in his pocket before he realized he hadn't been to the store.

Smith brought out a pack of chewing gum. He held it out, the end of a stick poking up. "This what you want?"

Early pulled the stick out. He examined the wrapping as he peeled it away–Teaberry . . . Teaberry. He folded the gum over and pushed it into his mouth. "Thanks. I've got a deputy chews tobacco. Always carries a spit can with him." A shiver ran through Early's shoulders at the picture those words brought to his mind. He watched Smith peel away the wrapping on a stick of gum, fold the gum over, and stuff it in his mouth. To Early it was like watching his own actions in a mirror. "Something you said, about knowing something about Garret, you wouldn't happen to have been out at the ranch house when he was murdered, would you?"

"No. No, when he died. Well, not exactly when he died. A few minutes later."

Early stopped chewing. He tongued his gum into his cheek. "You saw who did it, didn't you?"

Smith shook his head, his long hair moving in an easy wave, as if it were water.

"Then what did you see, and why were you there?"

"I saw what you saw when you came, Mister Garret dead at the kitchen table . . . and Missus Garret . . . and the children. I could tell you I came to collect their souls, but you'd only laugh at that."

"I expect I would."

"Then I'll tell you he wanted to talk to me. He'd gotten himself into deeper trouble than he could get out of."

"And what would that be?"

"He'd gambled away a fortune to some men in Kansas City–left a lot of IOU's, and they wanted their money."

Early's face clouded. Ever the skeptic, he wondered how Garret could be so dumb.

"You never bet on anything?" Smith asked.

"Nickels at cards."

"How about your ranch?"

"Wait a minute, you're going to far here."

"The mortgage, right? And you lost. You felt it ruined you, so maybe you can understand where Mister Garret was."

"But that time, Preacher, I bet on rain and grass and cows doing well, not some game."

Smith shrugged. "Maybe you can't understand where Mister Garret was. Well, that's your problem, and I can't help you with that."

"Let me get this right, you're saying some unknown gamblers from Kansas City killed Garret and his family over a debt?"

"A big debt. That's what I know because Mister Garret told me."

"Why would he tell you that?"

"People tell preachers a lot of things about the bad in their lives, things they'd never tell a sheriff. I expect they're looking for help in finding a way out, maybe in the process finding some forgiveness. Forgiveness, my job requires that of me."

"You're telling me I couldn't have helped Garret?"

"Apparently he didn't think so, or he would have come to you, now, wouldn't he?" Smith stood as if to leave. He gave Early the pack of gum. "Enjoy it. I've got to get over to Kimeo."

"Not so fast, you were out at the Garret ranch."

"Yes."

"Tell me one more time exactly what you saw."

"Why?"

"I've found people usually leave something out."

"Not me."

"I'll ask it anyway, did you see a car or a pickup leaving or going down the road as you came in?"

"No."

"Did you see a gun?"

"I did."

"All right, what kind and where was it?"

Smith squinted at Early. "A revolver come to think of it, on the floor near Mister Garret's chair."

"Had the gun been fired?"

"There's no way I'd know that."

"Preacher, I'll tell you this, the gun wasn't there when I got there. Did you take it?"

"Of course not. Anything else?" When Early didn't answer, Smith turned away. He moved toward the door at a deliberate gait. "Be sure you close this when you leave," he said.

*

Early walked back into Buck Fleming's open-Saturdays-only barbershop. He shucked his coat after he closed the shop's door.

"Couple more minutes," Fleming said as he shaved the back of Walter Estes' neck. "Get your gum?"

Early held up the partially empty package of Teaberry. "Your preacher gave it to me over at the Methodist church."

"Preacher?" Fleming asked. "We've haven't had a preacher now for, what, going on five years."

CHAPTER 7

December 16–Saturday
Back to church

"Walter, there really was somebody in there," Early said as he and Estes hoofed it across May Day's main street toward the building whose weathered sign, poking up from the snow, proclaimed it to be the Methodist church.

"That may be, but the barber said it wasn't no padre."

"The man said he was. Gave me his name."

Early stepped inside, Estes behind him. The place still smelled of abandonment. And the dust–everywhere, even streaking the windows.

"He and I sat right here, talking, me in this chair, him in that one." Early gestured to a wooden chair turned away from the front of the church.

Estes squinted in the dim light at the two chairs. "You may have sat in this one, Jimmy, but nobody sat in the other. Dust hasn't been disturbed."

Early went forward, Estes meandering after him.

"The organ. He was playing the organ."

"And look at the dust on that old critter."

Early ran his gloved hand along the edge of the keyboard, then examined the dust his glove had collected. "You think I'm losing it, don't you?"

"Losing what?"

"My mind. Seeing people who aren't there. That happened to Thelma."

"Thelma, but not you," Estes said. "Jimmy, I believe you. There was someone here if you say so, but there's just no sign of him."

Early glanced at the pedestal at the side of the organ, where a lamp would sit. A scrap of paper laid there. He picked it up and held it label-side out to Estes. "Teaberry. I knew he was here."

"So?"

"So I don't know." He put the gum wrapper in his coat pocket. "But I'm thinking while we're up here we ought to go see Gilly Dammeridge, see if the barber was right, and he and Al were feuding over pasture land. You know Gilly?"

"No. He came here long after Nadine and I settled down by Leonardville."

"Well, I know him. He's on the county Democrat committee."

"Oh Lordy, that makes him the enemy."

"No, in politics Gilly's just misguided."

"And you're gonna guide him into the light, right?"

Early laughed at that, the first time he'd laughed at anything since the murders. He waved for Estes to follow him outside. There at the Jeep, Early released the button end of his whip antenna from its restraint at the top of the windshield. The antenna pulled upright to its full height as he pushed himself inside, behind the steering wheel, and Estes settled into the shotgun seat.

Early fired up the engine and the radio with it. After he got the Jeep rolling, he pressed the transmit button on the side of his hand microphone. "Anybody home?"

"Roger that, chief," came a baritone voice through the speaker.

"Big John, what you doing in the office?"

"Nan's little boy got sick, so I told her I would come in and watch the radio until my shift. Where are you?"

"May Day. Going out to see Gilly Dammeridge. Anything going on I need to know about?"

"Nothing. So slow I'm thinking of springing Woozer the Boozer from jail so we can play a couple hands of Sheep's Head."

"He in again?"

"Picked him up last night wandering the highway outside of Rocky Ford, half nekkid. If he hadn't had so much whiskey in him he would have froze."

"Yeah, well, have a good card game, but no penny bets, understand? Early out."

"And base out."

Estes giggled. "You sure get all the strange ones."

Early leaned forward and glanced at the Garret place as he drove by, then slowed for the side road that ran south to the Dammeridge ranch. "Woozer's got a good heart, just finds life difficult, so he drinks."

He made the turn, shifted down to second, and pressed on the accelerator. "Ninety-eight-point-three percent of those we haul to jail aren't bad people. Harmless like old Wooze, just do dumb things that get themselves in trouble." Early snickered as he shifted up into third. "I'll say this, they do keep us entertained at the courthouse."

"And that two percent?" Estes asked.

"Male or female, they can scare the umph out of you."

"And this Dammeridge?"

"First time I've ever had to call on him as sheriff."

The Jeep idled along at forty-five, Early on occasion turning the steering wheel to sweep around a rut in the snowpack on the road. He slowed again, shifted down, and took off on a long ranch lane that paralleled a line fence. After several dips and rises, Early and Estes came up on a set of ranch buildings, the house set back in a cluster of leafless trees. When they passed a barn, Early heard a blower. He twisted around and saw someone working under a lean-to. Early wheeled the Jeep about. He stopped near a man in a sheepskin coat and a handrolled Quigley cowboy hat.

The man lifted a tarp away from the motor of a Diamond Reo flatbed.

"Hey-yup, Gilly," Early called out as he stepped away from his Jeep. Estes stayed inside, in the warmth.

Gilly Dammeridge saluted. "Sheriff, come to help me get my truck started?"

"Nope, just to ask a question or two."

"Uh-huh." He turned back. Dammeridge tucked the tarp around the motor, then came away. "Engine's like a block of ice. I got a kerosene heater cookin' under it, so maybe I'll get the motor started before sundown. . . . Whaddayah want to ask?"

"About Al Garret."

"Shit." Dammeridge toed the snow with his boot.

"You and he in a range war of some kind?"

"You heard about that?"

"I hear lots of things, Gilly."

"The little bandit did a job on me while I was away."

"How's that?"

"Our line fence was getting a little ratty, so back in the summer we agreed to build a new one. You know how it works. You and your neighbor stand facing each other at the middle of the fence and whatever's on your right, that's yours, and whatever's on his right is his. Well, I went up to the Sand Hills for a couple weeks to deal on some cattle and pasture there."

"Yup, and Al builds his half of the fence on your land."

"You heard about that, too, huh? Didn't move much near the joining point, but eventually that fence sneaked up a couple, three rods. I figured I lost twenty-two, maybe twenty-three acres along the run of the fence."

"So you went to see him?"

"Sure did. He said he moved that fence to where it was supposed to be by the original survey of Eighteen and Sixty-Eight, and Al, he whips this paper out. I tell you it was nothing like the survey I had made in Nineteen and Thirty-Four that's on file at the courthouse."

"So why not sue and let the judge settle it?"

"My lawyer said that old document looked real enough that I probably wouldn't win. So I went back to see Al last month. I told him he had thirty days to move the fence or I'd do it for him and shoot him if he tried to stop me."

"He do it?"

Dammeridge laughed.

"So a month later, here it is. Al's dead. Gilly, that puts you in a real bad light, wouldn't you say?"

"You're thinking I did him in? Hell, I wasn't even here."

"You weren't?"

"No, Sal and I were up in Lincoln, for a wedding–her sister's daughter. Went up two days early, stayed two days after."

"And Sal will verify this?"

"Of course. Wait a minute. You think I'm lying, and, when Sal backs me up, you're gonna be thinking she's lying, too. Well, call her sister."

Early shucked his gloves for a pad and a pencil. "Her name?"

"Wilva. Wilva Bailey. Lincoln five-five-three-four-one."

Early finished his note and pulled his gloves back on.

"The ranch goes back to Hoolie, doesn't it?" Dammeridge asked. "He's an old man. You think he'd sell?"

"To you?"

"I've got a son at K-State–basketball player–tall drink of water. Maybe you seen him play. Delbert'll be coming home in May. I could put him on that ranch."

"Guess you'll have to talk to Hoolie."

"I just might." Dammeridge broke up some crusted snow with the heel of his boot. After he finished, he peered sideways at Early. "I should tell you, sheriff, you're likely to have some competition in the next election."

"It's a free country."

"Willy Johnson called me, you know, the car dealer? He wants to take you on."

*

Early stopped his Jeep beside the mailbox at the head of the lane leading to the Rocking Horse E. He thumbed the transmit button on his microphone while Estes hauled in a newspaper and a fistful of envelopes.

"Home again, home again jiggidy jig," Early said into the mic.

"Just in time," came back the voice of his deputy, John Silver Fox.

"Whatcha got?"

"The Super Trooper called. He found the car stolen from Fat Willy's lot. Says you might want to come over and look at it."

"Where?"

"On a bluff south of the airport. You take that twisty track across from the airport road, and it runs up there."

"Be a half-hour."

"Trooper Plemmons figured that, so he's gone on supper break. You want me to come out?"

"Why not?" Early hung the mic back over the rearview mirror.

"Guess your work's not done, huh?" Estes said as he sorted through the envelopes. "Here's one for you from the R.E.A. Want me to open it?"

"I'll read it later." Early shifted into first. He bucked the Jeep off the highway and onto the ranch lane.

Estes waved another R.E.A. envelope. "This one's for me." He opened it and read down the letter. "Whaddaya know, I've been appointed to the board of directors."

Early stepped up the speed of the Jeep. "Dink's a man of his word. S'pose I should bow down to you."

"Oh, that's not necessary. But you could call me 'Your Lord High Directorship.'"

"I could, but I don't think I will. You do the evening chores without me?"

"Sure. Drop me at the barn. How about supper?"

"I'm liable to be late. Better tell Nadine I'll get supper in town."

*

The beacon at the Manhattan airport swept the undersides of scud clouds as Early came through the cut along the side of Sunset Hill and down into the Eureka Valley where far-sighted leaders of Manhattan had placed the airport the year Charles Lindbergh flew the Atlantic Ocean. Almost no traffic on U.S. Eighteen. Indeed, the supper hour.

Early glanced up to the left–the south–at headlights several hundred feet above the highway, the headlights not moving. Had to be the bluff, his destination.

He slowed for the trail across from the airport road, where several sets of tire tracks turned off. Early turned, too, and followed them, downshifting, milling past a State Patrol car parked at the side. He rammed his transmission into four-wheel drive as the Jeep climbed out of the valley.

Early helped himself to his microphone. "Who's up on top?" he asked anyone who might be on his frequency.

The voice of John Silver Fox came back. "The Super Trooper and me."

"Big John, I thought I'd been everywhere in the county, but I've never been on this road."

"Isn't much of a road, is it? First time for me, too."

"Can't be the county's."

"Private. Belongs to the WD. Fence line is just beyond us."

"Is that Daniel's cruiser I passed?"

"Yup. He walked up here and back down the first time. I gave him a lift the second."

"Mighty good of you." Early wrenched the Jeep around a switchback, and the vehicle bogged down on the next part of the climb, the tires spinning, howling. Early stepped down on the clutch pedal. When the howling stopped, he hammered the steering wheel. That did it. Tension released, he leaned out the door. Early studied the rut in which his rear tire had found residence. If only he hadn't left the tire chains at home . . . so he shifted the transmission into reverse. Early gingerly, carefully rocked the Jeep back once, again and a third time, up and out of the rut. He shifted into first, floored it, and the war machine banged through the rut and others, fish-tailing on upward. Early glanced back, at the airport, at the beacon. He estimated he had to be near the top of the bluff and couldn't help wondering as he went on why anyone would steal a car and bring it up here. And leave it. It made no sense.

Early rolled out on top, Silver Fox and Plemmons in his headlights, leaning against the fender of Silver Fox's Jeep, the two drinking coffee. Beyond them smoldered a burned-out hulk.

CHAPTER 8

December 16–Saturday night
Thievery

Early stopped his Jeep, the charred carcass dead in his headlights.

"You sure that's Fat Willy's Hudson?" he asked as he stepped out into the snow.

Plemmons dumped his coffee cup. "Checked the VIN number. The plate got scorched, but you can still read it."

"What I'd like to know is, if you couldn't drive your cruiser up here, how the heck did the thief get the Hudson up here?"

"Brought it up before the last snow. That's my guess."

"If you're right, why wait 'til now to burn it, and why burn it at all?"

"Jimmy, you're asking questions I don't know the answers to."

"How'd you find out about this, anyway?"

"I stopped over at the fire department, for a bowl of their heartburn chili, when somebody at the airport called it in. The boys wrote it off because they knew they couldn't get a water truck up here, but I was curious." Plemmons sucked on his teeth.

"Curious Daniel."

"I wasn't the only one who walked up here. Two sets of footprints coming up. Two sets going down, and tire tracks where someone parked at the side of the highway."

Before Early could ask, Plemmons said, "No, nothing distinctive about any of them. You want the tour?"

He set his cup on the hood of Silver Fox's Jeep and strolled off toward the wreck, a Magnum flashlight in his hand and a canvas bag slung over his shoulder. Early brought out his own long-barreled flashlight, a handy thing should you have an unruly suspect, the state sheriffs association training manual said. He flicked on the light and cast its beam into the shadows created by him and Plemmons and Silver Fox as they walked along.

"When I was first up here," Plemmons said, "the place stank of gasoline. They really doused the car before they put a match to it."

"Gas can?"

The trooper swung the beam of his flashlight to the side and ahead some yards. "They threw it over there. Me? I'd have carried it out, got rid of it someplace else."

"Isn't it nice the bad boys aren't as smart as you?"

Plemmons grinned at that one.

"Maybe they left us some fingerprints," Early said.

"I doubt it. Have you been running around barehanded, today?"

"No."

"I don't think they were, either."

Early pointed Silver Fox toward the can, a rusty red in a field of white in the beams of three flashlights. Early then squatted down. He played his flashlight underneath the rear of the car. "Huh, the gas tank didn't blow up."

"I wouldn't expect Fat Willy keeps much gas in those cars of his," Plemmons said. "My guess is this car was about out, if not out, when they got it up here."

"All very strange."

"I'll say."

Silver Fox returned, carrying the can by a stick through the handle. "It isn't new. No name or initials scratched in or painted on. I doubt we'll find out whose it is or where it came from."

"Take it back to the office and dust it for prints."

Silver Fox started off, but turned back. He gazed down, to the side of the airport. "Headlights. What do you suppose they're doing off the road?"

Early came over. He sighted along Silver Fox's outstretched arm. "Isn't that about where Fat Willy's car lot is?"

"Are you thinking what I'm thinking?"

"One way to find out," Plemmons said, now beside them. From his shoulder bag, he pulled what appeared to be a small barrel with an eyepiece on one end and a ground-glass lens on the other. Plemmons peered into the eyepiece as he pressed a button on the side of the barrel. "My new toy, courtesy of a friend you'll never know in Uncle Sam's Army."

"What is that thing?"

"A night-vision scope. First generation and most experimental. . . . Oh yeah."

"See something?"

"Two spooks. They've got a door open on a car. Here, look." He passed the device to Early who squinted into the eyepiece.

"Unbelievable," he said.

"Imagine what we could have done if we'd had this back in the war."

"At night? Oh my."

"You could call the city police in on this, but we can get there faster."

Early thrust the scope at Plemmons and sprinted for his Jeep, with Silver Fox and Plemmons racing for the second Jeep. Early spun his vehicle around. His tires threw up a rooster tail of snow and shot the machine over the precipice, down onto the switchback trail, Early wrestling with the steering wheel to keep the Jeep in the trail's tracks.

He slurried the vehicle around one switchback, then another, and a third before he came out on the valley floor. There he rocketed his Jeep through a wash and over a double set of railroad tracks that flung him up against the canvas roof. When the Jeep slammed down on the far side of the train crossing, two sets of headlights come out of Fat Willy's lot, turning west toward Fort Riley.

Early grabbed his bubble light from beneath the passenger seat. He rammed the light into a bracket on his dash and hit the ON switch. At that moment, two cars passed through the beams of his headlights. Early whipped his Jeep up onto the highway, the rear end swinging. He dropped the transmission back to second, and the V-Eight howled as he tromped the gas pedal to the floor.

Clutch in, whang the transmission into third.

Clutch out, tromp the accelerator again, headlights and another bubble light in the rearview mirror.

The Jeep's speedometer ripped past sixty, past seventy, past eighty before Early topped the hill outside of Ogden. He shot through the three-block-long town, skirted to the far side of the highway when a car came away from a gas station. Early aimed for the open gates of Fort Riley. He blasted his horn when a sentry jumped into the road, his carbine at the ready. Early held the horn button down until the sentry bailed out of the way.

Clear of the gate, Early chewed into the distance that separated him from the taillights ahead, taillights that went up a rise and disappeared around a sweeping turn. He knew this section of the road. It meandered through low fields and came out near the one-time cavalry post's horse barns, limestone affairs each almost as long as a football field. Beyond, the road split. One fork ran up into the post's headquarters compound, the other south and west over the Kansas River and into Junction City.

Decision time.

Early bored left. He hauled his microphone down from where it swayed beneath the rearview mirror. "John."

"Go."

"I got the JC road. You cut to the post headquarters. They went one way or the other."

"Roger that."

Early pitched his mic aside as he slurred his Jeep around a bend. Beyond he saw the post's airfield–dark–and further on the silhouette of a web of girders, the bridge over the river. No headlights and no taillights. Early stomped hard on his brakes. He skidded his Jeep into a turn that sprayed gravel when he ran off onto the shoulder. He sped away in the direction from which he had come.

Early grabbed his microphone. "Big John, they aren't this way."

"Roger that, we're on the HQ road."

Early again pitched his mic away. He held his speed until he came up on the fork. There he slowed for the turn and again put his foot in the carburetor. He topped a hill several hundred yards short of the headquarters compound only to see a gaggle of revolving lights ahead. Early slowed, then stopped next to Silver Fox's empty Jeep. Two military police Jeeps rolled up behind him.

Early nodded to the two drivers as they all stepped out. "Trouble here?" he asked.

"Maniacs on wheels," said one. "We got called in as back-up. You got something to do with this?"

"Could be."

The three quick-stepped forward to where Silver Fox and Plemmons stood arguing with a half-dozen MPs, the deputy waving his hand in the direction the road ran.

"Problem?" Early asked.

Plemmons turned back. He squared up his campaign hat. "Came on a blasted roadblock. Would you believe it, these yahoos want to arrest us."

A flat-nosed sergeant stormed over, a hand on the butt of his holstered forty-five. "What the gawddamn right you civilians got trying to run down my sentry, racing like gawddamn wild men on the reservation's roads?"

Early raised both hands, as a show to the MP that they were empty. "Back it down a notch. I'm the sheriff of Riley County."

"I don't give a shit who you are."

"Now stop a minute here. We're in the pursuit of one, maybe two stolen cars."

"Makes no gawddamn nevermind. You got no authority here. You shoulda stopped at the sentry box, had my corporal call us."

"And by the time you'd have rolled your men out, they would have gotten away."

"You accusing us of dereliction?"

"I'm not accusing. I'm just a tad upset. If your men hadn't gotten in the way, my deputy might have caught the car thieves. Now they're gone, like mist on a wind."

"I'll give you this much, the sentry did say two civilian cars preceded you at a high rate of speed."

Early thrust a fist at the sky, as if to say I told you. "He get descriptions of the cars?"

"No, you got one?"

"They're dark, black or a blue. That's all I could see of them."

"Two-door? Four-door?"

"I'd be guessing."

"The drivers?"

"Men probably, and good at running flat out."

"Uh-huh. I think you and your deputy and this trooper had better follow me over to the stockade. I'm gonna let the provost sort this out come morning."

"Are you arresting us?"

"I got grounds. At least three charges and each will get you all prison time."

Early turned to Plemmons. "What do you think?"

"This pissing contest isn't getting us anywhere. You got your peacemaker?"

"Yeah."

"Time to bring it out."

Early turned back to the MP. "Sergeant—what's your name?"

"Brackman."

"Sergeant Brackman, I've got a bottle of six-year-old Scotch whiskey in my Jeep that my friend here liberated from one of your colonels too drunk to drive home. What say we drink a round to the Big Red One and freedom from the generals and the governors?"

Brackman rubbed at the side of his nose. After what seemed enough time that a train could have driven between him and Early, Brackman waved for his squad to follow him.

"Six-year-old scotch, huh?" he asked.

"That's what it says on the label," Early said, he and the gathering crowd hoofing it back through the light from his Jeep's beams. At the Jeep, he rummaged in the back until he found a padded box. Early lifted the cover and brought out a bottle and a sleeve of Dixie cups. "They hold more than shot glasses," he said as he handed the cups to Plemmons who passed them out.

Silver Fox shock his head at the offer.

Early followed Plemmons around the assemblage. He poured two fingers for each man.

Brackman held up his cup after it had been filled. "To the Big Red One, the best gawddamn division is this man's Army," he barked and threw the contents at the back of his throat.

"Smooth," he said when he came up for air. "God bless the black heart of the chicken-shit colonel you stole this from."

"Liberated," Early said.

"Whatever. Pour me another."

Plemmons held his cup next to Brackman's. "Sergeant, would you be open to a little friendly competition?"

"Drinking?"

"Maybe."

"Why?"

"Perhaps we could make this night go away."

"You mean if I was to lose this friendly little competition you're wantin' to propose."

Plemmons shrugged. "How about you pick the event, we assign the details?"

"You 'n' me?"

"No, the sheriff over there."

Brackman strode over to Early, butted belt buckles with him. "We're about the same size, huh? Whatcha good at?"

"Mumblypeg."

"Smart ass. What else?"

"I can hold my own at pinochle."

"Might as well be Old Maid." Brachman laughed and turned to his men, and they laughed with him.

"Well, I've been known to be a fair shot with a pistol," Early said.

"Pistol, huh? I tell ya I'd rather rassle you with knives, but I'll go with pistols."

Plemmons filled the two cups to the rim. "Drink up."

Brackman tossed his scotch back, but not Early. He sipped at his, wondering what the trooper might set out for details for this shooting match. Target range? Speed shooting? A gunslingers' duel at the side of the highway? Surely not that.

Plemmons pointed off in the dark. "You've got a pretty fair firing range over there."

"Right," Brackman said, "but no lights on it, so that's out."

"How about you and the sheriff shoot by the lights of your Jeeps?"

Brackman rubbed his empty Dixie cup against the side of his nose for a considerable moment, then nodded.

"While driving flat-out, in reverse," Plemmons said. "We set up a Figure-Eight course with four targets."

"Wait a minute–"

"Most hits win and speed breaks a tie."

"Yer nuts."

"Hey, the deal was you pick the challenge, and you said pistols. We pick the details, and we did. You want to forfeit?"

"Hell with you." Brackman pitched his cup away. He stormed off. At his Jeep, he took his forty-five from its holster and racked a bullet into the firing chamber.

"He's right," Early said. "You are nuts."

Plemmons stood polishing the toe of his boot against the back of his pant leg. "Thought I could bluff him."

"Bluff him, my fanny. How many targets do I have to hit?"

"One more than him to rule speed out."

"Daniel, we're gonna spend the night in the stockade."

"Come on, Cactus, you can do this."

"Do I have a choice?"

"Not now."

Early hitched up his pants. With reluctance, he swung into the driver's seat of his Jeep and watched Plemmons huddle with Silver Fox and the MPs, gesturing this way and that as he talked. When they broke, the MPs and Silver Fox ran for their Jeeps, and Plemmons walked over to Early. He waved for Brackman to join them.

"Here's the way it works," the trooper said after Brackman drove up. "There will be a flashlight tied above each target. You see the light through your back window, drive to it, swing around, shoot the target when your headlights hit it and drive on in reverse to the next one. You stop to shoot and you're out. Any questions?"

"Sheriff," Brackman said from his Jeep, "modesty forces me to tell you I'm captain the division's pistol team. We, uhmm, we took the trophy last fall at the All-Army Shootout."

Early grimaced. He leaned toward Plemmons. "Better draw me a picture so I see what I've got to do."

The trooper took his notepad from an inside pocket. He opened to a blank page, and, with a pencil, made four X's, each about a quarter-inch in from one of the corners of the page.

"Sergeant, you better look at this, too," Plemmons said. He placed his pencil's point midway between the two X's at the top. "You start here, back to the first target"–his pencil moved toward the X in the upper right corner–"swing a turn of a hundred thirty-five degrees–"

"Precisely a hundred thirty-five degrees?" Early asked.

Plemmons stared. "It can be a hundred, a hundred fifty, I don't care as long as you bring the target light around into your windshield and you don't run off into the boonies. Cactus, can I go on?"

"Sure."

"You see the light over the target, you shoot the target, then you back like Satan himself was after you to the catty-corner target"–his line scratched toward the X at the lower left of the page–"swing another hundred and thirty-five degrees, give or take, all right?"

"Fine by me," Early said. "How about you, Sergeant?"

"I'm career military. I live for precision."

Plemmons rapped on his pad. "Will you two stop this? You shoot the damn target number two and go on to number three"–his pencil line went to the X at the lower right–"make that turn again, shoot and back away for the last target."

The trooper drew a fourth line, a slash from the lower right corner of his page to the upper left, then a short slash to the starting point, completing a Figure Eight. "One shot at each target. You rapid-fire two and you're out."

"Who's the pacesetter?" Brackman asked. "Who starts this thing?"

Plemmons snapped his pencil in half. He stuck the broken ends in his fist and held his fist out to Brackman. "Longest half leads."

The sergeant reached for one. He tapped it a couple times with his trigger finger, then took hold of the other half. He pulled it out.

Plemmons opened his fist, and Brackman compared his piece of the pencil to the other and let out with a chortle.

"Jimmy, I'm sorry," Plemmons said.

"Well, I never liked going first anyway. Get in." Early gestured to his passenger seat. After the trooper settled himself, Early waved for Brackman to drive on to the shooting range. For himself, he followed at a casual pace.

Brackman, after he reached the starting place, wheeled his Jeep around until his taillights faced the first target. Early did the same and stopped next to the Military Police command Jeep.

Plemmons got out. "Lower your windshields, gentlemen. I don't want either of you shooting out the glass."

Early hunched forward. He undid the toggles at the top of his Jeep's windshield and pushed the hinged glass forward until it laid flat against a locking mount on the hood. Early turned that toggle and snapped it down.

Brackman, too, locked his windshield down. "We get a practice run?"

"'Fraid not, Sergeant. You drive the Figure Eight once and once only. Are you ready?"

Brackman shifted his Jeep's transmission into reverse. He hooked his right elbow over the back of his seat and locked his gaze on the first target. "Ready."

Plemmons held his watch in the light from Early's headlamps. As he did, Brackman spit to the side. "What are we waitin' for?"

"For the second hand to get to twelve. . . . Five seconds, four, three, two, one, GO."

Brackman's Jeep lurched away.

Early jacked a bullet into the chamber of his forty-five. He laid the pistol on the passenger seat.

One shot and Early heard Brackman's military four-cylinder engine wind up. He ignored it. He took a roll of black tape from the glove box, ripped off a strip, and tacked it over the light at the top of his speedometer, the light that not only showed speed but lent a faint illumination to the Jeep's interior.

"Dark in there," Plemmons said from where he leaned against a front fender of Early's Jeep. He talked to the open windshield.

Early pitched the roll back into the glove box. "I like it that way. No distractions."

A second shot, far fainter than the first because of the distance.

"Think he hit it?" Plemmons asked.

"If he's as good as he says, I expect he did."

"You going to hit it?"

"I hope–if I don't wreck my steering hand on the turns."

A third shot and the whine of the four-cylinder became louder as Brackman's Jeep raced backwards across the field as wide as a football gridiron is long, toward the last target.

"You got that big V-Eight, Cactus. You can outrun him."

"Into pep talks now, huh?"

"Nope."

"Well, if I miss the targets, speed's no advantage."

"So you're going to take your time."

"Daniel, are you trying to talk me to death?"

A fourth shot. A moment passed and Brackman's Jeep rolled up beside Early's, the MP sergeant grinning in the tepid glow from his speedometer. "I'd say that ride was worth a scotch."

"Not until the sheriff has his try," Plemmons said.

"My time?"

"Fifty-three seconds." The trooper stepped away from the Jeeps. He called out through his hands cupped around his mouth, "Sing out!"

"A miss!" came back a voice from somewhere near the first target.

"Hit!" from near the second.

"Hit!"

"Hit!"

Plemmons walked around to the front of the Jeeps. He held up three fingers. "Sergeant?"

"Not bad. Want to get on over to the stockade now for the late-night snack or a minute from now?"

"That's up to the sheriff, wouldn't you say?"

The MP peered at Early. "Want to forfeit?"

"It's tempting." Early flexed his fingers before he gripped the top of the steering wheel. With his other hand, he worked the shifter into reverse. That done, Early picked up his pistol and twisted around until he saw clearly the first light out his back window.

"Ready?" Plemmons asked.

"Let's do this thing."

The trooper brought his watch into the light. "Eight seconds . . . five seconds . . . three, two, one . . ."

On GO, Early released the clutch pedal. He floored the accelerator, and his Jeep raced away, jolting across the uneven ground. As he neared the light, he spun the steering wheel with the palm of his hand, whipping the Jeep into a turn–foot off the gas. The light flashed by the side of the Jeep to the front, Early's gaze following it. He spun the wheel back. A spoke caught his fingers and his face twisted at the pain, yet he ripped off the first shot. The smell of cordite filled the interior of the Jeep as Early sped away.

Mid-field the vehicle slammed through something, a groundhog's hole? Early lost his grip on the wheel, and the Jeep veered off course. He got hold of the wheel again, over-corrected, and the Jeep shot too far to the other side. Early slowed. He straightened up and once more floored the accelerator, the whole business eating up time.

The second light flashed up, dead-on in the rear window. Early again threw the Jeep into a turn. He fired off the second shot when the light came around front. Early glanced over his shoulder for the third light, got it, and steered toward it, turned sharp, watched the light come around to dead over the radiator. Early aimed. In the instant he pulled the trigger, the Jeep bucked over something.

Shot go wild?

He twisted around. Early sighted on the final light and stepped down on the accelerator. He whipped wide around the middle of the field while he held the gas pedal to the floor, the transmission screaming, the light growing in the rear window. He spun the steering wheel, banged off the final shot and, foot off the accelerator, rolled up beside Brackman's Jeep.

Early clamped his injured steering hand under his arm before he forced himself out.

Plemmons hustled over. "You all right?"

"Caught my frickin' fingers in the wheel."

"Man, you were all over that field."

"Don't I know it. Did I hit anything other than chuckholes?"

Plemmons stepped toward the firing range. He called out, "Any hits?"

"Number one," came back a voice.

"Number two."

"Miss on three."

"Hit on four."

Early didn't like it. He shook his head. "Tie," he muttered. "What was my time?"

"Tie there, too. What happened to your third shot?"

"Banged into something. Gimme your light."

Plemmons handed over his black Magnum, and Early turned to his Jeep. He played the beam over the hood shimmering with heat. He halted the light when it crossed a hole just forward of where his windshield laid toggled down.

Brackman stood across from Early. "Shoot your beast?"

"Appears so."

"Tied on hits, tied on time," Plemmons said.

"I heard." The MP hooked his thumbs in his belt. "You didn't win, so it's the stockade for you all."

"No, you don't. You didn't win either." Plemmons came over to Brackman. He put an arm around the sergeant's shoulders and pointed off. "Those two flashlights out there, what are they, a hundred, a hundred-ten yards out? A shoot-off to break the tie, and the sheriff gets the first shot."

"If he misses?"

"We'll agree it's the stockade, unless, of course, you miss. Then it's game over and we all go home."

Brackman rubbed at the side of his nose. "Guess I can go with that." He stepped toward the field and, in a bullhorn voice, called out, "Boys? Get away from the targets. Get yerselves the hell behind a berm. We're gonna shoot the lights out."

He came back to Early. "What say we make this interesting, put a ten-spot on it?"

"The night's already been more interesting than I like."

"All right, your shot then."

Early reached inside his Jeep. He brought out his forty-five, stood tall, peered along his arm and over the gun sight at a dot of light that barely filled the notch. He squeezed the trigger. The resulting bark and recoil brought the pistol up in the same instant the light winked out.

Brackman drew a hand down his face. "Gotta tell ya, sheriff, that's one damn fine shot. But if I get my light, you still lose."

He caressed the steel of his weapon as if it were a lover. Brackman brought the gun up. He sighted in and squeezed the trigger.

The hammer clicked.

Brackman squeezed the trigger again.

Again the hammer clicked.

"Got a jam?" Early asked.

"Been known to gawddamn happen."

"Well, while you field strip your pistol, I'm for ending this thing." Early turned toward the second light. He squeezed off a shot, and, as his gun and hand came up, the light winked out.

Plemmons punched Brackman's arm. "Sergeant, he whupped your butt, didn't he?"

CHAPTER 9

December 18–Monday morning
Gamblers all

Early, elbows on the red-and-white checked tablecloth of the Brass Nickel, the diner in Manhattan he favored, finger-combed his mustache while he gazed at the man across from him, the man stirring a stream of sugar into his coffee. "You making syrup there?"

"This?" Wilferd Randall set the sugar jar aside, next to an ashtray where a Meerschaum pipe laid, a wisp of cherry-scented smoke wavering up from it. "Never can have too much of a good thing, I say."

"How can you drink that?"

"How can you drink yours without sugar?"

"Because I like it."

"Same for me." He sipped at his sweet brew. "Nectar of the gods. I hear the county's gone ripe with crime while I've been away."

Early took a swallow of his own coffee. He grimaced and brought the cup down so hard the silverware rattled.

"Problem?" Randall asked.

"Tastes like wheat paste."

A food-laden waitress, a brunette cracking her chewing gum, came hurrying up to the table. "I heard that," she said as she slid a plate of eggs and sausage in front of Early. "It's a new brand and, yes, it's got wheat in it. The Wheat Commission's backing it."

"Good Lord."

"Don't you ever get tired of complaining?" She set a plate of pancakes and bacon down for Randall.

Early gestured at him. "You know this man?"

"Surely do." She patted Randall on his bald spot. "He knows how to leave a respectable tip. A half-dollar, sometimes a whole dollar, not like your yuny-puny dime."

"Aren't you supposed to be in class up at the college?"

"It's Monday. Late classes today."

"Oh, lucky me." Early handed his cup to the waitress. "Tell Nelly this isn't gonna go. Bring me a buttermilk."

"Anything for you, sweetpea," she said and whisked away.

Randall slathered butter over each pancake in his stack. "I think she likes you."

"You really tip her a dollar?"

He flicked a speck of tobacco ash from his houndstooth vest. "Hey, I sell Meerschaums like mine, bent billiards, Kaywoodies, you name it, the best smoking pipes to the top retailers from Kansas City to Denver. Jimmy, I make a pile of money and I share it. Shared some with you, as I recall."

"I should repay you."

"No, you've got a baby girl now." The pipe peddler winked as he reached for the syrup pitcher. "Baby girls get real costly. I know, my Beth and me, we raised six of them."

"And every one the best."

"It is nice of you to say that. I stopped at the Mercantile in Clay Center, Friday," Randall said as he cut a bite of pancake and forked it into his mouth. "The murders up at May Day, it's the big talk there."

Early prodded at the food on his plate.

"Everybody's got their ideas who did it," Randall said, "and you know what that means? Nobody knows. It was pretty bad, I'm told."

"About the worst I've seen."

"The gunner, do you have an idea who?"

"Yup." Early shoveled a forkful of eggs into his mouth. He said no more as he chewed.

"You're not going to tell me, are you?" Randall said.

A bell jingled over the door. Early's night deputy strode in, head swivelling, as if he were looking for someone. When he spotted Early, he came over. "Chief," John Silver Fox said, "the judge sent me to find you, says you're late for a meeting."

"Oh Lord." Early glanced at the Coca Cola clock across the way, above the cash register. A sign pasted beneath the clock read IN GOD WE TRUST, ALL OTHERS PAY CASH. He pushed back from the table. "Wilferd, I'm sorry."

"Don't worry about it. We'll get to talk another time."

"Be in town long?"

"No, I'm driving up to Omaha, then Lincoln and work my way southwest to the big O-Kay City. I should be back home for Christmas."

"You drive safe then, huh?"

"Always do."

Early tiled his head toward the cash register. "I'll pay for the both of us."

"Won't hear of it. It's my turn."

"Wilferd, you always buy."

"And that's the way I want it."

Nels Arneson, the cafe's short-order cook and owner–built like a wrestler and wearing a grease-stained apron and a square hat made from a newspaper page–barged between Early and Randall. He glared at Early. "Sue tells me you don't like my coffee."

"It's not your best, Nelly."

"Made with Kansas wheat to cut the bitterness."

"Well, bitterness is what makes coffee coffee. What Sue poured, that was wallpaper paste with licorice for color."

"What you got against your home state's product?"

"Nothing. I just want coffee in my coffee."

Arneson shoved a glass into Early's hand. "Your gawddamn buttermilk, and may you choke on it."

Early watched him storm back to the kitchen. "I guess I'll take this with me," he said as he gathered up his cattleman's hat from where it resided on a chair at the side of the table. He and John Silver Fox walked out.

"Shouldn't you be home?" Early asked after they were on the sidewalk, hustling for Poyntz Avenue that would take them another block to the courthouse.

"Chief, there's always paperwork at the end of the shift. I was on my way out when the judge caught me."

"I suppose he's upset."

"Actually, no."

"Odd." Early finished his buttermilk without slowing his pace. He stuffed the empty glass into the side pocket of his winter jacket.

"He asked me where we were on the murders."

"And you said?"

"That he'd have to talk to you. As nasty as this was, you'd put a lid on it."

"I did not."

"I know, but I wasn't about to risk saying something I shouldn't."

They made the corner and walked on, the morning sun warm at their backs, turning the snow on the sidewalk to slush. Half-way along the block a grocery truck, coming up the street from behind the two lawmen, hammered through a pothole, showering Early with a great splatter of muck.

"For cripes sake, would you look at this," Early said, a sour expression taking up residence on his face. He raked the worst of the mud and water off, all the while muttering how blind drivers were a threat to mankind. Someone stepped out of the front of Kestler's Five-and-Dime. The man banged off a photo. Early jerked up when the flash went off.

"Sheriff," Red Vullmer said, "this is gonna be a fine Page One picture."

"I thought you were doing radio."

"The Mercury owns the station, so I do everything. We've been after the city to fix that street, and this'll get it done–'prominent county official splashed by city negligence.'"

"Gimme that camera. I don't want any part of this."

"Not a chance."

"Red–"

Vullmer spun away. He ran, his coat flapping behind him.

Silver Fox held out a bandana to Early. "The side of your face."

"I felt it. How come you didn't get showered?"

"Just lucky."

Early took the bandana. He mopped at the mess dripping down into his collar, burning at the thought of how Vullmer would twist the story on his noontime broadcast.

"Look at the bright side," Silver Fox said.

"Darned if I see one."

"A front page picture. Chief, that's free publicity and you're up for election in the spring."

"He's gonna make me look the fool."

"Do you want me to talk to him?"

"Talk, no. But if you happen to be near him and your gun goes off–"

*

Early dragged a hard chair over to where Judge Hanover Crooke and county attorney Carl Wieland sat visiting on a horsehair couch.

"Sorry to be late. I was over at breakfast and–" Early sucked in a breath "–well, let's say it's just not been my best morning."

Crooke motioned at Early's hair, and Early's hand went up to above his ear. He brushed and his fingertips felt wet. Early rubbed. He turned his fingers to where he could see them.

Muck and grit.

Early pulled out Silver Fox's filthy bandana and wiped his fingers. "This is what I get for trying to wash my own hair. What's the meeting about?"

"The court docket," Crooke said. "Three cases Carl wants to put on Wednesday. Can you have your deputies there?"

"Which cases?"

Wieland, at ease without his suit coat, red suspenders prominent, opened a file with his lone hand. "That high school kid, Robby Walker, on a traffic case. Got an assault from out at Leonardville–Mort Billdag. And our county drunk, Kendall Martin."

"Woozer? You're not going to prosecute him, are you?"

Wieland scratched at his empty sleeve. "How many times have your deputies arrested him?"

"Ten, maybe eleven in the past couple years. We don't usually write it up."

"Twelve times, Cactus. Worse than being a drunk, the other day Martin dropped his pants in front of my wife."

Early covered his face with his hand.

"He's a nuisance and a hazard," Wieland went on.

Early pulled his hand down. "I'll grant you Wooze is a nuisance, but a hazard? Judge, help me out, here."

"Carl says we're getting laughed at because we don't do anything about him."

"You want to lock him up?"

"Look, go talk to him. Tell him he's had his last free pass. He quits the sauce or it's jail and for a hell of a lot longer than overnight. And he keeps his galluses over his shoulders."

Early stared at the toes of his boots.

"Jimmy, he's your friend. Fix it."

Muck there, too. Early brought out the dirty bandana and scrubbed it away.

Crooke scratched at his Abe Lincoln beard. "Where are you on the May Day murders? I couldn't get anything out of that damn Indian of yours."

Early brought his head up. He peered sideward at Crooke. "That damn Indian is a fine deputy. If you want us at your side, Judge, you treat John with respect in what you do and what you say."

"Do I hear a threat?"

"No sir, consider it a just a bit of advice from one friend to another."

"So noted. So where are you on the murders?"

Early leaned back. The joints of his chair squeaked. "As it stands now, the number one suspect—or there could be a couple for all we know—is one or more unknown gamblers from Kansas City. It appears Al played away his ranch."

"Killed for a debt?"

"Could be."

"You don't really believe that."

"Doesn't make any difference what I believe. I've got to check it out."

"And how are you going to do that?"

"Go to Kansas City, I guess."

Crooke tugged at his beard. "Maybe I can help you there."

"How's that?"

"I could get you in with some people."

Early glanced at Wieland, and Wieland shrugged.

"I play stud poker in the big city once a month, high-stakes," Crooke said. "Mister Garret sat in on our game a few times."

"Judge, I've considered you only a fair hand at cards."

"I'll have you know I paid my way through law school at the poker table. The Kansas City players are far better than law students. With them, I come away about even, but I have a good time."

"And Al?"

"As I recall, he played conservatively. He lost maybe a hundred dollars." Crooke pushed up from the couch and went to his desk. He scribbled on the back of a bench warrant. When he finished, he came back and handed the note to Early. "This man will get you in the game. I'll call him and vouch for you."

"You're not going to tell him I'm a sheriff, are you?"

"Oh-no-no-no-no. I'll tell him you're a rancher. That's not stretching the truth by much."

"Why don't you stretch it a bit more? Put me out-of-state."

"Where do you want to be from?"

"I've always liked Oklahoma, the Claremore area–Will Rogers country. And go with my middle name. Make me James McBride. I can call down and get a driver's license."

"How quick?"

"Friday I expect."

"So a Saturday night game, then, huh?"

CHAPTER 10

December 18–Friday
Securing a stake

Early abandoned his Jeep in the Big Blue River Valley, at the side of the county road not far from where his wife had died in the autumn. The precise spot he avoided. So much had changed and not just the season and the temperature.

He pulled his sheepskin jacket's wooly collar up around his ears as he plunged off into the brush, the sumac barren of their fiery leaves of fall. He moved on, tramping through the snow, his eyes searching, and then he saw it–a thin curl of smoke rising from somewhere in a wild thicket near the tracks of the Kansas & Nebraska Railroad and the river beyond.

A rich baritone voice came drifting from that direction, crooning *Drink to me only with thine eyes / And I will pledge with mine. / Or leave a kiss within the cup / And I'll not ask for wine.*

Early pushed on and out into an opening–a camp–where a hobo continued his ballad, waving a bean can to the rhythm as he sang to another hobo, the second sitting on a stump, his back to Early . . .

The thirst that from the soul doth rise / Doth ask a drink divine; / But might I of Jove's nectar sip, / I would not change . . .

The singer cocked his head in mid-lyric, as if he'd heard something. He swivelled to the side, saw Early, and winked at him, flashed a lugubrious smile that showed a gap where a canine tooth should have been.

"Like it, Jimmy?" he asked.

"Wooze, you drunk again?"

"Just sampling the most delicious of wines." He raised his bean can. "A toast to thee, ol' frien'. You know this 'un?"

The other hobo glanced over her shoulder—a Potawatomi woman, her graying hair in heavy braids pulled back under a railroad cap, a none-too-clean blanket keeping her warm.

"Gertie," Early said in greeting.

Woozer Martin swilled down the contents of his bean can, then plunked himself on a log. He patted the bark beside him. "Come, sit."

Early hunkered down, and Martin nudged him, waving his can at a pan on a trivet over the fire. "Join us in our noontime repast? Mighty fine crappies Gertie's frying up. An' I did my part—caught the little shavers an' filleted 'em."

Early leaned forward. He inspected the meal. "Does smell good."

"Taters there, and, if you don't like my wine, got horseshoe coffee."

Gertie Thompson rustled in a pack by her feet. She brought out a trio of tin plates and spooned a cornmeal-crisped fish onto the top plate, then a modest pile of fried potatoes, all still sizzling. She held the plate out to Early.

He took it, and Martin handed him a fork and knife but only after he polished them on his trouser leg.

Thompson filled another plate. She gave that to Martin, then filled one for herself.

Martin broke a piece of johnny cake out of another fry pan. He plopped the johnny cake on top of Early's fish. "We eat like kings and queens out here, don't we, Gertie?" he said as he splashed Muscatel from a jug into his can.

She said nothing, just poured scalding coffee into two bean cans. She motioned for Early to take one.

Martin stuffed his mouth with fish, bits dribbling out as he talked. "How'd you know we was here?"

"The boys on the railroad keep an eye on this camp when they go by." Early took a bite from his johnny cake. He brushed crumbs from his mustache. "I want to know who's around, I just ask them."

"Yup, that Luke Blackwell and Oscar Miller, they are good fellas. Gertie and me, we want to hop a ride, they look the other way an' drive that train on."

"You ought to be home, Woozer."

The hobo scratched at the underside of his thigh. "I just like to ramble sometimes."

"Wooze, I got to ask you a favor."

"You didn't tell me if you liked my singing."

"You surprised me. I didn't know you knew anything other than maybe the Beer Barrel Polka."

"No, I go for the ballads, songs from the operettas, Merry Widow, things like that. 'Drink to me only with thine eyes,' didja know that started out as a poem?"

"No."

"Sixteen-and-Sixteen, written by old Ben Johnson, friend of William Shakespeare. Sir Walter Scott, you know him? History books say he used to sing that poem to a tune I don't know what of."

"How do you know this stuff, Wooze?"

Thompson glanced up from her plate. "Sometimes when he's sober, he goes over to the college, sits in the back of an English class or a music class. He's white, he can do that. Me–" She didn't finish the sentence. After a moment, she shook her head and returned to her fried potatoes.

Early put a hand on Martin's knee. "You think you could quit drinking?"

"You worried 'bout me?"

"I'm worried the judge will give you hard jail time if you don't."

"Wouldn't be so bad in the winter, Jimmy. Now jail for the summer or fall I wouldn't want it."

From his can Early sucked in a mouthful of coffee. He choked it down and blew out his cheeks, his lips puckering.

"Good, huh?" Martin asked.

Early mopped at tears forming in his eyes. "Lordy, that's horseshoe coffee, all right. You could float two horseshoes on it, eat the rust off them."

"Gertie likes it that way."

"Wooze, if you won't quit drinking, would you promise me you'll at least stay out of Manhattan? Good Lord, man, you dropped your britches in front of the county attorney's wife."

"Iszat who it was?"

"What were you thinking?"

"I wasn't. I was dancin', an' I just wanted some fresh air around my hinder parts while I was doing it."

Thompson beckoned Early to lean in. "Suppose I put him on a short string."

"Gert, he's got to go home sometime. He's a married man."

"Not much of that marriage left. Martin's like me, a harmless old shit."

"Gert, you ought to go home, too. Your daughter's worried."

"How would you know that?"

"She called me."

"Next time you talk to her, tell her she don't need to fret."

"She thinks you're a bit whacked in the brain, wandering off."

"Aren't we all?" Thompson filled her mouth with potatoes and chewed. "Last couple years, it got hard to stay with my husband, you know that? I took to sleeping on the porch. Then when he died, there was no reason to stay."

"You can't stay here."

"Why not? I'm good at living off the land. And I got a little money, so if I need some fixin's, I can hike to a store."

"And when your money runs out?"

She held up a long-stemmed key. "I can go back home, or get me a job."

"Doing what?"

"I'm a good hand at herding cattle. I've heard that the ranchers out west in the mountains, they send someone with their cows up to summer pasture, and you're there all alone for months. Live out of a chuckwagon, sleep on the ground. I'd like that."

Martin sopped at the grease on his plate with his johnny cake. "That's not half bad, Jimmy. I might go along if Gert would have me."

"You two are a pair."

"Yup, that we are. I sing an' Gertie cooks."

"How long you figure you can hold out here once real winter blows in?"

Martin scratched at his shoulder.

Thompson again leaned in. "If it gets bad enough, we might trek in to see you. You'd let us sleep in the jail, wouldn't you?"

*

Early settled himself behind the steering wheel of his Jeep. He snugged the canvas and plexiglass door closed and, after he fired up the engine, turned on his police radio.

"Alice, you there?" he said into his microphone.

"Go ahead, sheriff."

"Call Gertie Thompson's daughter over by Riley, would you? Tell her I talked to her ma, and she's all right."

"Gertie going home?"

"No."

"Ruth's going to want to know where she is."

"Tell her it's enough that I know."

"She won't like that."

"Tough beans."

"Anything else?"

"I'm on my way up to Randolph, to see Rance Dalby at the Jayhawk. You need to reach me, call me at the bank."

"Fat Willy came by."

"What'd he want?"

"To know what you're doing to find his stolen car."

"Tell him we're checking all the fires."

"There haven't been any fires for a week."

"Isn't that wonderful? Early out."

He hung his microphone over the mirror and drove on. Where the county road crossed State One Seventy-Seven, Early turned north, the sun still high in its arc across the sky, pale though, veiled by a vaporous layer of clouds. The road, dirt in the summer and snow-packed in the winter–when there was winter–ambled along, paralleling the K&N tracks. A steam whistle whooped, and a Baldwin I-One-S "hippo" trundled Early's way, the early afternoon freight coming down from Maryville.

He waved as the locomotive and its string of cars rumbled by, a whoop of the whistle responding to his wave.

Ahead laid Randolph, once a business hub for the ranchers and farmers in the area. But the advent of the automobile and pickup trucks and better roads crippled the town, leaving it with a grain elevator, a bank, a grocery, a sometimes-used depot and little else. Early motored in.

He stopped across the street from a two-story wooden building, the paint peeling. Gold lettering in a top window read Knights of Pythius, in the plate-glass window at street level, Jayhawk State Bank.

The door squalled as Early pushed it open. "You listen to the radio on Saturday nights, Mavis?" he asked the teller at her cage. "Think this is where they got that sound effect for 'The Inner Sanctum.'"

Mavis Anderson, built to hold her own with any unruly customer, gave a jowly grin and waved toward the back where the president of the bank, Rance Dalby, sat at a rolltop desk, hunched over a stack of monthly statements. Early moved on back. When Dalby failed to notice him, Early leaned down. "One of those mine?" he asked.

"Just so happens," the banker said as he prodded through the pile. He pulled out a page and gave it to Early. Dalby pointed to the balance at the bottom. "Pretty thin there, Cactus."

"Yup, well, losing a wife and getting a baby girl sure crimps the budget."

"I'm sorry about Thelma."

"Yeah, I appreciate that."

"She made you look good."

"That she did." Early touched at a tear at the corner of his eye.

With his boot, Dalby hooked a hard chair. He pulled it up, and Early settled himself.

"While your accounts are thin," the banker said, returning to business, "you appear to be making it."

"That's what I need to talk to you about."

"Glory, I think I'm about to die and go to banker's heaven. You're going to hit me up for a loan, aren't you?" Dalby opened the bottom side drawer of his desk. He leaned back, put his feet on the drawer, and shoved his spectacles up onto the top of his head. "They turned you down at the big bank in Manhattan, didn't they?"

Early rubbed at his mustache.

"Well, piss on them." The banker tapped a stubby finger on the arm of his oak swivel chair. "You need help, you come to your friends."

"I didn't want to impose."

"Hey, loaning money is how I make my money. How much you need?"

"Well, how much am I good for?"

"Cactus, you answer my question first. How much do you need?"

"Ten thousand dollars for the weekend."

Dalby gagged. After he hacked his throat clear, he waggled a finger. "James Early, what the hell's a-foot here?"

"I'm investigating the murder of the Garrets."

The banker sucked in a breath through clenched teeth. "That was tragic, right tragic, but what's that got to do with needing ten thousand dollars?"

Early finger-combed his mustache. "Well, it's this way. I need some show cash so I can get in a poker game."

"Not the hell with my money."

"Look, Al was a gambler."

"Cactus–"

"He lost his ranch and maybe a whole lot more to a bunch in Kansas City."

"–like I said, tell me something I don't know."

Early stopped. He peered at the banker.

"Al came to me like you're coming to me," Dalby said, "for a loan, to get himself out of trouble, he said, but he didn't have anything to put up."

"When were you going to tell me this?"

"Whenever you got around to asking. So you think the gamblers did Al and his family in?"

"I've gotta find out."

"And getting in a poker game will do that?"

"It opens doors."

Dalby stared over Early's shoulder for the longest time, as if he were studying the jagged crack in the plaster of his bank's front wall. "If I were to loan you the flash–and I'm saying if–are you good enough at poker that I'm going to get it back?"

"I'm fair."

"No-no-no, you'll have to be better than fair. If you lose my money, you're going to be paying me back out of your county wage for seven, maybe eight years. You can live with that?"

"No. But I still need the money."

Dalby worried an ear lobe. He came up straight in his chair and hollered to his teller, "Mavis?"

She looked up from balancing the cash in her drawer.

"Get in the vault and count me out ten thousand dollars for the high sheriff of Riley County."

"And why would I want to do that?"

"Because I'm making him a loan. The why you don't need to know."

She gave her employer the hairy eyeball, but left her cage and went to the vault.

"Cactus," Dalby said, waving a hand in the direction of his teller, "you didn't see the look Mavis gave me, did you?"

"No."

"She doesn't like this, but Al was a friend of mine, so I'm gonna loan you the wad. Still and all, I've got a black feeling I'm going to regret this."

CHAPTER 11

December 19–Saturday
Taking flight

Early sat in the airport waiting room, reading yesterday's edition of the Kansas City Star. The headline at the top of the front page blared out TYPHOON STRIKES KOREAN FISHING FLEET, THOUSANDS DEAD. He ignored that story and instead turned inside and focused on a small item below the fold on page three. That headline read: GERMAN CAR A FAILURE.

"Would you believe it," he said to the man next to him, an Army captain in uniform, Albert Tyler on the officer's nameplate. "The Krauts want to sell cars here–Volkswagens, this story says. Hah, and only two people bought them. The head man says he now thinks his car company hasn't got a future in our country. I'm for that."

Early leaned to the side and held out the paper to the captain. "See the picture here?"

Tyler adjusted his steel-rimmed glasses. He pushed them up on the bridge of his nose. "Gad, that's one ugly thing, isn't it? Looks like a bug on wheels."

The airport agent, Pratt Eldridge–an officious little man, his hair parted in the middle and slicked back–hustled up. He handed a ticket to Early.

"This is as phony as a six-dollar bill," Eldridge said, "but it shows you boarded Flight Nine in Tulsa–Tulsa-Joplin-Kansas City Downtown. Anybody goes to checking, this isn't recorded anywhere."

The agent tugged at the front of his suit coat. Early wondered if it was an effort to look innocent, but still Eldridge's nervousness showed in the form of a tic beneath his right eye.

"Then I better make sure nobody checks," Early said as he pocketed the ticket.

The agent handed him a second. "For your deputy and just as phony as yours. Are you going to tell me what this is about?"

"No."

"I suppose I shouldn't be surprised. You're sure dressed up."

"Yup."

"You're just not going to tell me anything, are you?"

"Nope."

"Well, then," Eldridge said, handing on two more tickets, "these are the real ones, Manhattan-Topeka-Kansas City Downtown. I left the return open, and I've billed both to the county like you asked. You sure they're going to pay for these tickets? They're train people, you know. None of the county officers have ever flown that I know of."

"Pratt, if the commission turns the bill down, I'll dummy up an expense for the jail and get your money that way. How's that?"

Eldridge again tugged at the front of his suit coat.

"Hope the flight is on time," Early said, making conversation.

The airport agent visibly relaxed. He took a teletype sheet from his side pocket and read it to Early. "Clear and cold to the west. Flight Five departed Salina at Fourteen-Twenty-Two local time."

"And that means what?"

The agent consulted his wristwatch. "Your flight should be here in nine minutes."

"Friendly Neighbor says there's snow to the east of us."

"More than that," Eldridge said. He again read from his teletype. "Embedded thunderstorms between Topeka and Kansas City, extend south to Oklahoma City, north to Des Moines. Sheriff, you bring a change of underwear?"

"Why?"

"You could be in for an exciting flight."

That pained Early and the Army captain beside him.

"You'll excuse me," the agent said, "I've got to get the baggage out to the ramp."

With that, he gave a brisk nod and hurried away.

"I'm going to Illinois–Springfield," Tyler said. "Sure hope I don't have bad weather all the way."

A man in a brown double-breasted suit with a vest came into the waiting room from the outside front door. He carried a camel-hair coat over his suitcase and wore a ten-gallon hat with an eagle feather sticking from the band. He came up to Early and the captain and put his suitcase on a chair opposite them. "Chief," he said to Early.

Early rose. He inspected his deputy. "Big John, you've outdone yourself. But that hat."

"What about it?"

"It makes you look like a Navajo with money, not a Cherokee with money."

"Cripes."

"Well, we'll get you a fedora in Kansas City." He turned to the Army officer. "John, this is Captain Tyler. He's on his way home to Illinois. Captain, this is–"

"–John Silver Fox," Tyler said, rising with his hand out.

Silver Fox, grinning, pulled the officer in for a rough embrace.

"I gather you know each other?"

"Chief, we were in boot camp together, same platoon. We both became MP's. At the end of a year, they tapped Albert for OCS. Last thing I saw of him, he was boarding a train for Fort Sill."

"Sheriff," Tyler said after he extricated himself from Silver Fox's hug, "I was the runt at Fort Leonard Wood. More than once John saved my hide. You're darn lucky to have him."

"You married now?" Silver Fox asked Tyler.

"Two kids and a third any day."

"Good for you."

"Yes. Well, they're all with my wife's parents in Springfield. I'm trying to get there before the third is born. You?"

"Still rolling around alone."

"John, your time will come."

"That's what my mother tells me when I go home to the rez."

A voice, that of the airport agent, came over the loud speaker. "Attention, attention. Frontier Flight Number Five from Denver, Goodland and Salina now landing. It will continue on to Topeka and Kansas City. Everyone boarding, please wait for those coming off the airplane to get their bags before you go outside."

Early glanced around the vacant waiting room. "We're everyone?"

Eldridge, in a parka, earmuffs, and fleece-lined gloves, gave him a thumbs-up as he grabbed Silver Fox's suitcase and went out. He stopped next to a baggage cart on the ramp and waited while a silver DC-Three motored in, its tail settled back on a small trailing wheel and its nose in the air like some proud creature. The airliner stopped after it paralleled the waiting room. The engine closest went silent, its propeller windmilling.

The door near the tail of the airplane opened out and swung down. It revealed five steps built into the door. A massive bear came out onto the first step, a woman in a fur coat and hat. The airport agent reached for her and helped her down the stairs. A second woman, in a plainer cloth coat and scarf, followed. Out came a suitcase and then another. Each woman took one and hurried toward the waiting room while Eldridge tossed three suitcases from his cart up through the plane's open door. He turned and waved for Early, Silver Fox, and the captain to come on the run. He pushed the captain up the steps, then Early and finally Silver Fox in his ten-gallon hat. The top of the door frame raked it off when the deputy ducked inside. Silver Fox scrambled after his hat, caught it, and went on in.

A stewardess pulled the door up. She slammed and locked it as the propeller on the silent engine spun up. The big radial engine fired. It belched out a cloud of exhaust, and shook on its mounts as it came up to idle. A burst of power to the engines and the DC-Three taxied away with Early, halfway up the aisle, sliding into a seat. He fiddled with the ends of the lap belt but couldn't make them latch. The stewardess came by, a trim young woman whose smile said all was right in the world of airline travel. She saw Early's growing frustration and snapped the belt ends together for him, her smile never wrinkling.

She's gotta think I'm some kind of idiot, Early thought, and that thought repeated itself as she moved away. Silver Fox, grinning like a raccoon in a field of sweet corn, punched him. The deputy pointed to the window as the engine noise shot up to the roar of full power, the power pushing Early back into his seat. He managed a glance out the window and saw the ground fall away. His stomach lurched, and he grabbed his seat's armrests so tight his knuckles went white.

Silver Fox bellowed over the engines, "First time?"

"Maybe my last."

"Aw, you're going to like it."

"What makes you the authority?"

"My grandfather's spirit, it's with me." He laughed as he slapped at Early's shoulder. "Besides, I tossed back a whiskey before I got out of my Jeep."

"First time in an airplane, too, huh?"

"First time."

"Aren't we the pair?"

Silver Fox turned away, to Tyler in the next seat.

Early settled in. To work off the tension, he set about rubbing his hands on his trousers, and he gazed around. A fabric interior, something of the color of desert sand. He hadn't known what to expect, the aluminum skin and ribbing, maybe. Cushy seats, the seatbacks covered in a white sacking, as if the seatbacks were oversized pillows. A small light over each window and curtains that could be drawn. Two seats on one side of the aisle, one on the other. How many people? Early leaned out into the aisle and counted the rows–ten. Thirty people if every seat was occupied. He guessed only a dozen were.

He smelled cigarette smoke. Someone forward was smoking a Lucky Strike or was it a Pall Mall? And he heard snatches of conversations as the engines throttled back to a quieter cruise power.

Early peered out his window again. He wondered whether he might see some landmarks he knew–the rolling Flint Hills, those were a certainty. He could see the underlying rock structure poking out through the sides of the some of the hills, where the soil had eroded away and no snow clung. Something to the south, was that Council Grove? That's where it should be, but–well, Early couldn't be sure. Wamego? No, that should be on the other side of the airplane. The Kaw River though–there it was below, snaking from side to side. It disappeared beneath the plane and reappeared moments later, as the river meandered to the east, the water looking a sickly gray against the white of the snow on the flatlands that bordered it.

Cattle clustered around a hay stack in a field south of the river. Early couldn't resist counting the red-and-white cows–a dozen, fifteen, eighteen. And they disappeared.

Vanished.

Everything beyond the window glass utterly and absolutely gone, lost in a driving white. Early twisted toward Silver Fox across the aisle, deep in conversation with the Army captain. He didn't want to interrupt, so he looked to the stewardess coming from the forward area. Early was about to point out his window when the airliner banged upward. As instantly, it dropped, and all in the airliner that wasn't fastened down–magazines, business papers, and coffee cups–took flight.

Early's eyes bulged. He saw the stewardess ahead, her hair disheveled, clinging to a seatback, holding on like one would hold onto a wild horse. And he heard bells–three bells, a ding-ding-ding.

"Fasten your seatbelts. Fasten your seatbelts," the stewardess called over a racket that sounded like bolts being poured from one bucket to another

Silver Fox and Tyler scrabbled for their seatbelts, but not Early. He'd never unhooked.

A wing shot upward. It tipped the DC-Three, and passengers slid to the side in their seats. Early hung against his belt. He grabbed for the seat arm next to the window and, as he pulled against the arm, the stewardess forced herself into the seat next to him. She buckled herself in.

"What's going on?" he asked.

"Rough air."

"What?"

The driving white outside the window flashed.

"Izzat lightning?"

"I don't know," the stewardess said as she worked at straightening her uniform jacket. "This is only my third flight."

The airplane bucked, and Early felt his body lift from the seat, felt it haul hard against his lap belt, felt his stomach plummet, felt the bitter juices of an undigested lunch slosh up in his throat. Lord, not now.

He flounced back into his seat, and the stewardess leaned into him. "If we go down, I want you to put your head between your knees and hold your hands over the back of your head–protect yourself."

"We're gonna crash?"

"No, but if we go down–"

Three bells sounded, followed by three more, and three more, each series more insistent than the series before it.

"The captain wants me. Remember, head between your knees. That's what they taught us at stew school." The stewardess loosed herself from the lap belt that had tethered her next to Early. She pushed away and staggered up the aisle, pushing off seatbacks as the airplane rocked.

Early knew that rocking experience. He'd spent five of seven days on a troopship returning from Europe after the war, the ship rolling and lurching through storm after storm in the North Atlantic. Early and the men of his platoon hugged fire buckets and threw up until there was nothing left to heave, while Navy men stepped around them as they went about their business of running the ship.

A hard jounce and more bilious juices came up in his throat. Early clenched his jaws, fought the impulse–

And then nothing.

Just the steady thrum of the DC-Three's engines. Early eased a peek out the window. What had been the driving white of snow at the edge of a storm had become a gray soup. They were in thick cloud and he knew it.

Lights snapped on in the cabin. Early craned around the seat in front of him and saw the stewardess standing at the front, facing the passengers, righting her cap.

"Ladies and gentlemen," she said, "the captain informs me we've just flown through a thunderstorm. There may be more, but he can't see them because we're flying in heavy snow, so he asks that you keep your seatbelts buckled. This is Kansas, and the captain says thunderstorms happen every month of the year."

A hand went up from a seat forward of Early. "Isn't this dangerous?" someone asked, the voice a woman's, but Early couldn't determine her age.

The stewardess looked in the direction of the hand. "Not excessively so. The DC-Three is one of the best airplanes ever built, and our captain was a bomber pilot in the Pacific. Ma'am, they don't come any better than Captain Pearl."

"And you?"

"I'm a nurse. If anything happens to you, I can take care of you. If we have a serious emergency, I will instruct you on what to do, but for now, relax if you can."

The plane bounced, a sharp up and down that sent the stewardess grabbing for a strap hanging from the bulkhead.

For Early, his stomach twisted. His mouth filled with the sour taste of vomit as he spilled his lunch up and out onto the seatback in front of him and over his trousers. He heaved a second time.

The stewardess appeared next Early with wet towels and a pail. She set about wiping up the mess. "You didn't find the sick sack, did you?" she said.

"The what?"

"The sick sack. It's a paper bag you use if you have to throw up."

"Didn't know there was such a thing."

"We keep them in a pocket by each window."

Early borrowed one of the stewardess' towels. He swiped it at his face, wet with sweat. "Sorry about this."

She held the pail in front of him. "Spit here. I'll get you some water."

The stewardess disappeared.

Early hacked away as Silver Fox leaned into the vacated space. "Are you all right?"

"Death would be better," Early wheezed after he could spit no more.

Silver Fox motioned at Early's towel. "Give me that. I'll work on your trousers."

As he sponged away at the vomit, the stewardess leaned across the seatback. She held out a paper cup filled with water. "Wash your mouth out with this."

Early sucked in a mouthful. He slurried it around and spat into the pail. A second time and he passed the cup back, his hand shaking.

"These pants of yours," Silver Fox said as he wiped at them, "they're going to have to be dry cleaned."

"No time. I'll get me a new suit."

"You have something you can change into?" the stewardess asked.

"Now?"

"I guess you can go walking around like you are, but you smell like a pig pen."

"Tans. In my suitcase."

Silver Fox hauled himself out of the aisle, and the stewardess passed by, going toward the back of the plane. When she returned, she carried Early's suitcase and a blanket. She took out the tan trousers he wore on the job. She laid them aside, then held up the blanket. "To give you a little privacy," she said, "while you change."

"You're going to watch this, aren't you?"

"Only if you want me to."

"I'd rather you didn't."

Early peered up at the stewardess and, only after he saw that she had her eyes averted, did he struggle out of his boots, then his suit trousers. He stood up and got a leg in his tans, and, at the moment he raised his other foot, the airliner jounced. It threw Early against the side of the cabin, and he fell into the window seat. The stewardess reached for him.

"I thought you weren't going to watch," he said, anger tinging his voice.

"Those legs, so cute, I couldn't help myself. Are you all right?"

"What's another couple bruises?"

"You're hurt then?"

"No. Well, nothing that a good soak in a tub won't cure."

"You finish putting your pants on, and I'll move you to another seat."

Three bells chimed.

"The captain again," the stewardess said, and she hurried away up the aisle.

Early thrust his other leg into his tans. He pulled them up and, after he tucked his shirttail in, cinched his belt extra tight. Silver Fox went through the pockets of the stinking trousers. He handed the contents over to Early who deposited them in the pockets of his clean trousers.

"Excuse me," the stewardess said from the front of the cabin through a pasted-on smile.

Early and Silver Fox glanced up.

"The captain informs me we will not be landing in Topeka–it's snowing too hard–we instead will fly on to Kansas City. He estimates we should be on the ground in twenty-five minutes."

A hand went up.

"But I'm supposed to get off at Topeka." That woman's voice again.

"I'm sorry. We have a return flight tomorrow morning, or we can put you on a Trailways bus."

"Why not the railroad? It is more dependable, you know."

"If that's what you want, our ticket agent in Kansas City will work it out for you."

Early returned to filling his pockets. When he again glanced up, the stewardess stood before him.

"Have you ever wanted to choke someone?" she asked in a harsh whisper.

Early, his wallet in his hand, let the wallet fall open. His badge showed. "I'd have to arrest you. It'd just make a bad day worse."

"It would, wouldn't it? Let's move you back." She took him by the elbow and guided him out into the aisle, back to an empty row and into a window seat.

The stewardess collected Early's suit pants from Silver Fox, and the filthy towels, and the pail, and went forward. When she came back into the cabin, she worked her way along the aisle, stopping at each occupied row, visiting with the passengers. In time she got to Early and sat down next to him.

"Well, I've got the chickens settled," she said. She brought a miniature bottle of Jim Beam out of her jacket pocket and twisted off the top. "Got a thirst?"

Early shook his head.

She took a slow, easy swallow.

"Are you sure you should that?" he asked.

"Where I come from in Nevada, you aren't much of a woman if you can't drink with your father–not that you're my father." She screwed the cap back on the bottle. The stewardess slipped it back into her pocket and brought out another small bottle that lacked a label. "Listerine," she said as she took a swallow. "Now no one will ever know. By the way, my name is Maddy–Maddy Stansworth."

"I'm–"

"James Early, I know. I have a passenger manifest. Are you really a sheriff?"

CHAPTER 12

December 19–Saturday
Looking for a game

Early and Silver Fox stood in front of a battery of full-length mirrors, Silver Fox towering over his boss, only not so much now that he modeled a fedora rather than a Stetson ten-gallon. He ran a thumb and forefinger along the edge of the fedora's snap brim, adjusting it just so, giving himself a raffish look.

A short, balding man, in a dark vest with white shirt sleeves pushed above his elbows, leaned around Early. The man tugged at the bottom of the western-style suit coat Early wore. "Fine fit, don't you think?"

"I guess. The trousers, though, don't they look kinda long?"

"That's the style. It's a boot cut, so the legs flare a bit. But if you would rather I shorten them, I can do that."

"Guess it's all right."

"And what else may I get for you–shirts, neckties, stockings?"

"We're set. No, how about a small suitcase about like so?" Early asked. He held his hands about two feet apart.

"Luggage isn't a big ticket with me, but I keep a few pieces in the stockroom. I think I may have just what you want." With that, the tailor departed down the aisle.

"We've got suitcases," Silver Fox said.

"Ours, but I want one we can throw away if it comes to that."

"What do you have in mind?"

"I'm thinking we need an emergency kit with us tonight if this thing goes sour."

The tailor came bustling back, holding a black leather suitcase in front of him. "Mister McBride, I have it."

Early took the suitcase. He examined it. "Long way from the pasteboard thing I'm used to. Can I get two changes of clothes in this?"

"That and a pair of shoes, but not much more. So you'll take it?"

"All right."

"Well, then, follow me to the cash register, and I will figure up your bill." The tailor moved away, smiling, his hands folded in a gesture of satisfaction. Early and Silver Fox strolled after him, Early passing the suitcase off to Silver Fox.

"Was this really the president's haberdashery?" Early asked as he dug out his wallet thin from age and use.

The tailor studied it. "If you are wanting to make a positive impression on people, may I suggest you replace that? I stock a very fine line of hand-tooled leather wallets."

"No. The haberdashery?"

"Everyone asks. Yes, Mister Truman owned the store, after he came home from the First War–he and a partner, Edward Jacobson, my father. You probably know they went broke here. I've done a little better."

The tailor's smile confirmed it. And Early's gaze around the store confirmed it as well—the burl paneling, plush carpet, subdued lighting, the displays of suits and accessories all said quality. So did the eye-popping prices for his suit, Silver Fox's hat, and the suitcase listed on the bill. Early peeled a hundred-dollar note off his roll and received back just enough change that he could jingle the coins in his pocket.

"Would you believe it," he said when he got out on the sidewalk, a serious dusting of snow filtering from the sky, "a month and a half's pay for this suit?"

"It does make you look like you've got money." Silver Fox glanced at the clock on the bank building across the street. "Almost five. Do you think there's a game going?"

"Kansas City? There's a game somewhere no matter the time, but I'm hungry. How about the restaurant back at the hotel?"

Early and Silver Fox turned up their collars and set off at a brisk pace, eastbound, the crystalline sparkles thinning out, replaced by the first of half-dime sized snowflakes. As they swung up to the Muehlebach Hotel, a woman stepped out of the revolving door, she in strap heels, nylons, a wrap of silver lame, and gloves of a brilliant blue that matched her shoes and her cloche hat. "James Early?" the woman asked when she saw him.

His brow wrinkled, then relaxed. He put the face to a name. "Miss Stansworth. Took me a moment, you're not in uniform. I figured you'd flown on."

"No, our crew lays over here, then flies back to Denver." She looked up at the sky. "Considering what appears to be catching up with us, a layover's just fine with me."

"Fly out tomorrow then?"

"Monday." The off-duty stewardess appraised Early through the spiraling snowflakes, her gaze taking in every detail of his new suit. "Don't you look like the wealthy dude?"

"Cattleman, actually," Early said as he and Silver Fox moved out of the snow and under the hotel's awning.

"I thought you were a sheriff."

"I'm that, too."

"Well, whatever. I'm off, looking for a party."

"Without supper?"

Maddy Stansworth gave Early a second look, her chin tilting to the side, a dimple showing that he had not noticed before. "Are you asking me?"

"Oh no." Early flicked flecks of white from his suit coat's lapels. "It's just that Big John and I haven't had supper, and if you haven't had supper, maybe uhm–"

"You are asking."

"I guess."

"Where?"

"Here? The Muehlebach? It's got the best steaks in Kansas City or so I've been told."

"All right."

She slipped her arm through his.

Silver Fox, having brushed the powder and flakes from his suit coat, held the door open for them. Once inside, Stansworth signaled for him to take her other arm, and the threesome went up the steps into a grand lobby rich with mahogany paneling, leather chairs, ottomans and potted palms, cigar smoke drifting up from behind newspapers open in the hands of, Early assumed, visiting businessmen not yet ready for dinner. They crossed the lobby to the side, to glass double doors that opened into a dining room, Early and Silver Fox slapping their hats against their pant legs, to rid their hats of snow. There they stopped at the maitre d's station.

"Table for three," Early said.

"And the name, sir?" the maitre d' asked, his face lifting into a smile, a pencil-thin mustache above his upper lip.

"James McBride. You'll bill this to my room, of course." He passed a ten-dollar note to the man.

Early felt a curious look coming from Maddy Stansworth. Was it the name he had given or the money for a table?

"For you, Mister McBride, only the best. Follow me, please." The maitre d' turned so quickly that the tails of his tuxedo jacket flew out. He moved away with a smartness in his step, weaving his way through tables set with linen and crystal, candles, and flowers.

Early, Stansworth, and Silver Fox followed, Early wondering where they got roses at this time of year.

The maitre d' stopped at a table for four by at a window that fronted on Twelfth Street, a winter scene developing on the other side of the glass. "Normally, this would be the mayor's, but he cancelled tonight," the maitre d' said as he pulled out a velvet chair for Maddy Stansworth. Neither Early nor Silver Fox waited. They seated themselves and set their hats on the extra chair.

The maitre d' snapped his fingers. He beckoned to a waiter standing in the shadows.

The waiter, a black man Early guessed to be perhaps thirty years old, whisked over to the table. He handed out leather-bound menus. "My name is Andrew," the waiter said. "I will be taking care of you. Perhaps you would like a few moments before you order. Would you prefer to start with coffee or a drink?"

"Coffee," Early said.

Silver Fox nodded.

Maddy Stansworth raised a finger. "I think I would like a Manhattan."

The waiter smiled and moved away.

The maitre d', too, started away, but turned back. "Excuse me, Mister McBride, but you've been a guest here before, haven't you?" he asked as he tucked at the handkerchief in his breast pocket.

"'Fraid not," Early said.

"It was back in August or was it September, a table for four. Yes, this table. I have a very good memory for faces."

"Perhaps it was somebody who looked like me."

"Perhaps." Disappointment creased the maitre d's forehead as he returned to his station.

Stansworth, an eyebrow arched, leaned her elbows on the table. "What was that all about?"

"Beats me," Early said.

Silver Fox cupped his chin. "Weren't you–"

Early stopped him with a shake of his head. "So," he asked, opening his menu, "will it be Kansas City strip steaks?"

The waiter pulled up, with a carafe and cups and a drink on a silver tray. He set the drink in front of Stansworth. "Kansas City strips? How would you like them?"

"I want mine cooked so there's no bawl left in it," Early said. "Well done."

Andrew grimaced as he poured coffee for the men, the grimace so slight that only Early noticed.

"Medium," Silver Fox said of his order.

Stansworth handed her menu to the waiter. "Pass mine over a match. A baked potato with that and a house salad."

"And you gentlemen?" Andrew asked as he placed the carafe back on his tray.

"The same," Early said, and Silver Fox saluted with two fingers to his brow.

"Excellent." And the waiter departed.

Stansworth leaned back into the comfort of her chair. She picked up her drink and sipped it. "What's this name business, Mister McBride?"

"Guess I should be straight with you, after all, you have seen me in my shorts."

"I should say I have." Stansworth sipped again at her drink.

"I'm looking into a murder, and I don't want anyone to know I'm here."

"But you're out of your jurisdiction, aren't you?"

Early dropped the volume of his voice. "We think the killer or killers are from here, gamblers angry with one of our residents who ran up too big a tab with them."

"You don't mind if I say I don't believe any of this."

"No, I don't mind. Do you, John?"

Silver Fox shrugged.

The waiter came back, rolling a cart ahead of him. "The maitre d' has changed your salad order. He must think someone here is special because he would like you each to have a Caesar salad."

"What's that?" Early asked.

"Allow me to show you."

Andrew picked up two tall ebony pepper mills. He rapped the mills twice on the cart's chopping-block top, then flipped them into the air. The waiter caught them and rapped them twice more, set the mills aside, and brought up three bowls. Each contained chopped romaine lettuce. He placed the bowls on the top, on his preparation table–his stage.

"Do you happen to know how the Caesar salad came into being?" Andrew asked. He brought up a bowl that held a hard-boiled egg, chopped, and set this to the side.

"No," Stansworth said, in the pause left by Early's lack of a response. She leaned forward, engrossed in the action.

"The story goes that on a particular holiday weekend in Nineteen and Twenty-Four, a year in which I was but a wee child, one Caesar Cardini–" Andrew brought up some seeded tomato and red Bell pepper. He chopped and diced them with a speed that dazzled. "–a restauranteur in Tijuana, Mexico, ran short of supplies. Panicked, he told his salad chef to gather up whatever he had at hand."

Andrew swept the tomato and pepper into a small bowl that had white corn in it. This he set aside.

"Wait a minute," Early said, "where are you getting this lettuce, and the tomato and pepper? I know a thing or two. They're not in season."

"We have a man who has a greenhouse. He grows them for us."

"Really?"

"Would I tell you fine people an untruth?" the waiter asked, turning his hands up in a gesture of innocense. He went about cleaning his preparation table. "Cardini told his salad chef to take everything he found to the table in the dining room and make a show of making a salad–much like I'm doing–and, said Cardini, 'Maybe we'll get away with it.'"

Out came a bowl of dressing. "This is vinaigrette for your salad, miss. We make it ourselves. Would you like to taste it?"

"Certainly."

Andrew dipped a spoon in the dressing and handed the spoon to Stansworth.

She put it in her mouth. Her smile expressed her approval.

Andrew drizzled half the dressing over the lettuce in the first bowl. He took out two wooden salad forks, talking on as he tossed the chopped leaves to get all the pieces well coated with vinaigrette.

"That first salad was romaine lettuce, a little fresh garlic, some ground pepper, a little salt, a little olive oil, lemon juice, Worcester sauce, some homemade croutons, and Parmesan cheese."

In went the egg, the rest of the dressing, a tablespoon of grated cheese, and a handful of croutons. This the waiter tossed as well. "The salad chef worked all of this together, just as I'm doing, then brought out a block of Parmesan cheese and a grater."

As Andrew said that, he reached beneath the tabletop and brought out a block of Parmesan and a grater, and grated fresh cheese over the top of the salad.

"He added the cheese for color and for taste, and he tossed in a couple of anchovies. We don't do that. We puree the anchovies and put them in the dressing."

Andrew rapped a pepper mill twice, then flipped it over his shoulder as a juggler would. He caught the mill, held the barrel firmly in one hand and, with his other, gave quick twists to the top, dispensing spurts and dashes of ground pepper over the salad. The pepper's sharp fumes pierced the air of the room.

"Your Caesar," Andrew said to Stansworth as he set the finished product before her.

He cleared his preparation table of excess bowls and utensils, and brought up two new bowls of salad dressing.

"This, Mister McBride, is for you and for you, sir," he said to Silver Fox, "salad dressing for a man–a little mayo, some chicken broth, salty soy sauce, fresh-squeezed lemon, minced chipotle chilies in adobo sauce for a hot, smoky flavor, and a pinch of brown sugar all whisked together. Would you like to taste it?"

Early glanced at Silver Fox who reached for the spoon Andrew held out. Silver Fox put the sample in his mouth. He rolled it over his tongue. "Whoo, that's good."

"Mister McBride?" the waiter asked. He held out another spoon.

Early savored the dressing as he would a fine barbecue sauce. A smile tugged at the corners of his mouth.

"Would you like it with a bit more bite?" Andrew asked. "I could throw in a jalapeno."

"No, this is fine."

"Miss?" he asked, picking up another spoon.

"Why not?"

Andrew gave Stansworth a sample.

She tasted it and choked, grabbed for her water glass.

The waiter drizzled half the dressing from one bowl over the lettuce in the second bowl and proceeded to stir and toss the lettuce.

"What do you do, Mister McBride?" he asked, making conversation while he worked.

"I'm a cattleman from Oklahoma, here for a convention."

"At the American Royal?"

"Uh-huh."

"I've heard about it."

"I'm also something of a gambler. You wouldn't happen to know where I could find a card game tonight?"

"High stakes or low?"

Early brought out his roll. He held it so the top bill showed its value.

"Very good, sir. I might," Andrew said. He dumped the bowl of tomato, corn, and red pepper into the salad, tossed in a handful of croutons and a tablespoon of Parmesan. Over this went the remainder of the dressing, and out came the salad forks. "What's your game?"

"Stud poker."

"That is the preferred game in our fair city." Andrew grated cheese over the salad, then went into his act of juggling the pepper mill and the show of twisting out ground pepper over the cheese. He set the bowl in front of Early. "You sure you wouldn't want me to put a jalapeno or two on there?"

Early put a hand to the side of his face in such a way that he covered one eye.

Andrew grinned and poured the remaining half of the dressing over the lettuce in the third bowl, this one for Silver Fox. He went into his act, asking, "You a cattleman, too, sir?"

"The work's more than I care for."

"I see."

"I have a couple oil wells."

"You're pulling my leg."

"No." Silver Fox wriggled his fingers in a show that his hands were above the table.

"The man's a Cherokee," Early said. "They've got oil land."

"I didn't know." The waiter turned back to Silver Fox. "Are you a gambler, too?"

"I prefer to watch my friend." Silver Fox motioned at Early.

"Your salad, sir," Andrew said and set the finished dish in front of Silver Fox. As an encore, the waiter brought up something from beneath his chopping block top, something on a cutting board covered by a gingham cloth. He set this, a pot of butter, and a serrated knife in the middle of the table, then, with a magician's flourish, whipped the cloth away. "Cinnamon apple bread, warm from our ovens."

"Looks wonderful," Stansworth said between bites of salad.

"I hope you enjoy it," Andrew said and wheeled his salad cart away, to the far side of the dining room, and out a studded leather-covered swinging door that Early thought surely led to the kitchen.

Stansworth stabbed a bit of well-oiled lettuce and tomato. She ate it. "An Oklahoma cattleman and an Indian with oil wells. I am amazed."

"If we have to prove it, we can." Early tried his thumb against the blade of the serrated knife. Satisfied with its sharpness, he set about slicing the small loaf of bread. "So tell us about yourself."

Stansworth reached for her drink. She held it while she leaned on her elbows. "What would you like to know?"

"On the airplane, you mentioned Nevada and drinking with your father. He a rancher?"

"A miner. He died trying to make enough money so he could buy a little ranch."

"I'm sorry."

"Thank you."

"Recent?"

"No, seven years ago."

"Mother?"

"A hash slinger. We never had enough money after Dad died, so she moved us to California and became a Rosie-the-riveter for Douglas Aircraft. She worked on the DC-Three line."

"She still there?"

"No, she's in the cemetery, next to Dad."

At that bit of information, Early released a slow stream of air, his cheeks puffing out.

"The war ended," Stansworth said. "We were all thankful for that, but then the men came home and she lost her job." Stansworth took a long sip of her drink. "Mom went back to slinging hash, and one night someone killed her for her pay. I don't know why I'm telling you this."

"Because I asked," Early said. "The police find the man who did it?"

She shook her head, then tossed back the rest of her drink.

"Brothers? Sisters?"

"Just little old me. By this time I'm in nursing school, working two jobs to pay my own bills. Taking Mom back to Nevada and the funeral, I had to drop out of school for a year."

"But you made it through?"

"That I did." Stansworth balanced her glass on the side of its base and made a business of playing with it. "Mom said I was a hard baby to be born. She could never have another and cried a lot about that. All those nights of listening to her sobs, that decided it for me–I was never going to cry. So I make it my job to have a helluva good time."

Andrew glided back in. He slid a folded paper onto the table, next to Early's hand. "The information you requested. I called someone. You can buy your way in."

Early held out a twenty-dollar bill, and Andrew took it. He slipped the money into his pocket.

"You wouldn't happen to know a friend of mine," Early asked, "from Kansas? Stayed here a couple times? Al Garret?"

"Yessir. Like you, he's a very generous man."

"This wouldn't happen to be the game he played in?"

"The very one."

CHAPTER 13

December 19–Saturday night
Five-card stud

Early, Stansworth, and Silver Fox walked away from the
Muehlebach, arm-in-arm, their boots and shoes kicking up snow
from the sidewalk, Early with the black suitcase in hand, the men
prepared with their winter coats for the cold of the evening and the
gathering storm, but not Stansworth. She dressed for show and not
for warmth, in her silver lame wrap over an equally lightweight satin
dress, the hems of both striking above her knee.

"So," she said as they moved into a pool of light cast by a street
lamp at Twelfth and Wyandotte, the light pierced by slowly falling
snowflakes, "you're hoping to find the people who killed your friend
at this poker game."

"That's the idea," Early said.

"How will you know who?"

"Maybe someone will let something slip."

"I want to go with you."

Early and Silver Fox stopped. Stansworth went on another couple steps before she twirled back to them, her gloved hands out, a smile wreathing her face. "It'll be fun."

"Fun, my foot."

"You want to look like a rich gambler, right? You need a girl on your arm, and I'm it."

Early shook his head.

"Come on."

"No, go to your own party or go back to the hotel."

"You need me."

"Like I need my grandmother here." Early thumbed over his shoulder. "Go."

He and Silver Fox went on, glancing at the only traffic as they crossed Wyandotte, a snowplow trundling along the roadway, slurrying its burden onto the sidewalk. They went on up Twelfth, leaving Stansworth under the street light.

Another plea of "you need me" came from behind them. Early and Silver Fox turned. They saw Stansworth still rooted to the corner, snow falling around her, a halo of steam rising from a grate behind her. Early, pacing backwards, thrust a gloved hand out. He pointed to the Muehlebach's awning overhanging its entrance a half-block beyond.

"Can you believe it?" he said after he and Silver Fox swivelled around and walked on.

"You would look good with her, Chief."

"Don't you start in."

Two blocks and, as they turned a corner, the plow passed them, splattering a roll of slush across Early's pant legs. He groaned as he raked the stuff away.

Ahead of them stood the Johnson, a handsome pile of yellow bricks, the hotel designed to present a brighter and livelier image than that of the staid Muehlebach. Early peered at the paper the waiter had given him, and he and Silver Fox trotted up the steps to the hotel's revolving door. They kicked their boots clean before they stepped into that wondrous unit that revolved them inside, into the lobby without an accompanying blast of cold air, revolved them into warmth and a space filled with hot jazz coming from a six-piece combo playing away on a raised platform in the corner. Early and Silver Fox went on, past the band and the hotel guests listening to them, to the elevators at the far end.

The doors of one slid open while they shook the snow from their coats and wiped it away from their hats. A smartly dressed couple stepped out, the aroma of coffee and something Early couldn't identify swirling after them. He and Silver Fox went in and turned back toward the closing doors.

"Eighteenth floor," Early said to the operator standing to the side of a stool.

The elderly black man, in a uniform of the hotel, did not respond, but merely swung a handle on the control panel from STOP to the UP position. Early heard the whirr of a motor and felt the car lift at what for him seemed a startling speed. But the smell of coffee distracted him—coffee and what was it? Early peered at a cup on the stool.

"Yours?" he asked.

"Yessir," the operator said, his voice a subdued bass. "A tip, gentlemen. The hotel coffee here will rot your plumbing."

"I noticed the thermos under your stool. You bring your own from home, then?"

"Yessir. Make it my way, not my wife's way, and sure not the hotel's way."

"How's that?"

"With a splash of rum. And I put a cinnamon stick in the cup." He swung the handle back toward STOP, and the car slowed. Early looked up. When the number eighteen lit above the elevator's doors, the operator moved the control handle fully to STOP and pressed a button, and the doors slid open.

"Eighteenth floor," he announced. "Please watch your step as you exit."

Early stopped in the doorway. "Room Eighteen-Twenty-One?"

"End of the hall and turn right."

Early held out a ten. "Would you keep this suitcase for me?"

"For a bill like that, I'll keep it all night. After nine, I'm the only operator here."

"And you're on until?"

"Six in the morning, sir."

Early handed his suitcase to the operator, and he put it down between his stool and the side wall of the elevator.

"Your name?" Early asked.

"Anthony. Anthony Howard."

"Mister Howard, there's another ten in this when I pick up the suitcase."

"Very good, sir." And the operator added, when Early and Silver Fox started down the hallway that appeared to stretch for half a block, "Hope you win more than you lose tonight, sirs."

Early waved an acknowledgment as he and Silver Fox went on.

At the end of the hall, they made the turn into a side hall and read the room numbers as they went along. At Eighteen-Twenty-

One, they stopped in front of a man seated on a hard chair, his suit and duffer's cap ill-fitting, the damage to his face suggesting he was a boxer who had known better days. Open containers of Chinese food rested next to a stained paper bag on the carpet to the side of the man's chair.

Early consulted his note. "James McBride to see a Frank Beldon."

"You dah rich cowboy?" the man asked, his voice wheezy. He snatched a napkin away from his shirt front and dabbed at grains of rice snagged in the corner of his mouth.

Early brought out his roll. He pulled off a ten. "Mister Beldon inside?"

The man helped himself to the money. "Lemme check," he said, and rose and rapped at the door.

After a moment, the door opened an inch, and Early watched the guardian carry on a mumbled conversation with a presence he could neither see nor hear.

The door opened fully, and the pug said to Early, "You're expected." To Silver Fox, he said, "Cost you twenty to get in 'cause I don't like Indians."

Early paid the fee.

"He's a friend of yours, huh?" the pug asked.

"Best friend, and you'll want to remember that."

The fighter stepped back, and Early and Silver Fox went on in. They raked off their hats as they moved. The air, heavy with cigarette smoke, choked Early and he coughed. He tried to mask it with the back of his hand. The short hallway spilled into a nondescript room with a table at the center littered with glasses and overflowing ashtrays. Around the table sat six men, each with a fistful of cards. A half-dozen chairs lined one wall, and a bar stood in the corner, an open bottle of Jack Daniels and some unused glasses on it.

The man at the far side of the table rose. "Sit in for me, Tom," he said to another lounging at the side of the room. He came toward Early, his hand out, a gold cufflink gleaming from beneath his suit coat's sleeve. "Frank Beldon," he said. "Andrew said you're good for a rich game like ours."

"How much to buy in?"

"Saturday nights, a thousand dollars."

Early counted off ten one-hundred-dollar bills.

"I like the denominations you use," Beldon said as he took the money. "Now I also want your wallets, both of you."

"I don't think so," Early said.

"Do you want to play?"

"Of course."

"Then gimme your wallets."

After a moment's hesitation and exchanged glances, Early and Silver Fox handed them over.

"Let's see," Beldon said as he read from the driver's license in Early's wallet, "James McBride, yessir, that's what it says right here." From Silver Fox's license, he read, "John Silver Fox. I see you're from the same county in Oklahoma as Mister McBride."

He passed the wallets to a mousey little man coming out of a side room. "Willy, make some calls. Check these gentlemen out, would you, please?"

After the small man went back into the side room, Beldon said to Early, "We just want to know for certain who's playing at out table. Mister McBride, you're good for a thousand to start. I understand your friend just wants to be a spectator."

"He might spell me if the night runs long."

"That's all right for as long as your money's good with us." Beldon waved to a player seated with his back to the bar. "George, let this gentleman have your chair, please, and why don't you go for a walk, maybe take in a movie, maybe that Orson Welles flick, The Third Man?"

The man called George rose and deflected into the side room. He returned a moment later snugging himself into an overcoat, a fedora slapped on his head at an odd angle. "At the Orpheum?" he asked.

"Think so. Anthony will know."

The man left, and Beldon turned back to his guests. "Gentlemen," he said, "I'll take your hats and coats, and, Mister McBride, you take George's chair. You just might pick up some of his mojo. He was up twenty-five hundred."

Early and Silver Fox slipped out of their coats. When Silver Fox handed his to Beldon, Beldon ran his hand over the camelhair fabric. He winked at Silver Fox. "If you play, I wouldn't mind winning this."

"It's too big for you."

"Oh, but I have a very good tailor." He studied Early's suit. "New?"

"Bought it today."

"Shame to get the pant legs splashed like that, isn't it?"

"That's for certain."

"Jacobson's?"

"And you know that how?"

"The quality, Mister McBride. You have excellent taste. Your shirt, though, doesn't do your suit justice."

"Big John said I should have bought a new shirt."

"I always do. In fact, I usually buy five with each new suit, but enough chit-chat about apparel. Enjoy the game."

Beldon eased into the side room, and Early worked his way around to the empty chair at the table of polished oak. He took notice of the reflections of the other players in the shine and the view of their cards when they tipped them just so. Silver Fox hauled a chair over to where he could peer around Early's shoulder.

"Call me James," Early said, glancing around the table as he sat down, "not Jim and certainly not Jimmy. The game stud?"

Tom, lanky and somber, with a haze of a mustache, gathered in all the cards. He tapped them on the table, squaring up the deck. "Stud is the only game we play."

He riffle-shuffled the deck. "Follow the queen. Five-ten-twenty, and, to make it interesting, double to bet the river."

Early rapped the table twice as a show that he understood.

The dealer held the deck out to him. "Cut?"

Early sliced off the top several cards and slid them beneath the deck. "Cut thin, sure to win," he said.

"An oooold saying. Now let's see if there's any truth to it." Tom dealt around the table.

Early peeled up a corner of the card that slid his way, his hole card–ace of hearts.

The next card came face up–a nine of diamonds.

The next–a four of spades.

The dealer looked around the table, tallying the show cards. "I'm the only one with a pair, so I guess I start Third Street." With that, he floated a five-dollar bill out to the center of the table, and the other players followed with fives of their own.

"Fourth Street," the dealer said. He flipped out a new card face-up for each player. "An eight for Bandy . . . nine for the old redhead . . . queen for Arnold there–next face card is the wild card . . . and there it is, a jack for Gib . . . and for the new guy–" he flicked a card to Early "–a nine for a pair . . . and for me, a six."

"Ten, huh?" Early asked. He put a ten-dollar bill into the pot.

Everyone else did, too, except for Arnold. "I haven't got shit," the dumpy man said. From the lip of the ashtray, he picked off a half-smoked cigarette and took a drag on it.

"Fifth Street and Arnold's out," the dealer announced. He flipped out the final card to Bandy whose shoulder muscles rippled under a too-tight shirt. "And it's a deuce for the big B . . . a nine for Red . . . a six for the man with the wild card showing . . . an ace for the new guy . . . and for me a six for two pair, sixes and fours."

He laid a twenty-dollar bill on the pot.

Bandy shook his head.

Red turned his show cards face down.

The man with the wild card up, hair slicked back, stroked his chin. "All I can make is a stinkin' pair. I'm out."

"That leaves you, James," the dealer said.

Early put in a twenty.

The dealer took two bills from his pile and placed them on the pile in the center of the table. "How much courage do you have, James? Forty on the river."

Early, with his thumbnail, lifted the corner of his hole card. He peeked at it. Aces and nines compared to the dealer's sixes and fours. A four up for Bandy, and a six and a four up for the man the dealer called Arnold. The dealer could have a six in the hole–slim chance of that. Or a jack–yeah, better chance. Or the card could be garbage. Early estimated the odds favored garbage and nudged two twenties toward the pile.

He turned over his ace.

"That's very good," the dealer said, "but not good enough." He turned over a six of clubs and reached for the pot.

From the hall, a woman's voice squalled, "Get out of my way or my boyfriend will pound the snot out of you!"

Scuffling followed and an "ooof", and the door banged against the wall. In hustled Maddy Stansworth, her wrap flapping open, showing a white satin dress with a most revealing neckline.

"Honey, your good-luck charm is here," she said as she hurried to Early. She fingered his two pair and glanced at the dealer's full house. "You really need me, sweetie."

Beldon came charging in from the side room, waving a hand at the woman. "Who the hell's she?"

Early, his gaze fixed on his cards, waggled a finger. "Guess I'll claim her."

Stansworth put her hand out to Beldon. "Jeannie Rae Thompson, little old gold digger from Wabbaseka, Arkansas. And you are?"

"Frank Beldon. Gimme your driver's license."

She giggled. "I don't have one."

"Look, show me some identification or you're out of here on your pretty little butt. What you got in your handbag?"

Stansworth giggled again and dumped the contents of her silver clutch purse onto the table. "Just the necessities–money, lipstick, and jewelry–and this." She laid down a twenty-two one-shot.

Beldon, startled, gabbed for it as did Early, but Early got his hand on the gun first. He cracked the barrel and extracted the bullet.

"It's a toy without this," he said and gave the shell to Beldon. "Suppose you keep that and she keeps the pistol."

The gambler eyed the debris on the table. He pawed through it, taking an excessive interest in a diamond necklace. He picked it up. "This real?"

"What do you think?" Stansworth asked.

"I've got a friend who knows stones. If he tells me this is worth something, I might let you gamble with it."

"No thanks," she said. She retrieved the necklace from Beldon. "This was my dear departed momma's."

He finished prodding through the stuff from Stansworth's purse. "It appears she's got only the one bullet for that one-shot. Okay, she can keep the pistol."

Early passed the gun to Stansworth and motioned for her to clear her things from the table.

She did, stopping to touch up her lipstick with the tube she recovered. Stansworth checked the gloss in her reflection in the glass that covered a picture behind the bar, a picture of the Kansas City Stockyards. She twisted around to Early. She hugged his shoulders, kissed his ear, and whispered, "Keep your cards close to your vest, honey. Too many ways for people to read them."

"Say, how'd you get past my Chuckie?" Beldon asked.

Stansworth patted her knee. "This, in the brass monkeys, really hard. Want me to demonstrate?"

He squared off to Early. "She's nuts. She really with you?"

"I'd deny it, but I don't care much to get kneed in the groin."

CHAPTER 14

December 20–Sunday morning
Upping the ante

Early leaned back. He yawned and rubbed the heels of his hands into his eyelids. "Gawd, I need a break. It's after four."

"Deal you out?" Tom asked. He squinted through the smoke wisping up from the stub of a cigarette pinched in his lips. "Your Indian friend's conked out on the bed in the other room."

Early gestured at Stansworth in a chair by the bar, paging through a Gideon Bible, her legs tucked beneath her. "How about she play my hand?"

"She any good?"

"Can't be worse than me."

"If you don't mind me saying it, you really are piss poor at this game."

"Shows, huh? Down almost sixteen thou. Doesn't Beldon ever play?"

"Few minutes at the top of the night."

"But it's his game."

"And for that he takes the buy-in money and ten percent of everybody's winnings, a fair price that keeps the cops away."

"Bribes them?"

"This game's not been raided in the two years I've played here. Now what do you think?"

Early reached over to Stansworth. He touched her hand, and she glanced up from her reading.

"You any good at this game?" he asked.

"Is Harry Truman president? I can hold my own."

"With the girls maybe, but with these guys?"

"How do you think I got the money for the necklace in my purse?"

"I thought it was your mother's."

"Just a story I tell."

"So, want to sit in for me while I stretch, hit the head?"

"I thought you'd never ask."

Early pushed away from the table. He went to the bar as Stansworth took his place.

Tom passed the deck to Arnold. "Deal me out."

"You be back?"

"After a bit."

Arnold, perking up, glanced at Stansworth. "Stay with the game, sweetie, or would you rather we play Go Fish?"

"Smart ass, stay with the game."

"Oookay."

Tom came over to the bar. He leaned on his elbows, a hand cupped around an empty glass. "A little tension there," he said, giving half an eye to Stansworth and Arnold. "Hope they don't break out in a fight. . . . You've been asking about Al Garret. What's your interest in him?"

Early massaged his aching temples. "Friend of mine. Said he lost about everything he had playing at your table."

"He accuse us of something?"

"Oh no, but I couldn't help wondering if maybe–you know– marked cards. If they're marked, I sure haven't been able to see it."

"They aren't. We buy the decks a carton at a time at the Five-and-Dime."

"Al–anyone have it in for him?"

"For losing money to us? We loved him." Tom stubbed out his cigarette butt and helped himself to a new stick from a pack of Lucky Strikes open on the bar. "Now Chuckie, our security on the door, he didn't like your Mister Garret."

"Why's that?"

The card player pulled out a Zippo. He flicked up a flame and sucked it into his cigarette. After he blew out a lungful of smoke, he said, "Let's just say your friend didn't show him proper respect."

"Enough that he might want to do Al some harm, say, in a back alley?"

Tom peered over the tip of his cigarette at Early. "What are you fishing for?"

Early helped himself to a bottle of branch water from under the bar. He poured himself a splash and sipped at it. "My friend's dead, did you know that?"

"Nope."

"Someone killed him."

"You're not thinking one of us?"

"No, but I'm thinking there's a cop or two in your city who'd like to check it out, someone who's not in on the bribe."

Stansworth let out a wahoo, and Early glanced over in time to see her rake in the pot.

"New game," she said as she followed that with corralling the cards. "Mississippi stud, aces and eights wild, ante up ten, twenty to bring in, thirty-forty-fifty and a C-note to bet the river."

Arnold snorted. "You're going for blood, missy."

"Damn right. I want to leave this table with all your money, and I want to do it before daybreak." She shuffled the cards.

Arnold leaned his chair back on two legs. He tucked his thumbs in his waistband. "You could lose all your boyfriend's money. You think about that?"

"That's why we call it gambling." Stansworth slapped the deck down for Bandy to cut. "You in?"

Arnold stroked the side of his nose, a grin picking up the folds in his face.

"I'm out," Bandy said and shoved the deck to Red. He cut and pushed the deck back to Stansworth.

"You all ante up," she said. Each tossed a ten-dollar bill into the center of the table.

Stansworth burned the top card–laid it aside, face down, out of play–then dealt a pair of hole cards to each player. She skipped Bandy who watched, his arms crossed and resting on his paunch.

"Her play is better than your conversation," Tom said. "Think I'll get back in the game on the next hand."

Stansworth flicked out the first show card, calling them as she did, "Jack of hearts to Red, three of diamonds to fat Arnold, king of spades to Gib, and a six of diamonds to the dealer . . . Come on, chubby," she said to Arnold, "you have the low door. You get to bring in."

Arnold lifted the corners of his hole cards. He studied them, then poked through his pile. He pulled out four five-dollar bills and waved them at Stansworth before he dropped them in the pot.

Gib tossed in a twenty.

Stansworth made a show of picking up her hole cards. She looked at them, holding them close, one corner of her mouth turning up. "Double," she said and pitched two twenties on the pot.

Red put in forty dollars. "Call."

"Me, too," Arnold said and put in a twenty.

Gib added a twenty without comment.

All stayed in on Fourth Street and Fifth Street. On Sixth Street, Stansworth again burned the top card and called the remaining cards as she dealt them face up. "A jack of spades to Red. With his wild card, he's got three of a kind. . . . Ace for the fat boy. With his three, four and six of diamonds, he's got the makings of a straight flush. . . . A red deuce for Gib, nothing but junk showing. . . . And a six of hearts for the dealer giving me one lonely, lonely pair."

"I'm in," Red said. He pushed two twenties and a ten to the center of the table.

Arnold counted out five tens and threw them to the middle.

Gib rubbed his sandpaper of whiskers, paused, then turned his cards down.

Stansworth put fifty on the pile. "All right, here comes the river," she said and once more burned the top card. The next card she dealt to each came out on the table face down.

"A hundred, huh?" Red asked as he peered at his hole cards.

Stansworth nodded.

He flew a hundred-dollar-bill onto the pot.

"Three of a kind up, you've got a boat with your hole cards, haven't you?" Stansworth said.

"Cost you to find out."

With his thumb Arnold rubbed the tip of his nose. "Double," he said and added two one-hundred-dollar bills to the pile.

Tom slipped into the empty chair, and Early took up watch from the bar where he could see over Stansworth's shoulder.

She counted out four one-hundred-dollar bills. Stansworth squared them up and laid them on the pot. "Redouble."

"Sonuvabitch." Red threw his cards down. He turned to the side and stared away as Beldon and Silver Fox came in from the side room, Silver Fox yawning. He ambled to Early and settled on an elbow.

"What's going on?" he asked.

Early leaned toward him. "She's got two pair or three of a kind, depending on how she wants to play the ace she's got up."

"Her hole cards?"

"I don't know."

Beldon, his arms crossed before his chest, took up a position behind Arnold.

"You're running a bluff," the fat man said.

With the corners of her cards Stansworth scratched at the tabletop. "Assuming you've drawn into a flush, you don't think I could beat it."

"Piss poor chance."

"Then bet away."

Arnold pulled ten large from his stack. He tapped them against the table and, with a defiant glare, shoved them into the pot. "See you and redouble."

Beldon lit a cigar, and Red turned back to the action.

Stansworth, chewing at the inside of her cheek, counted out sixteen bills, all hundreds.

Early leaned over her shoulder. "I wouldn't do that," he whispered.

She didn't pause, simply put the money on the pile. "Fold, call or redouble," Stansworth said over clasped hands to Arnold.

"No, ma'am. No, missy. You're not going to get away with it." He pushed sixteen hundred dollars into the center. "Call your fancy ass."

Stansworth turned up her river card–an eight of clubs–and placed it on her pair of sixes, then the first of her hole cards – an ace. She placed it on her nine and ace to make it three nines. With everyone's gaze locked on her second hole card, Stansworth turned it over. Another ace. She snapped that, too, on the nines.

"A quad with a six kicker," she said.

"Shit." Arnold pushed away from the table.

Beldon stepped in. He turned over the fat man's hole cards–a king and two eights, the eights wild cards. Beldon pulled the show card ace over. "A quad of his own," he said, peering at Stansworth. "You dealt this hand, didn't you?"

She raked the money in the pot to herself, not looking up.

"You stacked the deck. I don't know how you did it, but you did it. There's no way in God's world you could have gotten that hand by chance–four wild cards, three of them aces. You're out of here, pretty girl. Your boyfriend, too, and that damn Indian."

Early raised a hand, but Beldon cut him off. "It's my game, my rules. You're out, all of you, and don't you ever come back."

Stansworth stuffed her winnings and Early's money into her purse as Beldon's bookkeeper–Willy, the miniature man–came in from the side room burdened with overcoats and hats. He passed them around to Early, Silver Fox, and Stansworth.

After they silently suited up, Stansworth rebuckling the strap on her shoe. Early extended his hand to Beldon. "It's been an education. I just want you to know I don't bear you any bad feelings."

Beldon shot his pointing finger at the short hallway.

Early mouthed the words "all right" and backed away, following Silver Fox and Stansworth, she muttering and stomping on ahead.

Outside, in the hall, after they turned the corner toward the elevator, Silver Fox asked, "What are we going to do now?"

"Get the bank's money back, like we planned." Early hailed the operator standing in the doorway of his elevator. "Mister Howard, please, I need my suitcase."

He held it up.

"You wouldn't happen to be able to get us into a room where we could change?"

The elevator operator next held up a key. "Sir, a master key. Someone's always locking himself out, so all of us elevator men got us a key. There's a room on the floor one up that never gets rented 'cause somebody was murdered there."

All stepped into the elevator and, after the doors closed, the operator swung the control handle to UP. "Exciting evening?" he asked.

"You could say that," Early said.

"Lost, huh?"

"Very big."

"This room you're wanting to use wouldn't have something to do with wanting to get your money back?"

"Let's say I'd rather not comment."

"I'm good with that." The elevator man moved the handle to STOP and, after he opened the doors, led the three down the hall. He stopped at a room and there tried his key in the lock. It turned and he opened the door. He felt for the light switch, found it, and pushed it up. "I'll wait in the elevator," he said and left.

Early, Silver Fox, and Stansworth went on in, Stansworth closing the door.

"Smells kinda stale in here, don't you think?" Early asked as he laid the suitcase on the bed.

Silver Fox leaned into the bathroom. "He said they don't rent it much. Wonder who got it here?"

"Probably some card sharp."

Stansworth came to the dresser. She pushed a fingertip across the top. "Eeww. Dust."

Early opened the suitcase. He took out dungarees, blue chambre shirts, and jeans jackets, two sets of each. "You really stack the deck?" Early asked Stansworth.

"I have a friend. He's something of a magician with playing cards. He taught me very well."

"You got too aggressive there." Early stripped off his overcoat as did Silver Fox.

"Yes. I should have laid back. I should have been patient, but you'd lost so much money."

Early took off his suit coat and tie. He folded them and laid them in the suitcase. "Did it ever occur to you that that might have been the idea?"

Stansworth spun around.

He pulled the tail of his shirt out of his pants. "That's right. Are they going to be talking to me if I take every hand or every other hand or every third hand? You get it now?"

He hauled his shirt off over his head, and she snickered as she appraised his torso. "Interesting scars there."

Early fingered his side. "This one? A horned steer raked me when we were trying to get him on a truck. Good gravy, woman, turn away, why don't you?"

"Hey, I've seen your legs. You're not getting shy, are you?"

"No—yes—just turn away."

She did, but slowly, to the room's window glowing red from a neon billboard on the roof of the building next door, the sign proclaiming Drink Kansas City Select.

Early kicked out of his pants, as did Silver Fox. And they pulled on dungarees and blue shirts, and buttoned themselves into jeans jackets.

"All right," Early said, "you can turn around if you want."

When Stansworth did, he and Silver Fox were taking forty-fives from the suitcase. They checked the magazines of their weapons.

"My God, you're gonna steal the money," Stansworth said.

Early peered at her as he stuffed his pistol into his waistband. "We need your stockings."

"What? Why?"

"For masks. You think we're going in there with bandanas across our faces, like some old-timey bank robbers?"

"I don't believe this." She flounced down on the bed, her back to Early and Silver Fox. Stansworth undid the straps that held her shoes on and unsnapped her garters. "No looking now."

"Maybe you should check the mirror."

She glanced up at the silvered glass above the dresser. There admiring her and her exposed thighs were Early and Silver Fox, both in their jeans outfits and big hats, standing behind her. She burred out, "I'll get you for this," and stormed off, into the bathroom, her nylons sagging as she stalked away.

She slammed the door.

Silver Fox went back to folding his suit and shirt. He packed them into the suitcase. "Nice legs," he said.

Early only smiled, his droopy mustache lifting some. He, too, folded and packed, and they squashed their overcoats in. Silver Fox leaned on the cover of the suit case while Early snapped the latches shut. When they looked up, there stood Stansworth, nylons dangling from her fingertips.

"Going to pull these over your hats?"

"Clever, but no." Early took the pair. He handed one stocking to Silver Fox and kept the other for himself. The men stuffed the leg wear into their jacket pockets.

"You're going to stretch them," Stansworth said, "so I want new ones."

"That's fair. Let's go."

They left the room as they found it, Early smoothing out the coverlet on the bed with a few quick strokes of his hand. "Back to eighteen," he told the elevator operator.

Early wedged his suitcase between the stool and the wall. "Keep this for me," he said to Stansworth and handed her his cattleman's hat.

"Mine, too," Silver Fox said and passed his fedora over.

"But I'm coming along."

"You've come along one time too many," Early said. "This time you stay put, here out of the way."

"But—"

"No buts. You want us to tie you to the stool?"

The elevator stopped. The operator opened the doors and stared forward. Early put a hand on the man's shoulder. "Mister Howard, I expect we'll need this car in a few minutes. You wait for us?"

"If somebody rings, I can't."

Early wiggled his fingers at Stansworth. With reluctance, she took a hundred-dollar bill from her purse and placed it in his hand. Early tucked the money into elevator man's breast pocket.

Howard patted his pocket. "Don't think I can hear any bells ringing now."

Early and Silver Fox walked away, leaving Stansworth chatting with the elevator operator. When they turned the corner, they saw ahead an empty chair in front of the gamblers' room.

"Now where'd he go to?" Early asked.

"Maybe they've called it quits for the night," Silver Fox said.

"Be my luck, wouldn't it?" He took out his stocking and pulled it over his head. The nylon stretched his features, giving his face an otherworldly look. Early turned to Silver Fox who had done the same, only his hair in back extended from beneath the stocking to below his shoulders.

Early brought out his pistol. "Ready?"

Silver Fox brought out his weapon. "Let's do it."

Early rapped on the door.

He and Silver Fox waited, Early rocking on the balls of his feet, flexing the fingers of his free hand. When he heard the click of the latch, he banged his shoulder into the door, and from the other side someone howled.

Early pushed on in. He grabbed the howler–Beldon–rammed the muzzle of his pistol into the gambler's ear and pushed him ahead into the room, Beldon with his hand clamped over his nose, blood oozing from between his fingers.

"Paws where we can see 'em," Early said to the men at the table. To Silver Fox, he pointed his pistol at the door to the bedroom.

Silver Fox went around and inside. He returned almost as quickly, shaking his head.

"Gentlemen," Early announced, "this is a simple robbery if you do what we say."

Fat Arnold, a cigarette–half ash–sagging from the corner of his mouth, stared at Early, a quizzical look twisting at his eyebrows. "Who the hell you two yahoos tryin' to fool with those stockings over your heads?"

Early snickered. He pulled off the nylon that had been his mask and motioned for Silver Fox to do the same. "Was kind of silly, wasn't it? All right now, how about you fellas strip naked, huh?"

"The hell you say."

Early shrugged. "Well, then how about a choice? You strip, either the easy way or the hard way."

"Not gonna do it."

Early nodded at Silver Fox who stepped up behind Arnold. Silver Fox grabbed the man's collar and ripped his shirt away, startling Arnold and everyone at the table.

He got a fistful of Arnold's waistband at the back and hauled him up. "Drop 'em or I do it for you."

"You're gawddamn crazy."

"Drop 'em. Now." Silver Fox twisted the waistband, cutting into the fat man's gut.

"All right," Arnold said through scrunched-up lips. With trembling hands, he worked his fly open and let his pants fall to his ankles.

"You're shorts, too, then kick them under the table."

"You others," Early said, "you don't want my partner helping you, that's the hard way. So follow Arnold's example."

Red, Bandy, Gib, and Tom pushed away from their chairs, mumbling. They stripped to the buff, all the time glaring at Early, anger firing their eyes.

"You, too, Frank," Early said to Beldon.

"Gawddamn it, you busted my nose, man."

"Isn't that a shame. Strip with the others. Shoes and socks, too."

Silver Fox tore a sleeve from Arnold's shirt. He twisted the sleeve into a tight band of cloth and, with a hand the size of a baseball mitt, shoved the fat man down onto a chair. "Hands behind you."

When Arnold's hands came around, Silver Fox bound them together at the wrists. He pulled down on the knot until the fat man squalled. "We wouldn't want you getting away now," Silver Fox said.

In order, he worked his way around the table, doing the same tie job on each of the players. After he finished with Beldon, Early raked all the money on the table into the center and counted out fourteen thousand dollars.

"You're not taking it all?" Beldon asked, sniffling at a blood droplet slipping from his nose.

"Learned at my daddy's knee not to be greedy." Early folded the cash into his pocket and, as if an afterthought, he helped himself to four fifty-dollar bills poking out from the pile. He motioned toward the short hall, and he and Silver Fox dashed away, out the door. They pulled it tight shut to make certain it locked, then galloped off to a chorus of muffled yells emanating from the gamblers' room. Early and Silver Fox skidded around the corner into the main hallway and ran for the waiting elevator and on inside.

Wheezing, Early stuffed the fifties into Howard's breast pocket. "Down as fast as this thing'll go."

The doors slid closed.

The operator swung the control handle to DOWN, and the car dropped with a speed that had Early scrambling for the grab bar.

Stansworth took hold of his arm. "Well?"

He brought the wad out of his pants pocket, her eyes widening at the sight. "And they're not chasing you?"

"Seems they got themselves a little tied up and without their clothes."

"Shame on you, Mister McBride."

The elevator slowed and stopped, and the doors slid open onto an empty lobby, empty except for one man in an ill-fitting suit and duffer's cap, lighting a cigarette. He looked up, scowling. "What dah hell you three still doing here and in a change of clothes, for Chrissake? I thought Mister Beldon gave you dah bum's rush."

"We got delayed," Early said as he stepped out, black suitcase in hand. Stansworth and Silver Fox came with him, Silver Fox to the side closest to Beldon's pug.

"Like hell. We're goin' back upstairs." The pug brought out a revolver. Silver Fox clipped him hard in the side of the head, sending the one-time fighter sprawling and his gun skipping away across the carpet.

They ran–Early, Stansworth, and Silver Fox–for the front door, the revolving door. Silver Fox scooped up the errant revolver on his way. They whished through in order and outside, down the steps to the sidewalk, and out into a snowstorm. They dashed on into the street and across, Early and Silver Fox in the lead, Stansworth falling behind.

She yelled, and they turned back. There she stood in the middle of the street, struggling with something, unable to move her leg, a rotating light coming out of the storm.

"I've caught my heel!"

Early dropped his suitcase, but before he could plunge back, a snowplow swept Stansworth away, rolling her, tumbling her across its blade and out in a cascade of snow at his feet. Early's mouth gaped open as the snow before him reddened.

He and Silver Fox dropped to their knees. They pawed the snow away from the torn form–a foot gone, blood spurting from a sheared ankle, spraying Early. He whipped off his belt. Early wrapped it around the leg, just below the knee. He yanked the belt tight, then tighter and buckled it. "John, we gotta get her to a hospital!"

"I'll get us a car!"

Silver Fox levered up as headlights bore out of the snowstorm. He jumped in front of the lights, waving his gun. The vehicle–a Checker cab–slid, slurrying sideways on the slick pavement.

A window rolled down, but before someone inside could speak, Silver Fox hollered at the open window, "We've got someone hurt!"

As if in response, a back passenger door swung open. Early, up now, stumbled with his burden toward it, and hands reached out, hands that took hold of Stansworth's flaccid arm and pulled her inside, into an interior stinking of bourbon and barbecue. Early followed, settling Stansworth onto the middle of the bench seat.

"Mister," he said to a man on the far side of the seat, "we need your cab." Early looked up, his eyes wet as they adjusted themselves to the weak glow from the ceiling light, looked up and across to a rotund individual with flowing hair and no eyebrows. "Reverend Smith?"

"The very same, Mister Early." The man put his fingertips on the artery in Stansworth's neck, talking softly through a sweet smile as he did. "She's special, isn't she? You know she's dying."

"Not while I'm here." Early swivelled around to Silver Fox. "In the front. Come on!"

"Your suitcase?"

"Leave it." He grabbed hold of the driver's shoulder and shook it. "Get us to the nearest hospital."

"I got this other guy."

Early turned to Smith, but no one was there, only a crumpled gum wrapper on the seat. He swung back to the driver. "There is no other guy. Floor it, damn it."

CHAPTER 15

December 23–Wednesday morning late
Duty

Early, the collar of his sheepskin jacket pulled high around his ears and his cattleman's hat pulled low, dozed, a memory occupying his mind beneath his mind. Like a film, the memory replayed itself. And it always ended the same, with a snowplow looming out of a storm and Maddy in the street, and he screaming.

He gasped, and John Silver Fox leaned into him. "Are you all right?"

"Oh gawd–" Early, in that half world between sleep and wakefulness, felt sweat as ice droplets beading beneath the brim of his hat.

A bell pinged, and he peered up at the bulkhead of the DC-Three. Early drew a hand across his face and down. His hand stopped and cupped his chin. Then his fingers, beginning with his ring finger, rolled at intervals one after the other across the tip of his nose.

"Mister Early, Mister Silver Fox," a woman said from the web seat across the airplane from them, "we're landing. You may want to buckle yourselves in."

Early felt for his lap belt. He found it secure, but the shoulder straps hung loose. He pushed himself back into his seat and latched them.

The motor that drove the airplane's hydraulics hummed up. Early heard doors beneath the wings pop open, and he felt a sudden drag as the landing wheels forced themselves down into the slipstream. And then a thunk–the gear locking into place. He heard the great throbbing radial engines of the Frontier aircraft throttle back and a screech as the tires touched the concrete of the runway.

"Mister Early," the woman said, "we'll be changing flight crews for the last part of the trip, but I'm staying with you all the way, you know that."

He did. She was Jaime Nelson she had told him when they met at the Kansas City Airport, when others were loading the casket containing Maddy Stansworth's body into the freighter. They couldn't use a regular airliner. The exterior door was too narrow. And even if the door had been wide enough, they would have had to remove six seats to accommodate the casket.

This was easier, Nelson had said. And she said she'd asked to make this flight because she was one of Maddy's instructors at stewardess school, and they had become friends. Nelson wiped at a tear.

Early glanced out a window as the airplane swung onto a taxiway. He saw the sign over the passenger terminal–McCarran Field, Las Vegas. The DC-Three rolled off the taxiway and onto the tarmac and stopped, the engines going silent, the propellers whirling down.

"Do you want to get out, get some coffee?" Nelson asked.

Early loosed himself from his safety harness. "I'd just as soon skip it."

"Mister Silver Fox?" she asked.

He shook his head.

Nelson undid her shoulder harness and lap belt. "The handover takes about five minutes. If you don't mind, I'll go inside with the captain and the co-pilot."

The cargo doors swung open and at the same moment so did the door to the flight deck. A man in the uniform of the airline, gold braid outlining his epaulets, ducked down as he came through, and another man behind him. They stopped in front of Early.

The first held his hand out. "This is the end of the line for us, sir," he said. "Another crew will take you on to Tonopah. Wish we could have flown for you in a happier circumstance."

Early nodded. He pressed his lips together, unable to make them form any words of appreciation.

The pilot released Early's hand and went on. He squeezed past the polished mahogany casket and out the cargo door. The co-pilot followed, but not before he tipped his fingers to the bill of his cap in a casual salute.

Early responded with a wave that had no heart in it.

Nelson rose. As she did, she pulled her blue overcoat more tightly around her and left.

Left, departed, gone, almost as if she had vanished. Early did a double-take, wondering–Maddy?

Alone, the silence in the airplane increased with not a whisper of a breeze stirring beyond the open cargo doors. A faint smell seeped in, though. It wrinkled Early's nose–engine exhaust.

Silver Fox, in his own storm coat and cowboy hat, leaned back in his web seat. He stretched his legs well into the center of the aircraft.

Early hunkered forward. He rested his elbows on his knees. "You didn't have to come."

"You didn't either," Silver Fox said. "The airline people said they'd take care of it all."

"My daddy taught me, you make a mess of things, son, you clean it up. I made the mess."

"You told her outside the Muehlebach not to come."

"Didn't stop her, did it? The minute she showed up and let Beldon think she was with me, and I went along with it, she became my responsibility."

"Still and all—"

"John, what happened, it's on me. She's got no family living, so it's on me to see she gets a proper burial next to her mom and dad."

Silver Fox put his massive hand on Early's shoulder. "I suppose if I should get myself killed—"

"Not gonna happen."

"It sure be the ruin of a good day, won't it?"

Early chuckled. He knitted his fingers together and studied his knuckles scarred from working with lariats and barbed wire.

"I have to ask," Silver Fox said.

"About what?"

"Something you've been not wanting to talk about."

"Uh-huh?"

"The passenger in the taxi before I got in. There wasn't anybody there."

"He was. I just don't know where he went to."

"He? Who?"

"Preacher from up at May Day. Met him in this church that people say is abandoned. He told me then that he'd seen me before."

"Where?"

"In the war, when I was in the hospital. I don't remember that. Said he was a collector of souls."

"From the dead?"

"Maybe from the dying, I don't know. He said I wouldn't believe him."

"So in that taxi, with Maddy–"

Early twisted to look up over his shoulder into Silver Fox's impassive face. "A collector of souls, now that's crazy, isn't it?"

"Maybe. Maybe not."

"You can't have it both ways, John."

"Are you open to a story?"

"I s'pose."

"My father–he's a grand and very wise man–and his father and his father before him, they all believe there are those among us who are called to help the spirits of their brothers into the next world, when our spirits cry out for a freedom they can no longer have because our bodies are tired, hurt, used up, maybe at the end of their time."

"You believe that?"

Silver Fox shrugged. "I believe this, you should be real careful who you tell about this preacher. Few would understand."

A man in a leather flight jacket without patches or insignia hoisted himself in through the cargo doors. He adjusted the tan ball cap he wore, the Frontier logo sewn into the front of the cap. As he worked his way around the casket, another man, similarly dressed, followed in through the doors, then the stewardess.

"Mike Riley," the first said as he came up before Early, his hand out. "I'm flyin' you on to the queen of the silver camps. This is my co, Harlan Johnson."

The second man, chewing on something, gave a nod.

"You don't look like the others," Early said.

"Those fellas fly the passenger routes, so they gotta spiffy up. Harlan and me, we're the cowboys. We fly freight into places that would cause the line pilots to cream their pants."

"Tonopah that kind of a place?"

"Hardly. It's high desert country, a sweetheart of a stop." Riley winked. "Buckle up, my friend. We boogie out of here in two minutes."

With that he moved on to the cockpit beyond the door that kept the home of the pilots apart from the cargo bay. His partner went with him. And from the sweet smell that trailed after the second man, Early knew what he was chewing–bubble gum, a fresh wad. The crack from the cockpit confirmed it.

Three bells sounded and the stewardess, Jaime Nelson, settled back in her web seat across from Early and Silver Fox.

"Tonapah, how far is that?" Early asked her.

"Captain Riley says a hundred thirty miles."

One engine whined and fired, the cylinders shaking the airplane until they settled into a low rumble.

"How soon?" Early asked, pitching up his volume.

"A little under an hour."

The second engine whined. It, too, fired, the stuttering cylinders again shaking the airplane. That lasted only a moment, until the cylinders smoothed out into a rumble that matched that of the first engine.

Early felt the aircraft roll and the tail swing. He glanced out a window in time to see the terminal disappear.

"Buckled in?" Nelson asked.

Early, in answer, patted the latches of his lap belt and shoulder straps.

The rumble came up into a roar, and Early felt himself pushed to his side, toward the back of the plane. And he felt the lift that told him the freighter had broken free of the earth. There was a wonder to it, but a bell interrupted, one ding, then another.

Nelson unsnapped her safety harness and motioned at the cockpit door as she left her seat. She pushed forward and out of sight. The door closed behind her.

Perfume was that? Something of roses? Early hadn't noticed that before. He looked out the window, at the tan earth falling away.

Tan. Is that what winter is out here, just bare soil and leafless brush and colonies of cactus hunkered together, waiting for warmth and new life that comes with spring?

The cockpit door opened, and the stewardess returned. "Captain Riley would like you to come forward," she said.

Early wondered, as he thrust himself up, what this could be about. He pushed forward and through the door, blinking at the flood of sunlight pouring through the cockpit windows. "You wanted to see me?" he asked.

The pilot, without so much as a glance over his shoulder, patted the jump seat between his and the co-pilot's seat and slightly behind them.

Early worked himself onto what was little more than a padded stool.

"Get a better view of where we're going from up front," Riley said while he fiddled with the twin throttles. "Gotta get these just right and it sounds like one engine, not a wowing back and forth between the two. We call it gettin' them in sync."

He pointed ahead. "See that highway?"

"Yup."

"That's Ninety-Six. It wanders up to Tonapah. I could go direct over the mountains, but you see more history if you follow the road– like off to the left, just beyond those mountains, which are appropriately named the Funeral Mountains, that's Death Valley. And off to our right and a little behind us, if you look sharp you can see Lake Mead. Backs up behind Boulder Dam, the eighth wonder of the world and a helluva jobs project in the Dirty 'Thirties. Now south of us, the Dusters came through on their way to California. Any of your kin?"

"I'm from Kansas. We were on the rim of the Dust Bowl. My parents stayed put."

"Rain's a precious thing, isn't it?"

"Looks like you don't get much around here."

"We measure it by the thimbleful. Now up in the mountains, we can get some real snows. We got a forecast that calls for a hellacious one next week. May even blow into your area."

Early leaned on the back of the pilot's seat as he gazed forward over a bank of flight instruments at the horizon. "You didn't invite me up here for a weather lesson, did you?"

"No, just wanted you to see from up here, a mile above the terrain, what calls Maddy home, and Harlan and me, too."

"You knew Maddy?"

"Oh yeah. Had a mighty big crush on her when we were kids. Now Harlan, he only knows of Maddy by what I've told him because he grew up over by Goldfield."

"Where's that?"

"Good forty miles south of Tonopah, so he never met Maddy. And Harlan and I didn't know each other either until the war and Harlan found himself flying the Hump as my co."

"The Hump?"

"The Himalayas, India to Burma and on to China. We've been flying together ever since–I hear you were there when Maddy died."

Early rubbed at his face. How much should he tell?

"Yeah," he said.

"Word around the line is it was pretty bad."

"Hit by a snowplow."

"Gawd–how'd that happen?"

"Ahh . . . we were in a card game in Kansas City–poker–and it went bad."

"I see."

"We–uhm–we were running from the hotel, and she got caught in the middle of the street, and this big plow, it came ripping out of the storm. My deputy and I, we couldn't get to her."

"Poker, you say?"

"Yeah."

"Maddy sure was a sucker for that game. Loved it, and she could cheat the best. That how the game went bad?"

"I'd just as soon not say," Early said.

"Understand. Poker for Maddy, that's not a bad way to go out. Saw her some during the war, when I was home on furlough. We sure skinned a lot of old sharps out of their pay."

"So you're not upset?"

"I sure as hell could be, but no. Life's short any way you cut it, so live high while you can and go out in a flash. Appears Maddy did that."

Riley leaned forward. He studied the near horizon, his eyes shaded by his aviator glasses. "See that town up there beside the highway?"

Early peered through the windshield. "On the left?"

"Yup. That's Goldfield, although there's not been much gold mined there in the last twenty years," the pilot said. He elbowed his co-pilot. "Your momma home?"

Johnson gave a thumbs up.

"What's say we give her a thrill?" With that, Riley pressed the control wheel forward. He pushed the freighter into a steep descent. Early grabbed for his stomach with one hand and the side of the seat with the other.

Riley held the angle with the altimeter winding down out of seven thousand feet, through six thousand, five thousand, four thousand. At three, with a frame house, the paint peeling, dead on the nose, the pilot hauled back on the wheel. He pulled the airplane up into a hard turn to the starboard, Early moaning, and held the turn. After the pilot swung the DC-Three around and leveled out back on course, there below stood a woman in front of the house, waving an apron.

"There she is, Harlan," Riley said.

Johnson waved, and the freighter flew on.

Early's cheeks puffed out as he at last let loose of his breath. He mopped at the sweat dribbling down his temple. "That get you into trouble with the airline?" he asked.

Riley laughed. "Who's gonna tell? Look ahead. See that speck up there?"

Early looked, and there was something there. He felt sure that with winter on it wasn't a bug splat on the windshield.

"Tonopah," the pilot said. "Tonopah Summit to the lee side–see that? Eight thousand two hundred ninety-six feet of mostly damn hard rock. Maddy and me as kids, we climbed that sucker on a dare and caught the billy bejeesus for it from Maddy's aunt."

"Maddy never mentioned an aunt."

"Hard woman. The old gal could spit nails. They were never the closest."

"She still there?"

"Last I heard."

Oh gawd, what if she shows up? Early changed the subject. "Where do you put this thing down?" he asked.

"Airport's east of town, but the church Maddy and her mom and dad went to, and the cemetery, they're south of town, off a county road. We land on the road."

Early leaned forward. He spoke close to the pilot's ear. "I know a little about the law–"

"Me, too. Landing an airplane on a public highway is ill-legal," Riley said, finishing Early's sentence, "except, of course, in emergencies." He elbowed his co-pilot. "This is an emergency, wouldn't you say, Harlan?"

Johnson, nodding, laughed. His shoulders jiggled beneath his jacket.

Riley, grinning, slapped his co-pilot's arm. "A good co always agrees with his captain."

He pulled back on the throttles and aimed his trigger finger at a lever to the right of the control column.

Johnson pressed the lever down, and a hydraulic motor whirred.

"Gear going down," the co-pilot said. "I've got one green light, now two. Gear down and locked."

"Roger. Drop the flaps full on final. The straight section of road by the church is a mite short."

Johnson put his hand on a second lever as Riley banked the freighter to the right, shadowing a dirt road around a barren hill, the ground fast rising. "There's a lap belt on that jump seat. Appreciate it if you'd buckle up, Mister Early."

Early found the metal ends. He rammed them together and yanked the belt tight.

"Flaps, Harlan," the pilot said.

Early felt the airplane, still in the turn, hop–his stomach with it– as the flaps went out. He saw Riley pushing the wheel forward, forcing the freighter's nose down as the DC-Three rolled out of its turn.

Early's eyes bugged at what he saw ahead, and he sucked wind.

"Think the driver sees me," Riley said, "so relax."

A Model A touring car, coming down the road, veered off. It bucked across a ditch and into a patch of cactus as the pilot chopped power. The DC-Three's wheels touched and rolled, and dust from the dirt highway billowed out into a mini-storm as the freighter slowed. Just before it stopped, Riley stood on the left brake. He put power to the right engine and swivelled the big airplane a hundred and eighty degrees.

"We go out the way we came in," he said after he cut the engines. "There's our funeral party."

Ahead, two pickups drove out of the dust, four men in the box of one of the trucks, the box of the other truck empty. They wheeled, one behind the other, around the wing of the plane.

Riley turned back. He eyed Early's bleached face. "We're down, Mister Early. You can unbuckle now." He slapped Early's knee and pushed past him, out the door of the flight deck and into the cargo bay.

Johnson followed.

When Early got into the cargo bay, he found the doors open and Silver Fox and a clutch of men, strangers to him, muscling the casket outside into waiting hands.

Dust. Early tasted dust that had swirled in through the doors. No grit to it, not like Kansas dust. Nevada dust, just powder.

He stepped down and outside, and a meaty paw reached out to him.

"You James Early?"

Early shook the hand and found himself staring into the block-square face of the hand's owner, a squat man, a black suit beneath his duster, his head topped by a cattleman's hat that appeared never to have seen a cleaning, the hat resting at an easy angle.

"Hondo Drinkwater," the man said, "part-time preacher and postmaster. Thank you for bringing Maddy home. You want to ride with me?"

"My deputy?"

"There's room for him in the back."

The ride was an ancient Dodge pickup. If it had any paint left on it, Early couldn't tell.

Drinkwater reached through the passenger window for the door handle. He opened the door and, after Early got in, slammed it shut. Drinkwater then opened his door the same way, by reaching through the window, and, after he pushed himself in behind the steering wheel, he slammed his door with equal force.

"Those Dodge boys really know how to build trucks, don't they?" he said. "Solid fit for everything and engines that run forever."

"Your door handles?" Early asked.

"Now that is a problem." Drinkwater twisted around. He glanced in the back, at the casket. Satisfied, he hollered out his window. "You boys back there ready to go?"

The answer came as two slaps on the roof of the cab.

Drinkwater started the motor. He stepped the gas pedal to the floor. When he had the motor howling, he ground gears in a search for first. With effort, Drinkwater forced the shifter into place and let off slow on the clutch.

The truck crept away, the motor roaring.

Early hollered over the racket, "Clutch slip some?"

"Yeah, gotta get that tended to!"

Drinkwater guided the pickup around the wing of the plane and off through the ditch, the casket bouncing and banging in the back of the truck. Early saw it, horrified.

Drinkwater caught the look as he wrestled the truck up the other side of the ditch and onto a single-track road. "Hey, you don't have to worry about the action back there," he said. "The dead don't complain."

Ahead, on a rise, stood a clapboard building. Drinkwater sang out over the motor, "'At's the Pearl of Paradise Baptist Church. I baptized Maddy there, ohh, in Nineteen and Thirty-Eight. Beautiful young woman. Felt the call to Jesus at a camp meeting on the grounds. Sad times since." He waved off to the side, to a cemetery whose only vegetation was rank after rank of headstones. Drinkwater aimed his truck off toward an open grave and stopped.

He turned off the motor. Drinkwater learned on the steering wheel and peered past Early. "Sad times. We buried Maddy's father over there, then her mother, and today it's Maddy. Last of the family. No more Stansworths in Tonopah."

"I heard there's an aunt," Early said.

The preacher looked up. "Oh my Lordy, I'd forgotten about Bernice. Tough old gal. Desert crazy. She and her dog and her burro wanderin' the hills, lookin' for the next silver strike or gold or uranium. I hear she finds her enough to keep herself in groceries, but that's about all. Come on, what say we get this done?"

He pushed himself out, and Early slid off the passenger side of the seat. They met at the back of the truck where Drinkwater let down the tailgate, its hinges screeching. "Who's gonna be the pallbearers?" he asked.

Early and Silver Fox raised their hands, and Riley and Johnson.

"We need two more. How about you, Eddie? And Arlis?" Drinkwater waved toward a lanky gray-haired man in an overcoat and fedora and a shorter man in an Ike jacket and an American Legion cap.

Drinkwater worked Early and Silver Fox around the head of the casket and motioned for them to pull it forward. The pilots fell in next and the local men last. After the six eased the casket off the truck bed, Drinkwater led them on a slow walk. The men moved with a swaying gait that told Early they all had served on burial details before.

Beside the grave laid two ropes parallel to one another. The ropes came away from the grave at a right angle. Drinkwater nodded to them, and the pallbearers lowered the casket down onto the ropes and the tan dirt of a cemetery eerily silent except for the shuffling feet of a small group of mourners who had followed the casket.

The men stepped back.

At McCarran Field, the sky that had been the color of a coral sea, but it had gone to a slate gray on the flight north. Drinkwater pulled off his hat.

Early and the others did as well. A breeze–chill–came up out of the northwest. It stirred at Early's hair. He finger-combed it back into place but to no avail.

He heard Drinkwater say, "Brothers and sisters, it's a sad thing that brings us here, but for God this is a glory time. One of His children has made it through her appointed years upon this earth–"

Made it through, hardly, Early thought. Forced through, and I did it.

Mired in guilt, by itself that was enough. But he felt even worse because everyone who had known Maddy had been so accepting, so understanding, so sympathetic. Not one harsh word said.

The amen came, and Early stood fixed at the side as the Frontier pilots and the two local men, at the preacher's direction, picked up the ropes. They swung the casket over the earth's yawning mouth. On a nod from Drinkwater, they lowered the encasement in which rested the body of Maddy Stansworth to the bottom of the grave, and pulled the ropes away.

The preacher scooped up a handful of dirt. He dropped it into the grave, then motioned for the others to come by and do the same. Early and Silver Fox waited, Early taking a casual notice of a woman in work jeans, plaid jacket, and a flat-brimmed hat talking to Drinkwater, the preacher nodding and motioning in Early's direction.

After the last person passed, Early nudged his deputy into the line, and Early followed.

He dipped up a handful of dirt. As he let it sift down onto the casket, something hit his shoulder hard, sending the dirt flying.

A voice of gravel bellowed, "Where the hell you get off killin' my niece?"

CHAPTER 16

Early kicked up snow as he ran for a calf battered by its mother, the cow wanting nothing but to be free of this newborn. He scooped up the small one and, as he did, the cow, a slight, boney Hereford, charged Early. His Newfoundland dog threw himself at her, bit down on the cow's muzzle, and held on as she bellowed. The cow bolted backwards, shaking her head, trying to rid herself of this creature as angry as she.

Early tore off for his horse. He pitched the calf across the roan's shoulders, swung into the saddle, and spurred up the side of the ravine. At the top, Early let out a piercing whistle, and his dog unloosed himself from the cow. He raced away, she, blood streaming from her nose, hot after him, churning snow only to give up when the blur of black fur disappeared over the lip of the ravine and into the gloom of the evening.

Fifty, maybe a hundred yards on, Early reined in his horse. He studied the calf that laid before him, patches of frozen afterbirth still clinging to its hair. Early worked a gloved hand over the calf's ribs and legs, feeling for breaks.

"Malleable little critter, aren'tcha?" he said as he rubbed the calf's face.

The little Hereford flicked out its tongue in a languid attempt to catch Early's hand and draw it into its mouth, as if the hand were a teat to be sucked.

"Hungry? Well, we'll getcha home, get some milk in you. Gonna be a cold ride, though, and you're already chilled to the bone."

Early pulled off a glove. That freed the fingers of one hand, and he twisted around and undid the leather laces that secured a canvas roll behind his saddle. Early shook the canvas out. He swaddled the calf in it as best he could, the cold of the night making steam of his and his horse's breath as he worked.

Helluva way to spend Christmas Eve, Early thought, riding from haystack, to draw, to grove of scrubby trees, checking cattle, glad as all get-out to be away from Nevada, away from that witch of a woman who had attacked him. He had done what he had demanded of himself—saw to it that Maddy Stansworth was carried home and buried next to her parents.

Two yearlings stranded in deep snow broke him away from his mental stew. He roped first one, then the other, and dragged each out to keep them from becoming coyote food. This little calf faced the same fate had Early not stumbled on it and its momma.

Some momma, that wild one. Early figured he'd tell Walter Estes they should get her fat on grass come summer and ship her to the meat packer. Be rid of her.

He rubbed the calf's shoulders. This one he'd ask Nadine to hand raise because they lacked a dairy cow to put the calf on.

What are you anyway?

Early pulled the calf's tail up and checked.

Uh-huh, a heifer.

He kneed his horse, and she stepped out for home, the Newfoundland trailing behind, shagging along in the horse's track. The dog not breaking trail for himself, sure sign he's tired, Early thought as he glanced back. He looked up, too, at the sky swept clean of clouds by a front that had come through while he was in Nevada's high-desert country, at the moon a shade above the eastern horizon, the moon a coppery yellow, flattened on top as if it had been a ball of buttery dough slapped by a giant.

If Early had to be out, at least it was a nice night–no wind. As his horse plodded on, he watched stars spangle themselves out in the darker regions of the sky. Early could navigate by them. As long as he kept Polaris over his right shoulder, he'd eventually come out at home or nearby, striking the county road that would take him there. Half an hour he figured. Surely not much more.

Ahead, in the light of the guardian of the night, Early saw the spidery form of a cottonwood that grew by one of the two never-fail springs on the Estes ranch. A previous owner had cemented rocks around the spring to form a pool, so the cows wouldn't muddy the water when they came in to drink. Early also saw a bulky shape in the tree, and, when he neared the spring, the shape launched itself into the night–an owl. By its size, Early guessed a Great Horned or perhaps a Snowy that had come south from Canada to where it might better forage for rodents and rabbits.

Early guided his horse up to the pool and found it as he expected, iced over. He stepped down into the snow. Early hammered the ice with his gloved fist. He broke open a hole and pitched the chunks of frozen water away, and drank first. When Early moved back, mopping the sleeve of his mackinaw across his wet chin and his droopy mustache coated with ice, his horse pushed up. She drank long. The dog did not. He satisfied whatever thirst he had by gulping mouthfuls of snow.

Early rubbed his horse's face after she lifted her muzzle from the water. "Road's just over the rise, old girl. We've not far to go."

With that he swung back into the saddle, and the trio pushed on—quartet if one counted the calf. But the calf, stiff from the cold and hardly aware of its surroundings, lolled where it laid across the shoulders of the horse. When they topped the rise, tableland stretched before them, snow-covered bluestem pasture on Early's side of the county road, wheat and corn fields on the other, silvery in the moonlight. That road came over from State Seventy-Seven to the east and meandered on to Leonardville, the only things along the road a couple ranchsteads, three farms, and the Worrisome Creek Baptist Church where Early and the Esteses, on Sunday mornings and Wednesday evenings, sat in a back pew listening to Hubert Arnold preach, the man Early called the Great Bear of the Plains. Christmas Eve service, he could be preaching now.

A lone pair of headlights came Early's way from Seventy-Seven. He watched them as his horse walked along, watched them worm their way around two bends, then jerk to the north and go down. Into a ditch? Early wondered. He knew it had to be when he saw billows of steam piling up into the night sky. Early spurred his horse into a gallop. That jarred the calf, but he kept a hand on her back so she wouldn't be pitched off. Early hauled up on the reins when he neared his line fence and the ditch on the other side, the ditch that held an old Hudson captive, snow up to the vehicle's hood. He bailed from the saddle, jumped the strands of barbed wire, and plunged down, his chaps knee-deep in the snow. Early wallowed his way to the driver's door and wrenched it open.

In the light cast from the moon, he saw two people, a man behind the steering wheel and a woman beyond. She clutched something and whatever it was, it squalled. The man held a hand clamped over his nose, something dark and wet discoloring his fingers.

"You all right?" Early asked.

"Busted my beak."

"Your woman got a baby there?"

"Uh-huh."

"Your baby all right, ma'am?"

The woman leaned forward, rocking something in the blanket, shushing at it, cooing to it. "Just scared," the woman said. "I held him tight, kept him from hitting anything."

"You, ma'am, you all right?"

"Think so."

"What you all doing out here?"

The man twisted toward Early. "Going home," he said.

"And that would be?"

"Leonardville."

"Where you comin' from?"

"Manhattan. Mary Elisabet birthed our baby last week at the hospital. They let her out tonight."

Early leaned down. He peered at the man. "You Joe Davidson?"

"Uh-huh. An' my wife."

"Heard you'd had a baby–I'm James Early. You know me–Joe, this isn't the best night to be out and the worst night to be in the ditch."

"Hit something or a tie rod broke. I lost it."

"Not all you lost. That steam? Fella, you busted a radiator. Your car's dead."

"We gotta walk, huh?"

"Well, maybe not too far. Worrisome church is about a half-mile yon way. Service there tonight, so we ought to be able to find someone to drive you all to your place. First, we got to pack that nose of yours, get that bleeding stopped. Come out here in the moonlight."

Davidson slid off the seat, a big kid in jeans and a short jacket and a fedora that may have seen a lifetime on someone else's head before it came to him, the kid a couple years out of high school.

Early kicked the car door shut to keep whatever heat remained inside, then motioned Davidson to lean against the fender. Early pulled his gloves off and stuffed them in his coat pocket. When his hand came out, it held a bandana. Early bit the hem and tore a strip away, then a second. After he rolled each strip into a bean shape, he lifted Davidson's hand from his nose and studied it as he wiped away as much blood as he could.

"This is gonna hurt a bit now," he said. Early pushed one fabric bean into one nostril and the second into the other, Davidson wincing. "You got gloves to keep your hands warm?"

"On the seat by Mary Elisabet," Davidson said, his voice nasally, stuffed.

"Well, you wash your hands clean as you can in the snow, and I'll get your gloves, and your wife and baby."

Early, waving his way through steam and the smell of alcohol anti-freeze boiling away, slogged around to the passenger side of the car, a pre-war job, a coupe. He opened the door.

"Mary Elisabet," he said as he crouched down, "I got my horse on the other side of the fence. How about you and the baby ride, and Joe and me, we'll walk until we can get you someone to take you home?"

The woman–a girl now that Early saw her face more clearly–hugged her child to her chest. "I'm afraid of horses."

"You don't have to be. Molly's about as nice as they come, and she likes women and babies. Come on, let me help you to get out." He caught the girl by the elbow and drew her outside. He reached back in for Davidson's gloves, yellow work gloves like those Early wore around the barn. But when he rode, he wore fleece-lined leather gloves. Anything less in the cold was begging for trouble.

"You got gloves, ma'am?" he asked.

The girl shivered, giving Early his answer. "Well, here," he said, "take mine."

He stripped his gloves off and snugged the girl's hands into them.

Early started away, going ahead, kicking and tramping through the deep snow, breaking a path for the girl, but she called him back. "We got a suitcase in the backseat," she said. "It's got some things for the baby and a menorah."

"We could leave that and get it tomorrow."

"No, it's important."

"Well, all right." Early chewed at his mustache as he worked his way around the girl to the door. He opened it, pulled the front seatback forward, and reached in for a pasteboard suitcase. Next to it, Early found something far more valuable–a blanket. He pulled both out, banged the car door shut, and went on around the front of the crippled car and up to the fence line, the Davidsons struggling along behind him. He set the suitcase and blanket over, in the snow on the other side.

Hands free, Early pushed the top strand of barbed wire down. "Joe, you step across, and I'll hand your wife over, all right?"

"Yeah, I can do that."

Davidson eased over the wire. When he turned back, Early swept the girl and her child up in his arms. He passed them across to Davidson, but the hem of the girl's dress snagged on a barb and ripped.

"Whoa up," Early said. He caught the fabric and pulled it free of the fence, and he followed across, swinging first one leg over the wire, then the other. Early, with the suitcase and blanket, and Davidson, carrying his wife and baby, pushed on through the snow to where Early's horse stood waiting, the Newfoundland lying nearby.

Early peered at the calf already on the horse and all the cargo he wanted to put up there. "Not sure how we're going to do this," he said.

"What's in the canvas?" Davidson asked.

"Newborn calf. Her momma didn't want her. Help your wife up in the saddle, would you?"

Davidson moved up beside the horse. He slipped Mary Elisabet's foot in a stirrup and helped her lever up, she holding her child tight–helped Mary Elisabet to sit side saddle.

"I don't like this," she said as she settled on the seat.

"Hon, you'll be all right."

Early held the blanket out to Davidson. "She's gonna be cold up there. What say you wrap her in this?"

"Yeah, that's good." The kid flapped the blanket open. He lifted it at the midpoint of the long side up over his wife's head.

Early moved around to the other side of his horse. He caught an end of the blanket and, working with Davidson, tucked it around the saddle and brought the end forward, up and around the baby and the canvas-swaddled calf.

Early's hands felt the bite of the cold. He thrust them deep into his coat pockets and hustled forward. Davidson, toting the suitcase, came up the other side. The two met and moved along. And the horse followed, but the Newfoundland, instead of trailing behind, jumped out. He broke a trail of his own beside Early.

"Miracle for us you were out here," Davidson said.

"Some of us believe Christmas Eve is a night for miracles."

"I guess."

"Your wife says you got a menorah in your suitcase. I'm thinking that means you're not Presbyterian."

"Jewish," Davidson said as he gazed down at the snow he kicked before him. "Tonight's the first night of Hanukkah. Took the menorah to the hospital so we could celebrate, you know, light the servant candle and the first candle if they didn't let Mary Elisabet and the baby out. Know about Hanukkah?"

"A little."

"The rabbi says it's one of our lesser holidays, but I like to think it rates right up there with your Christmas. It's a freedom thing."

"How's that?" Early asked.

"Couple thousand years ago, fella named Mattathias and his boy led a revolt so we Jews could worship our God, and they won."

"Your temple, wasn't it destroyed in that war? Seems I remember that."

Davidson chuckled. "You do know something of us."

"Sometimes Herschel Weichselbaum and I sit in the back of his store. We visit and he takes it on himself to make this poor Gentile knowledgeable on a thing or two."

"Mister Weichselbaum's good at that. So he told you we rebuilt the temple?"

"That he did."

"Yeah, had to be some big effort. Mattathias dedicated the temple to God, and that first night he lit a lamp." Davidson smiled as he slogged along. Early wondered if it might be a memory.

"A miracle," Davidson said.

"The lamp?"

"Yeah. See, it burned 'round the clock for eight days, only our people had little enough oil to keep it going but that first night. Mister Early, Mary Elisabet and me, we wanted to celebrate that miracle, celebrate it at home now that we got a baby."

"Boy or girl?" Early asked, pushing along.

"Boy."

"Give him a name?"

"Christofer we're thinking, after my granddad."

"'At's a good name."

"Uh-huh, Christofer Davidson. Custom is to hand the generations down in my family. My granddad says we go back to early Israel days–the House of David."

"That is something. We Earlys hardly track back to yesterday."

"Family history is real important, my granddad says."

"My granddad never talked much of his life and nothing of his parents or brothers and sisters, if he had any. We can date him to the Civil War."

"How's that?"

"He rode with the First Nebraska Cavalry. My dad found a diary from that time tucked away in a trunk."

They came up on a rise and a gate in the line fence, a gate Early opened. He motioned for Davidson to lead his horse and her burdens through, out onto the county road. In the minutes Early had his hands out of his pockets, the cold made his fingers ache. He fumbled the gate closed and, when he caught up, he asked, "Missus Davidson, you and the baby doing all right up there?"

"As long as I keep a hand on the saddle horn."

"Well, the Worrisome church is down there by the creek. Lights are on, so people are still there."

They set out again, easier going walking in tire tracks, the only sound the crunch of snow under boots and the creak of saddle leather. And then they heard it–singing to the accompaniment of an old reed pump organ . . . *It came upon a midnight clear / that glorious song of old / of angels bending near the earth . . .*

"Pretty, isn't it?" Early said to Davidson.

"We won't be intruding, will we?"

"Door's open to everybody."

The straggly parade turned off at the driveway and made their way to the stoop. Early climbed the steps, stomping the snow from his boots as he went. When he opened the door, a rush of warmth and the smell of a cedar Christmas tree engulfed him, but no one sat in the pews and no one stood at the pulpit. Yet the singing continued . . . *Peace on the Earth / good will to men / all Heaven and nature sing . . .*

He turned back, eyeing Davidson and the girl. "Not a soul in there," he said. "Tell you one thing, we're all gonna get inside out of this cold. We'll figure it out later. Get your wife, Joe."

Davidson helped Mary Elisabet out of the saddle and into his arms. He worked his way up the steps and inside as Early pulled the calf off his horse's shoulders. He cradled the calf and its canvas wrapper and went on up the steps, his dog shagging behind him. After the Newfoundland cleared the door, Early reached back. He pulled the door closed.

The Rural Electric's lines had not yet reached the Worrisome church, so kerosene lamps illuminated the dozen pews and the front, the platform on which stood a wooden manger near a coal stove that warmed the building and, to the far side, a cedar tree decorated with strings of popcorn and chains of yellow and red loops made from construction paper. At the top of the tree resided a cardboard star wrapped imperfectly in aluminum foil.

The tree did not interest Early. He pushed up to the manger where he deposited his calf in the straw. He worked the canvas loose so the heat from the stove could get to the calf's hair and skin, the calf so cold Early felt she was less than an hour away from death if he didn't get her warm. He rubbed and massaged the calf, worked the heat into her body.

Near the manger stood a metal folding chair. Davidson hooked a foot around it and drew the chair closer. He lowered his wife onto it. "Feels some better already, doesn't it?" he said as he helped her open the blanket with which she had wrapped her child.

Mary Elisabet, smiling, gazed at the face of her boy. "Surprising he hasn't cried, what with all that's happened."

"You may have one of those peaceful babies, ma'am," Early said, "let you sleep through the night."

"You have children, Mister Early?"

"Little girl, three months old."

"That's nice."

"Yeah, it is," he said and rubbed the calf more briskly.

Early's Newfoundland nosed in. He peered first at the calf, then the baby. As if he were satisfied that all was well, the dog flopped down on the platform midway between the two.

"The people?" Davidson asked.

"All the cars and trucks out there in the side yard, they can't have gone home." Early looked up from the calf, his attention drawn by the sound of cooing–Mary Elisabet cooing to her child, the baby with his eyes open, waving a tight fist at the air around him. "Joe, looks like your family's all right."

From behind, at the far end of the church, the door swung open, and lyrics of another carol rolled in . . . *We three kings of Orient are, bearing gifts we travel afar* . . .

Early twisted around to see a burly man in a great coat and an earlapper cap lead a cluster of people inside–the man, Hubert Arnold. They all stopped and gazed at the manger scene, surprise on the faces of some, awe on others.

"Don't this just look like Christmas in Bethlehem," Arnold said, waving a hand toward the mother and child, the calf–alert now–and the dog and Davidson and Early, moisture dripping from Early's mustache as the last of the ice melted away.

"Where you been, Bear?" Early asked.

"Out back, all of us, singing to the Christmas star. Cactus, looks to me like Jesus sent you and your menagerie of friends and livestock to complete our manger scene."

"Hadn't thought about it. We're just trying to get warm."

"Is that a baby?" one of the women asked as she peered around the preacher.

"Oh my lands, it is," another said. She pushed past Arnold. So did a half-dozen other ranch wives. They hustled up the aisle to the platform and clustered around Mary Elisabet and the baby, leaning in, admiring.

One of them took hold of the child's tiny fist, cooing, "Isn't she just the prettiest?"

"She's a he," Mary Elisabet said. She gazed down at the child's face. "My baby's a boy."

"How old is he?"

"Six days."

Arnold made his way up to Early. "Bet we could rustle you and your friends up some gifts you all would appreciate on a cold night like this."

"Bear," Early said, "that isn't necessary."

"It is in God's house. It's Christmas. The wife's got a thermos of hot chocolate, a couple here've brought cookies, and I know in my pocket I've got some terrific divinity candy I'm dying to share."

*

Early sat on the edge of the platform, his hat on the floor between his feet, his dog lying beside him. Early stroked the great Newfoundland's face.

"Bear," he said as Arnold, in the first pew, chewed on a piece of divinity candy, "sure does get quiet when everybody goes home, doesn't it?"

"Quiet's good for the soul," the preacher said. "Lets one commune with God. You been doing that?"

Early shook his head.

"You thinking about Thelma again? Her death wasn't your fault, you know."

Early didn't respond, neither did he lift his gaze from his dog. He just continued stroking the Newfoundland's muzzle.

"If it's not Thelma, is it someone else?" Arnold asked.

"Yeah." The word came as a raspy whisper. "Death's grabbed up another."

The preacher leaned forward until his elbows rested on his knees. "Want to talk about it?"

CHAPTER 17

December 28–Monday
Those damn cars

Early strolled into the department's basement office to find Gladys Morton, his secretary with the ever-changing hair color–maroon, the self-inflicted dye disaster of this day–transcribing something from a scrawl on a notepad onto what looked to be an official report form.

"Morning," he said as he hauled himself out of his sheepskin jacket.

"You know what time it is?" she asked without slowing the clatter of her typewriter's keys.

Early hung his jacket and his cattleman's hat on a hook beside the door. "You're gonna tell me, aren't you?"

"It's ten-oh-seven and three-quarters. How do you get to take an extra-long weekend for Christmas and all the rest of us have to be here at eight o'clock?" Morton ripped the report from her typewriter before Early could answer. She held the paper out. "Cast your eye down this, then go see that big yahoo in your office."

A stolen vehicle report–two vehicles listed, a Nineteen Thirty-Nine Chevrolet four-door and a Nineteen Forty Nash coupe, both

stolen on Twelve/Twenty-five or Twenty-six or Twenty-seven from .
. . Oh Lord . . .

"Fat Willy," Early said as he stared over top of the paperwork at the man sitting in his desk chair, "get your size twelves off my desk and your yard-wide butt out of my chair."

Fat Willy Johnson, a toothy grin wreathing his face, threw his arms wide. "Your chair? Jimmy, this is gonna be my chair after I whup you in the spring election. I figure that gives me the right to try it on–and I must say I do like this chair."

"Get out of there or I'll have you trying on one of my jail cells."

"My oh my, you do get testy, don't you?" the used-car man said as he swung his feet down to the floor. He wrenched himself up. "Santy Claus put coal in your sock?"

"Fat Willy–"

"If anybody's got a right to be upset today, it's me, Jimmy Early. Somebody stole two cars off my lot."

"You ever think of putting up a security fence? Maybe getting yourself a big dog?"

"Hell no."

"What do you propose I do when those cars have been gone for maybe three days?"

"Find 'em."

"And what if I find you've been stealing your own cars just to make me and my deputies look bad?"

"Bull crap. You've got unsolved murders. I don't have to do anything to make you look bad." Johnson waddled to the door, his cheap cologne wafting after him. He turned back, holding up several folded papers he had taken from his inside coat pocket. "I want you to know how official this is, Jimmy. I took out my election papers this morning. First to do so the county clerk tells me. And now you have yourself a mighty fine day."

The used-car dealer turned once more and waddled on out through the department's outer office, chatting with Gladys Morton opening the morning mail, and the dispatcher–Alice–at her radio before he finally disappeared.

Early leaned in. "Anyone know where Big John is?"

The dispatcher swivelled away from her microphone. "May Day."

"Call him and tell him about the car thefts."

"Do you want me to send him down to Fat Willy's?"

"Waste of time, but tell John to ask around. And call Trooper Dan and tell him the same."

A knock came on the glass of the outer door. Early hollered to it, "We're here."

The door swung open, and a soldier in uniform–a slight young man–stood in the doorway a duffle on the floor beside him.

Early appraised him. "Sonny?"

"The same," the soldier said. "Can we talk?"

"I ought to jail you for bank robbery and all the other trouble you gave me last summer."

"I didn't get much from the Jay Hawk, sheriff," came a Whispering Smith response, "twenty-five dollars, and I sent that back. I'm not that fella anymore."

"Guess I can see that." Early went to Sonny Estes. He draped his arm around Estes's shoulders and hauled him inside, the soldier shagging his duffle bag with him. "Gladys, Alice, this is Sonny Estes, the guy I spent a bushel of time chasing but never did catch, the fella who saved my little girl."

"I didn't do nothing you wouldn't do," Estes said.

"Heckfire, I froze."

"It was only for a minute."

"Maybe. Sonny, this is Gladys, our department secretary, and Alice, our day dispatcher."

Morton smiled, and the dispatcher gave a small wave.

"Your folks know you're here?" Early asked after he had ushered Estes into his office.

"I thought I'd better talk to you first."

"Well, have a sit down." Early motioned at a chair beside his desk. "I expect you're about done with basic training."

"Finished the day before Christmas. Uncle Sam gave me a gift of a week's leave."

"I remember basic. You earned your leave." Early tapped his nose. "This. Tell me what happened."

"My nose?" Estes asked. "A guy from Georgia in my platoon said some unkind things about the parentage of Kansans and others who fought for the Union. He'd have you believe the South won the war, so I called him out. One punch and, man, he smashed me good. I didn't get a shot at him. Later, I find out he's a Golden Gloves champ."

Estes's gaze went up to the twin pictures of George Washington and Abraham Lincoln on the wall behind Early. "Isn't that a little old-fashioned, even for you, sheriff?"

Early twisted around. "It is. I've been thinking of retiring those two, maybe putting up a picture of President Truman."

"That's a bad idea in a Republican County."

"I suppose." Early turned back. He planted his elbows on his desk. "I could put up a picture of General Eisenhower. Word around Abilene is he's going to run for president sometime."

"Even if he doesn't, he's a Kansas, so you're safe."

Early pushed at a letter in front of him. "So what's next for you?"

"Fort Riley–tank school."

Early glanced up, surprised.

"Yessir, they got me in your back forty."

"Well now, Sonny, that leads me to ask, last summer, did you like living the life of a bad man?"

"I enjoyed beating you."

"I noticed. How would you like to be a bad man again?"

"Pardon?"

"Some soldiers at the fort are coming into my county, stealing cars. I just know it, but I can't prove it, and I sure don't know who they are. How about you find them and give them a hand?"

CHAPTER 18

December 29–Tuesday
Collection day

Early slammed the Sundowner's door against the fierce west wind, to keep the heat enriched by the smells of strong coffee and frying sausage inside and the slashing cold out. He rolled down the collar of his sheepskin coat and glanced around as he pulled off his gloves.

A dumpy woman behind the counter held up a burned coffeepot. "Want some, sheriff?"

"Angel, be mighty nice," Early said, and he pointed to a table where his deputy, John Silver Fox, sat talking with a wisp of a man in coveralls and a cowboy hat, smoke curling up from a cigarette pinched between the man's third and fourth fingers.

Angel Gibbs and Early converged on the table, he getting there a step before she did. "John," he said, acknowledging his deputy as he threw a leg across a chair. "Hoolie."

"Aye-yah, Cactus," the man in coveralls said, a bent smile lifting the corners of his mouth.

The waitress set a cinnamon roll on a blue china plate in front of Early and filled a cup with steaming brew.

The aromas of both enticed him, still he pushed the roll aside. "I didn't order this."

"Now, Jimmy, my Hermie baked these, new batch just out of the oven. You're not going to hurt his feelings by refusing one, are ya?"

"Well, put that way I wouldn't think of it. You thank him for me."

"Jimmy, you thank him yerself. He's right there looking at us over the swinging doors."

Early twisted around. He waved at Angel's husband in an apron tied up under his armpits and a cowboy hat more beat up and filthy than his. "Herm, nobody bakes better than you do. Thank you."

Herman Gibbs grinned, a gap showing where several teeth were missing, then he disappeared into the depths of the kitchen.

"Angel," Early asked the waitress, "you and Herm ready for the big blow?"

"Could be bad, couldn't it? That's what they say on the Friendly Neighbor. We're thinking of closin' after the noon trade and skedaddling for home an' the farm. Get the livestock in the barn. You, Jimmy?"

"I'm just hoping all of Walter's cows hunker up behind the haystacks and don't drift." Early clicked his cup against the cup of the man in the coveralls. "Hoolie, how about you?"

"County gave me that new road grader outside. Wing plow on it and a heated cab. Sure gonna beat ridin' that old open job I had for the last four winters."

Angel Gibbs patted Early's arm. "I'll leave you boys to chew the fat. I gotta help Hermie get the mashed pertatas and gravy whipped up for the hot-beef samwiches on the lunch menu."

After she left, Early peered up at Hoolie Garret. "You decided what you're going to do with your ranch–your grandson's ranch?"

"I was just tellin' Injun John here I sold it the other day."

"To Gilly Dammeridge," Silver Fox said.

Early bit into his cinnamon roll and chewed. "Sure will make for peace up around May Day."

"My grandson never shoulda moved that line fence on Gilly. But we worked it out."

"So what're you going to do now that you've got big money in the bank?"

"We didn't get all that much, but it's enough for the wife and me." Garret sucked on his cigarette. He held the smoke in, then let it out in a ring that floated away toward a ceiling light. "We're talking about gettin' us a place for the winters in south Texas. Hear it's really nice down there around McAllen–dry an' hot, not like the gawd-awful cold we get. Here now Mazie just keeps close to the stove, an' she's got a heart condition, too, you know."

"Couldn't you go now?"

"An' leave the country without a road patrolman up in my area? Won't do that to my neighbors. I told the boss I'd finish out the winter, but come spring he's gotta get somebody else." He sucked again on his cigarette. "If I'm gonna be a bum in south Texas next winter, I figure I'd better get in a couple months' practice here."

Garret stubbed out his cigarette in his saucer. "Gotta ask before I get in my new grader an' head up the road, you got anything on who did in my grandson an' his wife an' my great gran'babies?"

Early sampled his coffee. "Whoo, hot. . . . Hoolie, I could feed you a line of hope, but no."

"This long an' nuthin'?"

"I didn't say that. John and I run down every lead we get. Just so far there isn't anything that looks good to us."

"Even them gamblers? One of them called the other day, said he wants his money."

"Hoolie, he's got no legal standing."

"He says he's got my grandson's IOUs."

"Look, let me make some calls."

"'Preciate that, Cactus. Well, I gotta go." Garret pushed away from the table. He said to Silver Fox as he stood up, "Injun John, see ya 'round the Christmas tree."

Silver Fox gave a wave.

"Injun John?" Early asked after the café door banged shut. "See you 'round the Christmas tree?"

"Guess Mister Garret just likes me."

"How so?"

"I stop in on him every time I get up his way, so he and Missus Garret know we haven't forgotten them. Sometimes in the evenings Hoolie and I just sit outside and howl at the moon."

"John, you're a good man. I keep thinking there's something we've overlooked on the Garret killings, but I don't for the life of me know what it is."

"I suppose some murders do go unsolved."

"State statistics, about half, and most of those are in Kansas City and Wichita. Rural counties like ours, we do a lot better." Early finished his roll and, with his finger, raked up blobs of sweet white icing from the plate. He sucked his finger clean. "Why don't you take a room at the Wareham tonight? If this storm rolls through, you take the office tomorrow because I don't think anyone else'll get in."

"And should I need you?" Silver Fox asked, "You don't have a phone out there at the Esteses yet."

"Call the constable at Riley. Mose will come get me. He runs in the awfullest snows with that little Chevy of his."

Silver Fox hunched forward. "How about I go into the office now?"

"Fine by me."

"I'll spend the day on the telephone and call all the car dealers and garages in Junction, Ogden, and Manhattan. Someone may have seen one of Fat Willy's latest rash of stolen cars."

"Can't hurt to try." Early collected his plate, coffee cup, and spoon and pushed up from the table. "As for me, I'm going over to Bala. Haven't spent much time there in the last couple months, and I don't want anybody there to forget me come March."

"Right, the election."

Early, followed by Silver Fox, shuffled over to the counter. He handed his dirty dishes to the waitress.

"Jimmy, you didn't have to bring these over," she said.

"I just like to be helpful. What's the bill for John and me?"

"It's on the house."

"If I was ranching and not wearing a badge, I'd say thank you. But John and me, we've got to pay our own way."

"Well then, sixty-five cents."

Early dug in his pocket. He pulled out a handful of change and counted it out. "That do it?"

"Do it just fine."

"You and Herm, you take care now."

Early turned up his collar and pushed out into the wind. He went to his Jeep and Silver Fox to his.

The drive out of Randolph and the Big Blue Valley to the high ground went with little more than some buffeting from the wind. On the high ground, Early stopped at State Seventy-Seven. He waited for a car coming from the south to clear the intersection.

A Missouri license plate. Odd, Early thought. He turned not south, the direction in which he intended to go, but north. Early fell in behind the green Packard that had whistled past him. A mile on and curiosity became too much. He flicked on his dashboard-mounted bubble light and tapped his horn button.

The Packard–a coupe–slowed and Early with it. Both slid over onto the shoulder and stopped.

Early got out. He trudged forward, a hand on his hat to keep it from whipping away in the wind. He motioned at the driver to roll down his window already open a crack.

"Trouble?" the man asked.

Early leaned down and surprise flickered in his eyes. "Oh my Lord. Frank? Frank Beldon? What're you doing in my county?"

"James McBride?"

"It's James Early. I'm the sheriff here."

"Where's your Indian friend?" Beldon asked between puffs on a black cigar.

"He's my deputy. I expect he's at the county seat by now."

"Well, James McBride or James Early or James Whatever, I'm here on business. Your buddy, Al Garret? I hold twenty-six thousand dollars of his IOUs and his granddaddy's got the money–sold the boy's ranch."

"How do you know that?"

"I've got my sources. Anyway, I'm here to collect."

Early shook his head. "It pains me to have to tell you–"

"Tell me what?"

"–that debt, it went to the grave with Al."

"The hell you say."

"I do say. You can't collect it. Now if you go up to May Day and you bother Hoolie, take this as gospel: I'll arrest you for Al's murder."

Beldon fumbled his smoke. He dived down for it and, when he came back up, cigar once more in hand, he scowled at Early. "I'm a businessman, not a killer, and you know that."

"Do I?" Early leaned an elbow into the open window while he kept a hand on his hat. "Frank, let me tell you how this works in my county. I find me a couple solid citizens who will swear before the judge that they saw this car, with your license plate on it, at Al's ranch on the morning he and his family were killed. I don't need a murder weapon or fingerprints or anything else. My judge just loves witnesses."

"You wouldn't."

"You got brass knockers big enough you want to try me?"

Beldon studied the ash end of his cigar. His scowl grew more ugly.

"Frank," Early said, "I think this'd be a real smart time for you to turn around and go home. You might even make Kansas City before the blizzard."

He stepped away from the Packard and waited. Early counted off the seconds. At twelve, the car rolled, Beldon, scowling still, cranking the steering wheel into a hard turn that headed the car south, the way it had come.

Early put his shoulder into the wind and made his way back to his Jeep. He wondered why the gambler had given up with so little fight. After he buttoned himself inside, he picked up his microphone and squeezed the transmit button.

"John, you there?"

"Coming up on Fogertown," came back Silver Fox's voice through Early's radio.

"Wait there. Should be a green Packard coming down Seventy-Seven to Twenty-Four—Missouri license plate. Shadow him to the county line, wouldja?"

CHAPTER 19

Early bounced his baby daughter on his knee, going "booga-booga-booga" to her and she, grinning, burbled bubbles back at him. His nose wrinkled.

"Oh, Barbie Sue, you mess your diaper again?"

Walter Estes glanced over from his Capper's Weekly. "Babies do that, Jimmy. Isn't it wonderful being a pap?"

"I guess." Early held his daughter out at arm's length as he made his way to the back bedroom the two of them shared in the Esteses' ranch house. He laid her down on the top of the bureau and proceeded to unpin the diaper.

"You sure can load it up, little one, huh?"

He stripped away the diaper, folded it, and dropped it in a porcelain pail. Early rescued a washcloth from a pan of clean water on the bureau. He wrung out the excess and washed his child's bottom clean. A fresh diaper became a drying rag, and, with a liberal powdering, Early clouded the air. As he brought out a second fresh diaper–for the new covering–he sneezed. That diaper became a handkerchief. Early tossed it and brought out another.

"Just like your momma, huh? Never do cry, do you," he said as he pierced the fabric with a safety pin.

The baby squalled. She flailed her arms and kicked out her legs.

"Oops. I'm supposed to keep my fingers between you and the diaper, aren't I?"

"What're you doin' in there?" came the bellowing voice of Estes from the front of the house.

"I'm jabbing pins in my daughter!"

Early tried again. This time he yelped. Early whipped his hand away from inside the diaper and jammed a finger oozing blood into his mouth.

"Now what?" Estes hollered.

"I stabbed myself!"

"Three months' practice, I'd think you'd be better than this."

"I would, too."

Early attacked the diapering job again. He pinned one corner, then the other. Early tugged at the sides. "A little loose, but not bad for government work, I'd say."

He hoisted his baby up against his shoulder and marched back to the front room, she pawing up wrinkles in his shirt and gumming on them.

Nadine came in from the kitchen. She wiped her well-floured hands on her apron as she surveyed Estes at his paper. "Walter, why don't you have the radio on?"

He looked up.

"The radio. Why don't you have it on?"

"Don't want to run down the battery."

"If you run down the battery, you bring the battery in from your truck. I want to know what's going on out there."

"It's snowing," Estes said.

"Well, la-de-dah. It's about done. I saw a patch of sky among the clouds out my kitchen window."

Estes glanced at Early. "Jimmy, you hear that?"

"What I hear is the wind around the corners of the house."

"Oh my–" Estes twisted toward the Crosley on the table by his chair. He turned the ON knob and cranked up the volume.

. . . *Five and Dime closed today as are most downtown businesses, but Seth over at the Quality Market says you can get groceries and milk at his store if you can get there. He's going to stay open into the evening. City Hall closed as is the courthouse, although there is one deputy in the sheriff's department and one patrolman in the police department to take calls. The fellas at the city firehouse have hunkered down, and the managers over at the city garage and the county garage say they won't send plows out until tomorrow. On the north/south roads drifting is bad. Wilton James up by Randolph tells The Friendly Neighbor he's measured drifts three and a half feet deep on the county road out in front of his place. Ministers at every church in Manhattan have called in to tell us no services tonight . . .*

"I suppose that means no church for us, either," Nadine said.

Early patted his daughter on the back as he rocked her. "I sure can't picture it."

. . . *This off our news wire . . . Snowfall across the northern half of Kansas is pretty uniform, eighteen to twenty-four inches. It peters out south of Salina, but gets some deeper north of us, particularly in Nebraska. Snow in Goodland ended six hours ago, four hours ago in*

Hays, and an hour ago in Abilene. We still have a little snow falling outside Mighty K-M-A-N Radio. Topeka and Kansas City, blizzard conditions continue. . . . This is Red Fulmer at The Friendly Neighbor. We're coming up on four o'clock in the p.m. I'll be with you until we sign off at six, and then I'll be back at six in the morning. If you'd like to tell us how things are out your way, give us a call at Pleasant Four-Five-One . . . Here's a call now. Go ahead, you've got the old redhead.

Red, this is Gilly Dammeridge up by May Day. I've been out searching for my cattle and they're gone.

Drifted ahead of the wind you think, Gilly?

Must have. I've found fences trampled down.

Talk to your neighbors?

Not yet. I just got in and the wife said you wanted callers.

Well, your cattle sure won't cross the Big Blue River.

That's a lot of miles from here. If they get that far and pile up in the valley with other cattle, it's gonna be a helluva mess to sort out. Guess that's why we brand 'em.

How about feed?

My cows oughta be good for a couple days, then I've gotta get hay to them wherever they are.

And you're gonna do that how?

Red, you ask some tough questions.

That's my job . . .

Early handed his daughter to Nadine. "Walter, I'm going to get my horse and go out and look for your cattle."

Estes pushed himself out of his chair. He shook the stiffness out of his legs. "Guess I'll hitch up old Norby and Jack," he said. "We can move some hay with the bobsled if we have to."

*

Early, a muffler tied down over his ears and the affair topped with his cattleman's hat pulled low, broke open a bale of prairie hay. He kicked chunks of it out into the snow as a half-dozen cows crowded in.

"Think you girls had never seen feed," he said. He scratched the back of the nearest cow, and she swung her head up toward him, strands of hay dribbling from her mouth.

Estes whoaed at his team as they came lunging up through knee-deep snow, the bobsled swooshing behind them.

"Six is all we got here, Walter," Early called out. He waved a gloved hand toward the east, where the white-blanketed pasture fell away and a cluster of Osage orange trees poked up. "I expect we ought to find a bunch of them over there, in the draw."

"Jimmy, pitch some bales on the sled, and we'll go ready."

Early stepped back to the haystack. He hefted a bale up and arched it over to the sled. The bale banged down. Estes straightened it and the next and the next, then stacked and rearranged the incoming bales that continued to bang down until he had a pile of fifteen.

"Enough," he hollered.

Early stopped in mid-pitch. He wheeled around and toted number sixteen away to the cluster of cows where he broke it open for them. While they ate, Early twisted the wires that had held that bale and the first together. He tossed the wires to Estes.

"How many you think we'll find in the draw?" the old rancher asked.

Early swung up into the saddle. "Wouldn't it be great if there were thirty?"

"Sure would."

"Be lucky if it's a dozen."

Early clicked his tongue in his cheek, and his horse bounded out toward the east.

Estes guided his team and sled alongside. "Sure do like a bobsled for gettin' around in the winter," he called over to Early. "I 'member back in 'Forty-Two for a month that's how I took care of the cows and got Sonny to school. Sundays we'd load up a couple neighbor families and all of us'd go to church on the bobsled. Get the bearskin out and a couple quilts, you know."

Early slowed his horse as they neared the draw. "I can do without," he said.

"The bearskin?"

"The snow. I may have liked it as a kid, but now I just put up with it knowing spring's out there somewhere."

Early and Estes halted their horses at the top of the draw, and Early stood in the stirrups. He peered down at cattle, snow well up on their sides. Early counted them, moving an index finger over each one. "I get eleven. No, wait. Couple over in the brush. Walter, did you bring the grain scoop?"

Estes held up an aluminum shovel.

Early stepped down from his horse. He took the shovel from Estes and plunged down into the draw, snow going up to the knees of his chaps. Early scooped and pitched as he dug out a path down to the larger gang of cows, all with snow crusted on their backs and faces. They eyed him as he came.

Early, at the bottom, worked his way around the nearest cow. He grabbed her tail. "Call 'em up," he hollered.

Estes broke open a bale of hay and sang out, "Hey, boss! Come, boss! Hey-up, feed time! Comeboss, comeboss, comeboss."

"Come on, girl, git!" Early said, and he rammed his shoulder into the cow's haunch.

She lunged. The cow broke free of the snow and stumbled into the path that led up out of the draw. Early gave her a swat with the shovel, and she bolted away. The other cows struggled out of the deep snow, Early whistling and hooting at them. They made for the side of the draw and up toward the hay Estes scattered.

Two had trapped themselves in a thicket. Early broke the brush away and whacked their rears, and they, too, bolted off. Early followed, high-stepping over blotches of hot manure the cows dropped as they climbed their way toward the high ground of the pasture and feed.

"Twenty cows when you count those back at the haystack," Early sang out when he came over the lip.

Estes rubbed at the long hairs on the back of his neck. "Should be fifteen more in this pasture."

"We go on then and look for them."

Early tossed the scoop to Estes. After Early walked among the cows, eyeing each for chills and weakness, he climbed back into the saddle. He reined his horse around the far end of the draw and on across the pasture. A ten-minute ride and he came to the fence. Early studied it as he leaned on his saddle horn. He twisted back toward Estes driving his team up.

"The cows," Early said, "they piled up against the fence here until they broke a couple posts over."

"Walked away, huh?"

"How stout's your next fence?"

"Not the best."

Early reached around to his saddlebags. He brought out binoculars and peered through them at the haystack in the middle of the next field. "Nothing moving around there."

"They could be on the backside," Estes said.

"We're running out of light. What say you head back to the house and I'll go on? If the cows are there, I'll feed 'em and come on home."

*

Early eased the door open. He slipped inside, a chill wind pushing him.

"Needn't try to be quiet," came a voice from the dark. "I'm awake."

Early heard the scratch of a match and saw a flare of light and Walter Estes as the old man touched a flame to the wick of a kerosene lamp. A new flame jumped up. Estes twiddled with the knob on the lamp until he had the light casting a soft glow around the front room of the ranch house.

Estes rubbed at his thatch of white hair. "Know what time it is?"

Early pulled a railroad watch–his father's–from his pocket. He opened the cover and sucked in a breath when he saw the hour.

"Well?" Estes asked.

"Four twenty-three."

"Ohmy." The old rancher stretched. "Be sunup before long, won't it? Take it the cows weren't at the haystack."

"Three were," Early said as he shelled himself out of his sheepskin coat and his chaps. "I trailed the rest by gosh and by golly, picking up their trail where they trampled through somebody's fence."

"Get kinda far, did they?"

"You know that extension of our county road that runs down to the Big Blue, goes under the K&N viaduct? They're piled up in Sim Peters's cornfield beyond, out of the wind–cows from a couple other ranches and a few unbranded beasts." Early sagged into a chair.

"We can get 'em back?"

"When the roads get plowed out."

CHAPTER 20

January 2–Saturday afternoon
The old Red Rooster

Early stood on the porch, bundled for chores in the cold and snow of the second day of January, the sky a cobalt blue. He surveyed the white desert that was the Rocking Horse E. Nothing moved other than the black Newfoundland that leaned against Early's leg. Early bent down and rubbed the dog's ears.

The Newfoundland perked. He swivelled his head toward the ranch lane.

"Arch, I hear it," Early said. He, too, peered off and saw a black car, its paint faded, churning up out of a wash. The car came on, its engine whining, a tell to Early that first gear was the best the driver of the car could make. He recognized it, the elderly Chevy coupe.

Early kicked his way out to where the lane came past the front yard, the dog shagging along with him. A flurry of horn beeping came from the car, and Early waved.

Mose Dickerson, the Riley constable, stopped in front of Early. He cranked down his window. "Jimmy, you not been out yet?" he asked.

"Only on horseback."

"They're startin' to get some of the roads open. Still an' all, I had to buck the better part of three miles of drifts to get here. Good thing I got chains."

Early leaned an elbow on the roof of the car. "Big John call you?"

"Yup. Says the state co-man-deer of the National Guard wants you in Salina, something about guiding a crew that's to drop hay to stranded cattle around the area."

"Heard something on that on the Friendly Neighbor."

"According to the governor, we're in a first-class disaster here. The Guard's to help. John says they've flown big planes into the old air base at Salina, an' they're trucking hay up from Okla-dang-homa."

"Mose, I can't get over there without the roads open."

"'At's what I told Deputy John, but he says he's rustled up Jenny an' the Old Red Rooster to come get ya."

Early kicked at the snow. "Jenny Collins? There's got to be some way I can get outta this."

The distant drone of an airplane's motor wedged its way into the conversation, and Early looked off in the direction of the sound. He shaded his eyes.

A speck crept over the horizon, a speck that became increasingly larger as it came on, skimming the fences and the few trees on the high ground. It circled over Early and Dickerson–a red Piper Cub on skis. The pilot of the Cub swung the airplane back down the lane, turned the two-seater once more, and put down parallel to Dickerson's track, the Cub shuushing along, its propeller blast billowing out the snow.

The roiling crystals settled after the Cub came to a stop short of the Rocking Horse E's corral.

Arch bounded out, and Early and Dickerson slogged after the dog, Dickerson moving with a hop-step that had been a part of his life since he injured his leg as a child.

The airplane's engine sputtered and quit, and the propeller windmilled down. In the new silence, the Cub's clamshell door swung open, the top half going up underneath the wing, and the bottom half going down. The pilot hefted herself out, she in coveralls, boots to her knees, leather gloves and a flying helmet. She shoved her sun goggles up onto the top of her head.

"Get the word, Jimmy?" the pilot called out.

"Jen, I don't want to fly with you."

"They want you in Salina, and I've been hired to by-God get you there." From a back pocket, Jen Collins drew out a calf-tying rope. She came over and dangled it in Early's face. "Your deputy says I'm to use this on you if you don't hop up in the backseat on your own. Jimmy, if you run, I'm faster than you, plus I've got you by thirty pounds. What's it gonna be?"

"I don't like little airplanes, and I particularly don't like you."

"Aw, just because I beat you out of forward on our high school basketball team–git in the backseat."

Early turned to Dickerson. "You got your gun?"

"It's in the car, Jimmy."

"I want to shoot this woman."

"I don't think that'd be smart. After all, the governor and the co-man-deer–"

"Oh heck." Early huffed off to the Cub. He hitched a leg up through the open door and hauled himself into the second seat–behind the pilot's seat.

"Mose," he said as he struggled with the lap belt and shoulder harness, "take Arch to the house. Tell Walter and Nadine that Jenny Cee's kidnapped me and I may never get back."

Collins loomed up in the doorway. Early smelled the Lifesaver she sucked on. Collins took hold of Early's shoulder harness and cinched it tight and his lap belt even tighter. He groaned, but before he could loosen either, she kissed him hard on the mouth.

Early, wide-eyed, spit.

Collins merely patted his cheek. "Always wanted to buss you, Jimmy. And now that you're a widower an' in the market for a wife–"

"Jen!"

"Oh, quit yer yapping."

"I got no interest in you."

"Yeah, yeah. Gonna play hard to catch, aren'tcha?"

As she talked, she flipped a couple switches on the airplane's dash and checked the bobber wire in front of the windshield for gas in the tank. Then she strode to the front of the Cub. Once there, Collins snapped the propeller down through a power stroke, and the engine caught. It burbled to life, dribbling exhaust out its stack that the propeller wafted back to Early. He coughed.

"Love this little airplane," Collins said as she horsed herself into the front seat. She twisted around and looked to the sides and then ahead. When Collins appeared to be satisfied that there was no one and nothing that she would hit, she pulled the two halves of the clamshell door closed and pushed forward on the throttle.

The airplane jumped as its skis broke free from where they'd sunk into the snow. Collins stepped hard on the rudder, and the Cub swung around. It scuttled away to the south, the two-seater lifting into a slow climb skyward, the engine in a full-throated bellow.

Collins tapped the headset she had slipped over her ears. She hollered back, "Jimmy, there's one there for you. Put it on. Want to talk to me, use your microphone."

Early searched around his area until he unearthed a headset and a microphone in a pile of junk under his seat. He chucked his cattleman's hat and worked the headset over his ears. In the process, Early risked a peek over the side of the Cub while Collins eased back on the power. He brought the microphone up and pressed the transmit button. "You hear me?"

"Five by five," came back Collins's voice in his headset.

"What's that mean?"

"I can hear you loud and clear."

"Is Seventy-Seven open?"

"Parts of it. I'm told a plow's working down from Blue Rapids and another up from Manhattan."

"Fly me over there."

"Can't. I'm to get you to Salina."

"Fly me over there, Jen. And swing out over the Big Blue, by the viaduct. I want to check on Walter's cattle."

"They that far from home?"

"Drifted with the storm, and they're not the only ones."

"So his cows are going to need hay from the sky, too?"

"I expect. Sim Peters hauled over all he's got, but that wasn't much. Soon as the roads are open, Walter and I'll cut his cows out of that herd and drive them home."

"You've been there then."

"Couple times on horseback."

"Lip of the valley ahead. Going down."

Collins pushed forward on the control stick. That nosed the Cub over, and Early grabbed his stomach.

She glanced back. "Don't go gettin' sick on me now. I don't want you messing up the Rooster."

Early moaned as Collins banked the plane up onto its wing. She swung the Cub into a circle over a herd of reddish-colored cattle in a field of white between the viaduct and the river.

"That them?"

"Yeah."

"I can see they've had some hay, all right. Think there's more in the valley?"

"Ooooo –"

"Jimmy?" Collins passed a paper sack back over her shoulder. "Burb bag. Put 'er there if you have to."

Early pressed the open end of the sack around his mouth. He heaved his lunch before Collins leveled the Cub onto a north-bound course.

She banged a side window open. Cold wind and the blat of the Cub's engine roared in. "Get rid of the bag."

His hand shaking, Early pitched the sack overboard.

"Bombs away. . . . Suck in some of that air, Jimmy. You'll feel better."

"Easy for you to say."

"Do it."

Early inhaled as he mopped at a watery eye.

"How you doing back there?"

"Some better."

Collins yanked the side window closed. That shut out the hurricane and some of the racket of the Cub's engine. "We're coming back over Seventy-Seven."

Early leaned toward the window. When there, he forced himself to peer downward. "That a road grader?"

"Aye-yup, cutting his way toward a car in a drift there."

"Can you land?"

"Why?"

"That car, see it? It's on its side. Can we land?"

"You know how late this is going to make us?"

"Jen, I don't like this. Get us on the ground."

Collins pulled back on the throttle. She put the little plane into a descending turn that took the Cub away from the highway. After the two-seater came fully around, Collins paralleled Seventy-Seven a short distance to the west as she herded the Cub in a fluttering glide down to the snowfield. The skis touched soundlessly, kicking up snow that the propeller's wash swirled back.

She let the plane run out its speed, ski to a stop. Collins then turned off the ignition. She set her headset aside, opened the two halves of the clamshell door, and stepped out. Early followed.

He loped off. At the fence, he hopped the wires and plunged down into the ditch, chilling snow shooting up his pant legs. Early mushed his way on over to the highway ridged by drifts. There he met the road-grader operator clambering down from his machine.

"Hoolie," Early called out to the graderman.

"Yup. Cactus, you've taken to airplanes to get around the county now?"

"Hardly. Jen Collins is flying me over to Salina. We saw the car in the drift and your rig."

Hoolie Garret took the stub of a cigarette from the corner of his mouth. He waved his smoke toward the car, as if the cigarette were a pointer. "What damn fool you suppose coulda been out here during the big blow?"

"We better find out, wouldn't you say?"

"And look what he's done to his car, tipping it up like that."

Early turned away. He waded to the car, a Lincoln four-door, more than half its body buried in a drift, two wheels and their fenders and part of the undercarriage exposed. Garret moved along at Early's side, the graderman with the lappers of his checkered cap pulled down over his ears.

Early leaned around the car. He peered through the windshield, but frost inside blocked his view. He worked his way to the rear and tried the back window. Same problem.

Garret pounded on the exposed floorboard. "Anybody in there?"

Silence answered, silence and a muffled breeze that raised errant snowflakes into a twisting dance.

Early hauled himself up onto the side of the car. He tried the handle on the driver's door, but it didn't yield. So he braced himself and gave the handle a hard yank. Something gave, Early felt it. He pulled hard and again, and the door's frozen hinges let go. The door squalled open.

The smell of burnt tobacco rolled out.

Early peered over the door and down, inside. A man there at the bottom of the mess–had to be the car's driver–the man on his side, collar up around his ears. Hat askew. Frost on the side of his ashen face.

"Well?" Garret called up.

"Hoolie, I know who this is."

Early jammed his pocketknife into a hinge so the door could not fall closed. That done, he lowered himself inside the car. Early crouched down and shook the man's shoulder. "Wilferd?"

No movement other than the fabric under Early's gloved hand. He stripped off his glove and put his bare fingers against the artery in the man's neck.

A moment.

Two.

"What's going on in there, Jimmy?"

"I can't get a pulse."

"The man, he's dead then?"

"I'd say so."

Early pushed himself up, out of the driver's door. A scrap of paper came out with him. It clung to his trouser leg. The paper–green with yellow printing–fell away. Early saw it seesaw over the side and down to where Garret stood, mittened hands parked on his hips.

Early waved at the paper, and Garret picked it off the snow.

"It's a gum wrapper, Cactus," he said after he looked at it.

"Jesus H. Christ."

"Mean something, does it?"

"Yeah." Early sat down on the side of the stranded car. He dangled his legs over. "The man, he's Wilferd Randall. Sells tobacco pipes around the country. Must have been pushing it to get home from a sales trip up in Nebraska. Got a wife and three girls. Girls all grown, thank the Lord for small favors."

Garret studied the snow drifted around the car before he looked back at his idling road grader. "Well, I can cut a lane along here, I guess, enough to get people by."

"And go on?"

"Cactus, the road up ahead, I gotta get it open."

"No, we can't leave Wilferd here." Early stepped back up onto the side of the Lincoln. He called across the ditch to Collins standing next to her plane, "Jen, can you get a police frequency on your radio?"

"Sure can."

Early jumped down off the car, into the snow next to Garret. He put an arm around the graderman's shoulders. "You got a shovel in the cab of your rig?"

"Always carry one."

"Here's what I want you to do, Hoolie. You plow up and around the car, then dig it out. Got that? I'll call for a wrecker from the plane–and a hearse–and you stay with Wilferd until they get here."

"But the road goin' north, it's my job to get it open."

"Hoolie, the living up that way can take care of themselves. The dead, they don't deserve to be left alone."

"Well, I s'pose if that's what you want–"

"That's what I want."

Early and Garret waded back to the grader. Early went on alone from there. He crossed the ditch and worked his way up onto the snowfield where Collins and the Red Rooster waited.

"What do you have over there?" Collins asked.

"Did you know Wilferd Randall?"

"Sure. That his car?"

"Yeah."

"That him in it?"

"'Fraid so," Early said.

CHAPTER 21

January 2–Saturday, late afternoon
Operation Hay Lift

Early stared out the window of the Red Rooster, at Wilferd Randall's Lincoln on its side, the road grader, and the undulating drifts that barricaded the highway going north, all falling away. He pressed the transmit button on his microphone.

"Big John, you out there somewhere?"

"In the office," came back John Silver Fox's voice through Early's headset. "And you?"

"In the sky. Jen Collins's got me prisoner."

"Really," Silver Fox came back, laughing.

"John, I'm going to remember you did this to me."

"It was the only way to get you to Salina."

"That may be. Look, I need you to do some things."

"Go ahead."

"On Seventy-Seven, six miles north of Twenty-Four, there's a car–Wilferd Randall's–tipped up in a snowbank. Hoolie Garret's plowing it out. Would you call Brownie and tell him to get his hearse up there? The road's open from Manhattan up."

"What happened?"

"Wilferd's in the car. If the accident didn't kill him, I expect he froze to death waiting out the storm. And call Brook Evans. Tell him to get up there with a wrecker and get Wilferd's car back on its wheels. Have him tow it to his place."

"What about Missus Randall? You want me to break the news?"

"No, but do go out to her house. You put Beth Anne on your radio. It's my job. I'll tell her. Sheriff out."

Jen Collins' voice came through Early's headset. "You get the crap work, don't you?"

"Yeah, having to fly with you."

"Jimmy, you do know how to sweet talk. . . . I'm switching to the Salina tower frequency, gonna tell 'em where you are."

Collins hunched down. Early leaned around and watched her crank the frequency selector on her coffee-grinder radio, a whistling coming through his headset as the dial moved through frequencies. He squerinched at the sound. Then the whistling faded.

"Salina tower, Salina tower, this is Piper One-One-Two Delta. Do you read?"

"One-Two Delt, go ahead."

"I have Sheriff Early on board for the haylift people. Would you tell them I'll have him on the ground in thirty minutes?"

"Roger that, sweetheart. Call when you're five out."

"Hey, fella, I'm not your sweetheart. Piper out."

Early picked up his microphone. "Little testy, aren't you?"

"I worked damn hard to get my ratings, and I can fly circles around most men. Sweetheart. I'm tempted to grab him by the balls and twist until he sings soprano."

"Now, Jen—"

"Don't you start in on me, Jimmy."

Early thought about it for a moment and concluded some things weren't worth pursuing, that it would be better to shift the subject. "Thirty minutes to Salina did I hear you say? Last summer, I drove over there. Better part of two hours."

"That's the way it is, Jimmy. When you have time to spare, go by road. Now when you need to get somewhere fast, you call me."

"No-no-no, not a chance. I love my horse, my Jeep, and trains in that order."

"Listen, you and me, we're the same age. You're too young a fella to be an old fud."

Early gazed out the window. "Jen, my feet are ice. You got any heat in this thing?"

"Not a lot." Collins glanced up at a dial in the wing root of the Cub. "Well, isn't that interesting?"

"What is?"

"The outside air temp. Minus five. Sure glad I'm wearing two sets of long johns."

Early stamped his feet.

"Stop that."

"I'm trying to get the blood moving."

"You stomp a hole in the Rooster, you're gonna find out what real cold is."

Early settled himself, and Collins cranked the frequency selector on her radio. The cranking launched an ear-blistering howling in Early's headset. "How can you stand that racket?"

"What racket? I've got your frequency."

The howling faded. As it did, a sizzling, like the sound of bacon frying, replaced it. Early leaned back. He resumed gazing out the window. "With all this snow, I can't tell where the heck we are."

"Fort Riley off the left wing there, you see it? And ahead, that's Wakefield in Clay County we're coming up on."

"Man, it's flat around here."

"Good farming country."

"Well, if Fort Riley's as snowed in as the rest of us, Fat Willy Johnson's cars ought to be safe for a while."

"How's that?"

"Somebody's been rustling cars off Fat Willy's used car lot, and don't tell me you haven't heard about it."

"What's Fort Riley got to do with it?"

"I've come to think maybe some soldiers are the rustlers."

"Word is Fat Willy's telling everybody he sees you're not doing anything about it."

"I got a little something underway."

"You have? . . . You gonna tell me?"

"Nope."

The Rooster mumbled along, its propeller chewing a track through the cloudless sky to the southwest. If it weren't for the cold, not a half-bad ride, Early thought, though he was loath to admit it. He pressed the transmit button on his microphone. "My dad told me you flew in the war. That true?"

"Anything with propellers on it. Mostly bombers–B-Seventeens and Twenty-Fours–ferried them to Maine where the guys flew them on to England. I was a Wasp–Women Airforce Service Pilot."

"Miss that, do you?"

"Sure do, but then no one was shootin' at me like they were shootin' at you."

"Sheriff, you out there?"

Early twisted in the direction of Manhattan as he spoke into his microphone. "Go ahead, Big John."

"I've got Missus Randall here."

"Give her your microphone."

A crackle of static, then Silver Fox's voice came back, more distant. "Now, Missus Randall, you want to talk, you press this button like I am, see? And when you want to listen, you take your finger off the button, all right?"

"Let's see, I press this button in. I think I understand. . . . Sheriff?"

The new voice, high-pitched and a shade off-key, reminded Early of Eleanore Roosevelt. He pressed his transmit button. "Go ahead, Beth Ann."

"Jimmy, scared me to death your deputy coming to my door like he did. This have something to do with Wilferd? I haven't heard from him for three days."

"Beth Ann, I'm sorry."

A sizzle of static answered.

"Beth Ann, you there?"

This time Early thought he heard someone, but it sounded more like snuffling than anything else.

"Beth Ann, I am truly sorry. I really am."

The tiniest of voices, pinched, came back. "Where is he?"

Early felt the freezing in his feet creep up his ankles and into the lower portions of his legs. There was no part of his job he hated worse than being the death messenger. "In his car–in a snowbank up by Randolph, heading home. We found him about an hour ago. I'm guessing he's been dead maybe two days."

"Jimmy?"

"Go ahead."

"What in God's world am I going to tell the girls?"

"Beth Ann, you tell them the truth. Tell them their father loved them."

"Do you . . . do you know how he died?"

"Not for certain. I can ask for an autopsy if you want."

"Cut my Wilferd open? No, I'll not have that."

"I can tell you what I think when I get back to Manhattan."

"When's that, Jimmy?"

"A day, maybe two."

"Can I see him?"

"Brownie has him. You let Brownie lay him out proper first. Why don't you pick out a suit and a shirt for Wilferd, and John will take them down to the mortuary."

"I guess. . . . Jimmy, I'd like you to be with me when I see Wilferd."

"I'll surely do my best, I surely will. Right now John is my stand-in. You need any help with anything, you ask him, understand? . . . I am truly sorry, Beth Ann, I really am. Wilferd was a good man."

"Jimmy?"

"Yes?"

"Thank you. It would have been awful this coming from a stranger."

"Wilferd and you, you've been family to me. Now would you give the microphone back to John? I need to talk to him."

"Deputy, he wants to talk to you. Here's this thing."

"John here."

"You heard everything?"

"All of it."

"You help Beth Ann call her daughters, would you, then stay with her until they get there?"

"Sure. And you enjoy feeding the cows."

"What I don't have to do. Sheriff out."

*

"See it?" Collins asked, talking into her microphone, speaking over the drone of the Cub's engine.

"See what?" Early came back.

"The Salina airfield there."

"All I see is that line of concrete grain elevators."

"A half-mile long, you sure oughta. No, to the right, another mile. . . . Salina Tower, Salina Tower, One-One-Two Delta. We're five out."

"Got you in the glasses, One-Two Delt. Oh, you got skis."

"Roger that."

"We have a snow runway parallel to and west of Three-Six. Plan for that. Wind calm. Altimeter three-zero-point-zero-one. Your only traffic is an Air Force C-One-Nineteen on climb-out."

"That funny-looking thing with the twin tails?"

"That's him. He's turning northwest. Call me on downwind, sweetheart."

"Uh-huh. Hey, controller, what's your name anyway?"

"Albert. Why?"

"Albert, how about you meet me on the ramp? We'll talk a little."

"Are you looking for a date?"

"Maybe."

"Well, I guess my partner could spell me for ten. And One-Two Delt, you are now cleared to land."

Collins banked the Cub onto the downwind leg of the airport's landing pattern.

Early tapped her shoulder. She lifted her headset away from one ear as she leaned back.

"Jen, you're not going to—" Early said as he pushed himself forward.

"Just watch me."

"I'd rather not."

"Suit yourself." Collins hauled her ski plane around to the base leg and on to the final approach. She lined the Cub up with the snow runway and chopped power. Early's heart pounded as the frozen landscape came up at what to him was a horrific speed. He squeezed his eyes shut.

Seconds ticked by before he said, "Tell me when we're on the ground."

"We're on the ground," Collins called back.

Early opened an eye. He ventured a peek out at snow shooshing past his window, the powder rolling away as the Rooster glided along with the grace of a skater, glided to a restful stop to the west of a plowed ramp. There men in winter military gear worked at unloading bales of hay from semi-trailers onto pallets that skid loaders pushed through the open rears of Air Force cargo planes.

Collins cut the engine of the Cub, then motioned toward the ramp. "Jimmy, you should find a sergeant over there. Should be the crew chief. You check in with him."

She pushed open the airplane's clamshell door and clambered out. She helped Early untangle himself from his lap and shoulder belts, and he tumbled out, falling against Collins. She laughed.

"Jimmy, you love me, you know you do," she said.

A civilian in a black storm coat and knit cap came hustling away from the control tower's ground-floor door. He moved with deliberation toward the Cub, and Collins saw him.

"I do believe that is my dear Albert," she said, waving to the man.

He returned her wave.

"Jen, you really shouldn't do this," Early said.

"It's only a little talk. You go on and look after the cows."

Early raised an eyebrow. There are times, he thought, when the best thing to do is nothing, so he turned away. Early slogged off through the snow, across the runway, and out onto the ramp. He could smell the dry hay–the smell of summer come and gone, gone now for months–and a more pungent aroma–gasoline. He stepped across a spill.

From somewhere someone screamed, and Early spun around. He saw the man in the black coat writhing in snow, Jen Collins standing over him. She, grinning, waved a two-finger, V-for-victory salute to Early.

*

"Sheriff, you're gonna freeze your butt in that civvy stuff," the flat-nosed sergeant said as he held up insulated Air Force-blue coveralls. "These look to be your size. Put 'em on."

Early kicked away some snow, but before he could strip himself out of his boots and ranch coveralls, the sergeant threw down a cardboard flat. "Don't want to get your feet wet, do ya?" he asked.

Early nodded his appreciation. He pulled off his boots and stood in his socks on the cardboard where he shimmied out of his coveralls. Early then stepped into the blues and was about to pull on his broken-over cowboy boots when the sergeant stopped him.

"Not those, huh-uh. You need ice packs–Arctic boots." He rummaged in the jumble in the back of his Jeep until he came up with a pair of felt-lined boots that had a barrier of goose down between the lining and the rubberized leather shell. "Two pairs of socks with these and your tootsies will think they're in heaven."

"Wool socks?" Early asked.

"You betcha." The sergeant held out two pair.

Early fingered them. "What I wouldn't have given for these five years ago. It was winter like this, and I was an infantryman in Belgium."

"Yeah, back then we didn't appreciate the value of really good cold-weather gear. We've come a long ways."

Early stuffed his civilian socks in his cowboy boots. He set the boots aside and pulled on the wool socks, first one pair, then the second. After that, he worked his feet into the insulated boots and laced them tight.

"Ah, I see a smile," the sergeant said. "You like those, huh?"

"Any chance I can keep them?"

"It's amazing the stuff we lose. If you were to walk away with them, I'd never know." The sergeant handed on a hooded parka and insulated gloves.

"So what am I supposed to do here?" Early asked after he pulled the parka over top of his coveralls.

"You're our big bad guide. You get our pilot over your county and point out where he's to make the drops. We've got five tons of hay to kick out the back door. Twenty pallets, eighteen bales to the pallet."

Early wiggled his fingers into the gloves. "So how many drops do we get?"

"One per herd."

"Sarge, that planeload will feed only a hundred eighty cows for three or four days."

"You sayin' two bales per cow then?"

"Yessir."

"Well, you're the authority. I'm from New Jersey, so I don't know nothing from cows. We get a big bunch somewhere, I guess we make several passes to get down what you say they need."

"You're going to make a lot of friends, you know."

"What's the Air Force for if not to help our neighbors?"

"And their cows."

"Yessir, that, too." The sergeant pitched Early's clothes, boots, and his cattleman's hat in the back of his Jeep. After he secured the door, he turned around. "Ready to go?" he asked.

Early gave a thumb's up and stepped out with the sergeant toward a mammoth cargo plane idling at the far side of the ramp.

"Do I see the back open?" Early asked.

"Yup. For your cargo drops, we take the back section off the fuselage so we can push everything out in a hurry. But having no doors means we can't keep any heat in the bay for the drop crew. That's why we dress like we do." The sergeant reached up for an outstretched hand. He caught it, and a crewman hauled him up and aboard. Early followed. He grabbed the hand of a second crewman. The four men packed themselves together in the narrow passageway between two lines of pallets, each stacked high with hay bales. The dust from the hay caused Early's nose to twitch, and he sneezed.

The sergeant took down a headset. He fit it over his ears and plugged a long cord from the headset into an overhead jack. He gave Early a push along. "Up to the front parlor you go. You're expected."

As Early moved away, he heard the sergeant say into his boom microphone, "Lieutenant, spin 'er up. We're loaded."

The engines that had been rumbling at idle rose in pitch and volume, and Early felt the floor of the aircraft shudder beneath his insulated boots. Ahead he saw steps leading up to a safety-paint reflective outline of a door. Early pushed against the hay bales, to steady himself, as the aircraft trundled along. He hefted himself up the steps, leaned into the door, and it opened. Early moved on, out of the gloom of the packed cargo bay and into the late afternoon's moldering light that illuminated the flight deck. The place smelled of factory newness. Early wondered how it was possible that this beast hadn't acquired the stench of work–sweat, hydraulic oil, stale cigarette smoke, and overheated electrical lines.

The pilot in the left seat twisted around, an unlit black cigar jammed in the corner of his mouth. "You Sheriff Early?" he asked from behind his silvered glasses.

"Yessir. Your ship?"

"Sweet thing, isn't it?" With a flame from a Zippo, the pilot lit his cigar. He sucked in a lungful of smoke and blew it in Early's direction.

Early wanted to wave the smoke away, but didn't. He instead gritted his teeth and fought the queasiness the acrid smoke brought on.

"We call her the flying boxcar," the pilot said, clouding the air with more smoke from his cigar. "Man, she can carry a load. Picked her up this morning at the factory in Maryland." He slapped the shoulder of the man seated next to him, the man intent on steering the aircraft. "This is David, my co-pilot. I'm Mack. We were humping for Tinker when they diverted us here to help the Guard. Hop up on the jump seat, sheriff, and buckle in."

Early found the two ends of the lap belt. He examined their fit as he sat down.

"Sheriff, my chart shows your Riley County to be northeast of here about seventy miles. Have I got that right?"

"Straight line, yessir."

The co-pilot leaned on his elbow toward the pilot. "We're cleared to take the active."

"Go ahead."

The co-pilot spun a wheel to the right of his right knee, and Early felt the aircraft swivel. Through the windshield, he watched the snowbanks of the near horizon sweep past as the aircraft swung off the taxiway and onto the broad, bare concrete of the north/south runway.

"Roger that," the co-pilot said into his microphone. He glanced over to the pilot. "We're cleared for take-off."

"Sheriff," the pilot said as he sucked on his cigar, "you'll have to excuse me. I have to go to work."

His hand went to two levers on his side of the console. He shoved the levers forward, and the cargo plane's radial engines came

up into a deep-chested roar that vibrated the walls, the seats–
everything–as the aircraft lumbered down the runway. The pilot
hauled back on his control wheel, and the nose came up. Early felt
the plane lift into the air.

"Wheels up," the pilot said.

The co-pilot's hand swept up a lever on the front of the console.
That set motors somewhere behind Early to grinding away, driving
the hydraulics.

The pilot called back over the noise, ash shaking from the end
of his cigar with each word, "Sheriff, do much flying?"

"Only when forced to," he shouted. "Came over in a little two-
seater this afternoon."

"Fun time, huh? Well, we're a shade bigger and maybe three
times as fast. We should be in your area in, oh, thirteen, fourteen
minutes."

"So what do we do?"

The pilot pushed forward on his control wheel and pulled back
on the throttles. That leveled the massive airplane and lowered the
noise level. "When we get to where we need to be, I'll drop us down
to a hundred feet. We set up on the first bunch of cattle we see and,
when we come over them, I yank this lady up into a steep climb, and
zip, zingeroo–eighteen or thirty-six bales of hay go sliding out the
back."

"What if it's a big bunch and more hay's needed?"

"I'm just the driver. My cargo chief'll tell me what to do. Is that
Fort Riley off there?"

Early's gaze followed the direction of the pilot's pointing hand
that aimed the smoldering cigar. "We're there all ready?"

"I told you we were fast. Sheriff, I'd appreciate it if you'd put your eyeballs out the front window and help us find some cows."

Early scanned the near horizon through the bluish haze in the cockpit. Open pastures didn't interest him. He searched instead for clumps of trees, creek bottoms, and ravines where cattle could escape the wind. "There," he said, pointing to the left.

"Oh, very good." The pilot tipped the C-One-Nineteen up on its wing, and Early's stomach lurched.

"What do you count, Davy?" the pilot asked.

"I'd say a dozen at least," the co-pilot said, gazing that way.

The pilot spoke into his microphone. "Sergeant, unstrap two pallets of bales on the tailboard and get ready to kick 'em off. I'm going to swing out, do a one-eighty, and set up on line. You kick when I hop this beast."

He leveled the plane, flew away from the cattle for half a minute, then put the plane into a broad, sweeping turn that reversed its direction. All the time the pilot let the aircraft slide out of the sky, down to the drop-run level. Early clutched his belt, his lips pinched shut, and his cheeks pooched out.

"Sergeant," the pilot said into his microphone, "fifteen seconds. Ten . . . five . . . hop."

The pilot hauled back on his control wheel. That pulled the aircraft up into an instant climb that sent Early's stomach plunging into his boots.

He moaned.

"You all right, sheriff?" the pilot asked, another explosion of cigar smoke wrapping itself around his words.

"No."

"How about you go back and get some cold air 'til you feel better? Be careful where you step, though."

Early released his lap belt. He slid off the seat into the door and stumbled down the steps of the cargo bay. Early grabbed a strap that held a stack of bales to a pallet. He pulled himself along from handhold to handhold, sucking in air that chilled and cleansed his lungs, until he hovered near the sergeant.

The sergeant eyed him. "Man, you look like the cat's breakfast," he bellowed over the engine racket.

"Feel like it."

"Don't care for it up front, huh? Well, I'm a man short. How about you work with me a while?"

"But you said I'm supposed to help your pilot find cattle."

"Time for straight talk. If you're gonna be sick up front, you're not gonna be any help to the Louie. He can pick out cattle in a snowfield same as you," the sergeant said. "Hell, I'm told a blind pig can find a few acorns in the forest." He took hold of the strap on the hay pallet nearest the open rear of the cargo bay and hollered over the noise of the aircraft into Early's face, "I yank off this strap, see, kick out the chock that holds the pallet to the rail in the floor. That done, I run like hell forward to throw the strap in an equipment locker, then run back here and wedge myself between this stack and the next so, when the Louie hauls the plane into a climb, I can kick this stack free and it goes shootin' out the back. How about you kickin' the stack?"

"Guess I could for a couple minutes."

"All right then, but you be damn sure to hang onto the strap of the pallet behind you. That's the only thing that'll keep you from shootin' out into the wild blue with the hay, understand?"

Early shuddered at the thought of falling out the back of the airplane.

The sergeant whipped off the closest strap. He kicked away the chock and shoved past Early toward the front of the cargo bay.

Early wrapped a gloved hand into the strap of the next pallet load. He wedged a foot between the two stacks and waited. A hand slapped his shoulder. "Fifteen seconds to hop!" the sergeant hollered.

Early felt his stomach pull down when the cargo plane nosed up, but he had a job he'd said he'd do. He watched out the back as the sky and the horizon rose up and gave way to the white blanket folded over central Kansas.

He saw a cluster of cattle in the snow, the cattle gawking up. Early kicked hard, and the pallet careened away. It slammed into the end of the track, and the impact sent the pallet's load of bales tumbling out. Early saw them fall and hit and burst and the cattle buck their way toward the loose hay.

"Good job!" the sergeant hollered as the plane settled back into level flight. He waved for Early to follow him, and the two edged toward the rear. The sergeant tipped the empty pallet up and motioned forward. "We stow and strap this out of the way, see, against that wall!"

The two wrestled the pallet into an open area of wall, and the crew chief snapped a strap across the pallet. He slapped Early's arm. "Let's do it again!"

The roar in the cargo bay made Early strain for every word of instruction. He pushed off for the passageway and wrapped his hand into the strap of the pallet two up from the rear of the line. He'd hardly gotten a good hold when the sergeant elbowed his way past.

Not bad back here, Early thought. The cold held his queasiness in check. And to see the stranded cows break for the feed falling from the sky, that was something.

Down went his stomach. And up went the horizon out the open rear of the cargo bay, up until the snow scape replaced it fully. He saw cattle there, yes. How many? A larger group. Early pushed his stack free as did the crewman to his side. Both stacks slid away and slammed out over the tailboard.

Early glanced back at the sergeant jabbering into his boom microphone. The sergeant threw Early an okay, hollering to him, "We're gonna make another pass. Come on!"

The plane banked. It threw both men into the wall. There they struggled back to the empty pallet, rescued it, and secured it while the plane settled back into level flight.

The sergeant pushed his face into Early's. "We've got half a minute, then we turn, and then we've got another half a minute to set up! Got it?"

He climbed past Early, and Early followed, slipping on some loose hay. When he caught up, the sergeant had hold of the strap release on the end pallet. Early leaned in. "You sure work up a sweat back here, don'tcha?"

"What?" the sergeant bellowed as he pulled the headset away from one ear.

"Hot work, isn't it?" Early hollered.

"Can be!"

The plane tipped up into another banking turn. Early braced himself, held himself in place until the plane leveled out and the sergeant went at his setup work. Early went at his. Already he knew the rhythm, the countdown. The sergeant pushed by him. . . . Fifteen, fourteen, thirteen, twelve . . . Early readied himself. Up went the nose of the plane and he kicked. The stack rocketed away faster than he anticipated. It sucked his body around. Early clung to the strap on his stack as he scrabbled to right himself. His load jerked and he felt it give way, felt it slide, slide toward the rear. The load pushed him ahead of it toward the great yawning open end of the fuselage and the howling cold beyond. Early hollered, but the cyclone roar of the engines masked his shouts.

He glanced over his shoulder. "Oh shit!"

Something slammed into his leg, whacked his head, and he shot out over the tailboard.

CHAPTER 22

Time unknown

Early felt nothing.

Neither warmth nor cold.

Nor pain.

It was as if he were suspended in a space without dimension, where there was neither up nor down, top nor bottom, nothing to either side, as if he were in a void.

With an effort of will, he moved a finger–an index finger–just slightly, he was sure of it, then a thumb. But which hand? Early intended it to be his right.

He forced up an eyelid.

Was it extraordinarily dark or had he lost sight in that eye? And his other eyelid, it would not lift.

The darkness birthed a nascent niggling of fear. Where was he? What was out there beyond the reach of his one hand, the fingers of which he could move?

A crust of something chillingly cold fell against Early's face.

Fell?

Or did it push up from below, against his face?

He turned away. He forced his gloved hand down–at least he thought it was down–into a pouch pocket on the leg of his coveralls. His fingers felt something cylindrical–oh God, yes, a flashlight, where the sergeant told him it would be. He worked the flashlight up and out, pushed on the ON/OFF slider. The movement ignited a burst of light that pained Early's one open eye. He squinted and peered in the direction the flashlight pointed. A brilliant white, so close that he–snow?

Early let the flashlight lay on his chest.

On his chest.

Yes, there is an up and a down. The light didn't roll off. It didn't fall away. I must be on my back.

On my back.

In the snow.

But there was no snow overhead.

Early twisted his face to the side. Snow there, and to the other side. He could see it with his lone eye.

He picked up the flashlight. He aimed its beam up, rotated it along the sides of a white tunnel that extended upward.

To where?

Early pulled his thumb against the slider switch until the light extinguished itself. Then he peered into the darkness, and he saw above him the spike end of a crescent moon.

What time was moon rise? And for the moon to be there, in relation to this tunnel, it must be–it must be–midnight. Maybe one o'clock?

The plane–

The hay–

What the heck–

I can't be dead.

But he hurt. Early's leg now fairly screamed at him.

He elbowed himself up, relit the flashlight, and aimed it down toward his foot. Below the knee, the blue of his coveralls–maroon– and there was a whitish shaft, splintered, extending from the fabric.

Early reached down. He touched the shaft, pressed against it. And he howled.

Bone.

Broken bone.

The shank bone of his leg, the tibia Doc Grafton would call it.

Where did that scrap of memory come from?

Must've broke my leg when I went out the back of the plane–I went out of the back of the plane?–yes, when the pallet of hay slammed me against something.

I must have.

The medic. What did he tell me about broken bones, the long bones in an arm or a leg? Immobilize them, that's it. Splint them. But I've got nothing.

Early rolled up on an elbow. He gazed around, probed with the light. To the side, far down, a splintered board thrust itself out of the snow–sure looked like a splintered board–and another jutted out from beneath the lower portion of his leg.

Busted pieces of the pallet.

Had to be.

The pallet had to have come out of the back of the plane with me.

Early inched first one piece of wood, then the other to either side of his broken leg, an effort that beaded sweat out onto his forehead. He pulled his belt free. He wrapped it around the splints and his lower leg, pulled the belt tight–Gawd–secured it with the buckle.

Now the upper part of the splint.

Early laid back, to rest.

To think.

The cold dulled the pain in his immobile leg.

Can I rip a sleeve out? Not the insulated coveralls, my shirt sleeve?

He worked a hand out of a glove and inside his coveralls, to his shoulder. Early grabbed the chambray fabric. He pulled.

He yanked.

The damn thing didn't tear.

Again Early fell back.

Pocketknife.

He felt for it, found it. Got it out. Opened a blade, snagged at and cut his shirt sleeve at the shoulder, cut the fabric enough that he got his fingers into the hole and ripped.

Ripped.

And ripped again.

The sleeve tore free.

Early worked his fingers up inside the sleeve of his coveralls, from his wrist. He got hold of his shirt sleeve's cuff and pulled the sleeve down, off over his hand, got the sleeve out where he could work with it, moved it around under his upper leg, tugged the ends of the fabric up together.

He tied them.

Hauled down hard and tied them again.

How long had it taken?

Hours?

He flopped back.

His mouth tasted of old rags. He'd done it before, that winter in the Bastogne forest when the Germans were out to kill him and everyone else in his battalion, Early scratched a bit of snow into his hand. He felt its chill before he dribbled the snow into his mouth.

Gawd, it was cold, but it melted. Became water.

He swallowed the dab and ate more snow.

As his thirst eased, his belly ached for food.

Chocolate bars, that greatest of all G.I. survival food. The sergeant had said there were two bars in a pouch pocket. Early felt for them, found them. He fingered one out of the pouch pocket and brought the bar up where, like an otter floating on its back, he could tear at the wrapper. He bit a corner off and spit the paper away, broke a square out and, too tired to chew, just let the chocolate dissolve in his mouth.

It tasted good. Gawd, it tasted so good.

Early swallowed the buttery-smooth liquid.

Chocolate and snow.

Snow and chocolate until half the bar was gone.

The rest he wrapped and pushed back in his pocket.

Early caught himself drifting along the thin edge of exhaustion. He couldn't let it claim him. Sleep in this measureless hole open to the frigid cold above was a passageway to death. A sergeant from the Colorado mountains had drummed it into him that long winter past– dig a snow cave.

Dig a snow cave. Pull yourself in. Wait it out.

Death can't get you in a snow cave. Your body will warm it.

Early rolled on his side, grimaced at the pain from his leg. He punched at the snow, punched and hammered a hole into the wall half his length, an arm deep, and an arm high. He rolled to his other side, grimacing again, and, using a chunk of board, fashioned a cave into that wall. He passed the waste snow over himself and packed it into the hole behind him. When he had that hole packed tight, he punched and pummeled the walls of his cave back and the roof up, hauled himself into the space.

The effort warmed him.

And exhausted him.

His mind wondered. Where had the hay fallen? Could some be near?

He wriggled out of the cave, back into the shaft. With a Herculean effort Early elbowed his way up the side of the shaft until he stood on his good foot. He could smell it, the sweet, dry aroma of prairie hay. He reached out for what he could get, raked it into the shaft and pushed it down and into his cave. He twisted back down, around and inside and made a nest for himself.

Oh, his leg.

As a kid, he'd slept in the hay in the barn and in the stacks in the fields. Nothing better if the critters left you alone . . . nothing better . . .

*

Early felt something moving on his leg. A spider?

An ant?

A mouse?

He swatted at it without opening his good eye.

The movement continued, and he swatted at it again.

"Any way to greet an old friend?" a voice asked.

Early snapped his good eye open. In a glow at the end of his cave hunkered a man whose face was devoid of eyebrows, whose skin had the sheen of pearl, whose longish hair swept back, then forward around his collar and down.

"Preacher?" Early asked.

The man waved an open hand.

"Am I dead?" Early asked.

"Hardly."

"Then why?"

"Just happened to be in the neighborhood."

Early cocked his head to the side for a better look.

"Really," the man said. "The old boy who owns this land, he's– what shall I say–"

"Gonna die?"

"Uh-huh. Heart attack. He's digging out a path to his barn, so I've come for him. And, well, I've got a bit of time on my hands until–you know." The Reverend Legzeligs Halcyon Thanatos Smith, sitting Indian-style, leaned forward, his forearms on his thighs. "So what would you like to talk about?"

"Talk?"

"I expect there are things you'd like to know."

Early thought, thought long. His vision blurred, and he blinked to clear it. There was something. "If you aren't taking me," he said, "why are you taking those around me?"

"Thelma?"

"And Maddy."

Smith reached into the pocket of his duster. He brought out a small black volume. "Manufacturer's handbook," he said as he turned into the pages. He stopped after some moments, his finger on a section. He read it. "To every thing there is a season, and a time to every purpose under the heavens."

"Ecclesiastes," Early said.

"Ah, you know your Bible."

"Some."

"When was the last time you read this section?"

"The Bear preaches on it about once a year."

"You listen?"

"Most times."

"Then you know there is a time for birthing and dying, planting and harvesting. A time to weep and mourn, and laugh and dance. You've been doing a lot of mourning, James Early. So I'm not telling you anything you don't know. I'm just relaying a message that, if you've got what it takes to endure, there's a time of laughing and dancing ahead."

"When?"

"You're not the first, nor will you be the last to ask, my friend."

"You're not going to tell me."

"I can't tell you what I don't know. I'm labor, you see, not management. It's the God I work for who ordains. I think the old Calvinists had it right. He predestines, but He doesn't share His timetable."

"Bear says it's a hard world, that those who have not been born have it much easier than the rest of us."

"You've lived through war. You know what hard is. It's better for you now."

"Not without Thelma."

"Ah yes, Thelma." Smith came forward. His breath smelled of Teaberry gum. He reached out with his hand, laid it on the side of Early's face.

Early's eye closed. His breathing eased. It slowed. A warmth from far back in his mind brought forth a memory, of Thelma. He saw her, so vibrant and alive, her face–beautiful. Her eyes gazed at him.

He wanted to reach out to her, to touch her, to–but he couldn't. But he heard himself saying her name. "Thelma?"

"Yes, Jimmy?"

"Are you really here?"

"Not in the way you understand 'here'. I've gone from the world we shared, but I've not forgotten our time together, the little house we had in Keats–worrying would it wash away in a spring flood. And I've not forgotten our baby. How is she?"

"You know she's a girl? How? You died before–"

"A mother knows these things. How is she?"

"Growing. She's got all her fingers and toes. She's a happy one, like you were."

"I wasn't in those last months."

"I know. And I couldn't help you."

"Jimmy, you did in your way. You cared. You truly cared. I often wonder how many wives can say that of their husbands. But I'm not here about me. I'm here about you. I'm here to assure you that, no matter how dangerous your work as a sheriff is–and you know it is–you will have a long life."

"But alone?"

"You have our child."

"I don't have you."

"There will be someone else."

"There was a time–a brief time–I almost thought so."

"It was an awful accident."

"And my fault."

"It was no one's fault, Jimmy. It was her time, just as it was my time."

"Who then?"

"I can't tell you that."

"When?"

"When you least expect it."

The warmth cooled, but it lingered long enough that Early absorbed every bit of Thelma's smile.

Smith again laid his hand on the side of Early's face, moved his hand up along Early's temple. He pressed against it, humming.

Music enveloped Early. Violins and cellos. Horns and drums.

"Do you hear that?" Smith asked, an ethereal quality to his voice.

"Hear what?" Early heard himself ask.

"That music. It's called 'Death and Transfiguration'. A fellow named Richard Strauss composed it."

"Knew it waddn't Bob Wills."

"Nothing like him."

"I hear a pulse."

"It's in the music."

"It's getting weak, isn't it?"

"It's the composer imagining death."

"Preacher, you said I wasn't dying."

"You aren't. Six months ago, as you accord time, it was Strauss' time. He was eighty-six. He lay there a-bed, and I sat with him,

waiting. In his mind he relived this composition–he heard it clearly–
and he said to me, 'Dying, it's just like I imagined it when I was a
young man, when I wrote this music.' He lay there, quiet for some
time, then beckoned me close. 'I now know,' he said, 'I don't have to
fear death. And what comes after–the transfiguration–it shall be
wonderful.'"

"Was he right?"

"You saw Thelma."

Early eased. He asked no more questions. The music that had
wandered the nether regions of his mind faded.

And he drifted.

CHAPTER 23

Snowfields

Early woke to a twilight from beyond his cave. He wriggled out, out into the shaft, ooching as he twisted his leg. He peered upward at pink-tinged ripples in the bottom of an otherwise winter-gray cloud.

Pink?

Dawn?

Could it be?

Early elbowed his way up, taking care not to twist his leg a second time. He hauled himself out onto a snowfield that spread to the near horizon in all directions, one of the horizons lightening. Had to be east.

Early had a direction and knew it, but which way to the nearest ranch or road or–

Four sticks of gum–Teaberry by the wrappers–laid on the snow, two sticks together in a point, the others back, like the shaft of an arrow. Gum doesn't fall out of a pocket and form itself up like that, Early thought. Not possible. The direction of the arrow, in relation to east–south-southwest.

He cast his gaze that way, at a field of gray white that rose. He gathered up the gum, then horsed himself to his feet. Early stood there, one leg stiff with its splint. He teetered–teetered forward–took a step and spilled, his face contorting from the pain that shot through his broken leg.

He wanted to scream, and why not let it rip? No one around to hear him, not even a cow to be spooked, but screaming, yelling, howling wouldn't get him an inch toward help or help an inch toward him.

Anyone even looking for me? Early wondered. And how would they know where to look?

The crew chief must have reported me going out of the back of the plane–must have–but they'd only have a general area, maybe ten miles square. Not a pinpoint. Not a dot on a county map.

Early massaged the upper part of his injured leg. The pain eased as a curiosity passed through his mind–what is over there, beyond that rise?

He swivelled toward it. Not half a hundred yards in that direction he saw it for the first time–a lone tree–an Osage orange from its squatty, gnarled shape, hay from the heavens in its branches, prairie hay stringing downward. But how'm I gonna get there?

Dumb question. Crawl on your belly, fella.

Early reached out. He pulled himself along, elbowed his way, pushing with his good leg, the broken one dragging like so much dead weight.

Five yards.

Ten.

Fifteen.

Twenty-five.

Dammit I give up.

Early stopped, so close to the tree that he could see chunks of a broken pallet beneath it and branches that must have sheared away when the pallet and its load hit the tree.

Early rolled onto his back. He panted, threw an arm across his eyes.

How long can I stay here? Give myself a couple minutes, I guess. Gawd, the front of my coveralls–they're soaked, I can feel it. And the cold. Oh hell–

Early forced himself back over onto his belly. He reached out a gloved hand, pulled himself on, pulled himself into the mess beneath the tree, grasped a broken branch.

A broken branch.

Early turned it over. He studied it, became fascinated by the branch's shape–a Y, and a stem from the base of the Y. Thicker. Suppose I've got me a crutch?

He snapped away a mass of prickly twigs, then looked again at his find.

Length about right. Tops of the Y a bit raggy and the base of the branch where it broke out of the trunk. I could whittle the ends some–I've got a knife–but why waste the time?

Decision made, Early inched his way to the tree trunk. He pulled himself upright, fitted the crutch up under his arm. He leaned on the crutch, hopped with his good foot.

One step. Then another.

He hopped, hopped and hobbled toward the horizon, the crutch never sinking more than a couple inches. Snow can't be too deep here, Early thought. The land rising and the norther whipping the snow during the storm, snow that should be here has gotta be piled up on yon side of the hill. Could the hill be steep enough that maybe I could just roll down the other side? Wouldn't that be something?

The sun broke over the horizon, and Early felt a warmth growing on the side of his face.

Thank you, God, for no wind. If you keep it quiet, God, maybe I've got a chance.

He topped the rise. The exertion drained him, and Early flopped down on the crusted snow. He went mining in a pouch pocket for the half a chocolate bar. He found it, and brought it out. Early broke off a square. He gnawed on the sweet, alternating squares with half handfuls of loose snow, slaking both his hunger and his thirst.

A glint of light far down the hill interrupted his meal. Sunlight on glass? A building down there?

Early stood for a better look.

Yeah, there is something. Bleached gray, a line shack, maybe. And scrubby bushes.

He took a halting step, then another, testing the snow, pain twinging at his leg. On the third step, Early's crutch sank like a stick in soft mud, and he fell forward, sprawled on his face, broke through the crust. Early laid there, anger at himself rising. He knew better than to trust the strength of snow that had frozen over. It was treacherous to walk on and hell to walk in it. But one could slide on it if you got on your butt. And this was downhill–not a steep grade, but still downhill.

Early yanked his crutch free of the snow. He worked himself back up on top of the crust and sat, his feet aimed downhill. He laid his crutch across his lap and pushed off. A short distance and the splint dug in. It twisted Early's bad leg. He howled as the momentum of his slide swung him around. But it freed his leg, and he slid on backwards down the hill. Early grabbed at the thighs of his coveralls and held on–bouncing, sliding, careening. He hit something that spun him into a sidewards roll that threw his crutch free, that rolled him until the hill played out into a flat field of white.

He laid there, the world inside his head spinning. Early hated merry-go-rounds. Riding them had the same damn effect.

His inside world slowed, and the cold of the snow that had gone down the neck of his coveralls and up his sleeves chilled him. He felt something new–a pain in his hip wherever he hit whatever he hit. A gawd-awful bruise, he was sure of it, but it didn't feel like a break.

And his leg. Early opened an eye. He peered down along his side, at his broken leg. No odd angles. The splint musta held.

Early twisted his head to the other direction. He stared at a weathered building just beyond him, at a door and windows and a faded sign over the door–GREEN RANCH SCHOOL.

Early knew where he was–the old Howard Green ranch, the school not more than four miles from his parents' ranch, when they owned it. Where he'd grown up. The country school he'd attended, on a day like this as warm as home from the fire in the coal stove.

No kids now. No teacher to throw open the door and ring the bell. The school had been abandoned years ago. There never was a trail in from the county highway. Everyone, even the youngest kids, rode in on horses cross-country from wherever. Old Man Green had offered the site for the school because there was a good spring and later a hand-dug well. And he had five children of his own.

Early let out with a "Hallelujah! Lord, the arrow," he said, "it pointed here. I can hole up here. They'll find me."

He scratched his crutch out of the snow, dragged himself and the crutch to the school. A drift there in front of the step and the door. With the stem end of his crutch, Early broke a path through and heaved himself inside, into another drift.

Shouldn't be.

He turned. A sidewall gone, and rafters once attached to it hung like broken wings. Gaps showed in the wood shingles.

Early hauled himself up onto a bench. He sat there, sorrow flushing through him.

Can't stay here. Just couldn't stay.

Absently, his fingers gripped the underside of the bench, and they squeezed, and, as they did, the tips of the fingers of one hand felt something odd, like grooves. They traced a J and an E.

My bench.

He moved his finger tips to the side and traced another set of initials–his kid brother's–and a C and a W–Carl Weiland, a couple years Early's senior and now the county attorney. Would Carl think to look here for me? Naw, probably doesn't know there's anything left of the building standing.

On the far side of the drift, the teacher's desk. Early pushed himself up. He hobbled over, pulled open a drawer. Never know, you might find something useful.

Early poked around inside the drawer. Some attendance records there, faded, and the litter of an abandoned field mouse nest. He brought one of the sheets up–Nineteen Twenty-Six, sixth grade, and his name. Early scanned across, and he smiled–at the end of the year, B's in Reading and Math, a D in Deportment. Couldn't make out the grade for history or geography.

Early folded the paper. He stuffed it in one of his pouch pockets.

He turned to the blackboard behind the desk, a chunk the size of a cow's head broken away, a piece of chalk still in the tray. Early picked up the chalk and wrote in scrawling letters I WAS HERE. JANUARY ???, 1950. JAMES EARLY. He drew two lines under his name for emphasis.

A closet to the side caught his eye. He remembered that one, managed to stay out of it–jail for any kid who gave Miss Eldridge too much trouble. Early opened the door. Wonder of wonders, on the top shelf a blanket. He hauled it down and pressed it to his face. The blanket smelled of must. But he could use it. And leaning in the back, a by God half-pint American Flyer sled. Could still make out the name on it, the school's one piece of recess equipment–for winter, of course, for the hill out back. Who had left it?

And hanging from a peg on a sidewall, a coal oil lamp, some fluid still in the reservoir. Early reached his fingers into the metal box nailed beside the lamp, and he felt them.

Lordy, there's still some here–Lucifers.

Sulfur matches.

He took them all. He slipped them in a breast pocket.

Useful stuff here. Might come in handy.

So Early set the sled on the floor. He brought out the coal oil lamp and wound the blanket around it, and, with some cord he found, tied the wrapped lamp upright to the sled, and a ball bat–he didn't remember a ball bat being here–and an old Thorndike unabridged dictionary.

I can always burn the pages if I have to.

Had the light changed, darkened? Early glanced out through the missing wall. Fog. Where'd that come from?

And there was a temperature difference. It seemed a tad warmer and it wasn't from moving around, Early was sure of that. He hop-stepped past the drift and outside with his crutch, pulling his sled along. He closed the door, although he couldn't for the life of him think of any good reason for doing that other than habit. And out of habit, Early looked to the side as he had always done as a kid, looked for the big Martha Gooch Flour Company thermometer one of the first teachers had hung there. There it was still, most of the paint flaked away, the metal rusted.

But Early could still make out the stem of mercury and the lines. Thirty-four degrees.

Something about dew points stirred in his memory. Where temperature and humidity come together. The temperature must have risen enough. But, doggone, that fog is thick.

Which way?

It snapped back as if it were yesterday. Angle off to the left and stay with it a quarter mile. That's where the county road is.

Early set off, hop-walking when he could, wincing from the sharp stab of pain each time he stepped down with his broken leg, crawling when he couldn't walk, pulling himself and his sled across crusted drifts slick from the fog, the wet seeping through his coveralls. Banked up snow stopped him. Early felt his way up to the top. He determined its height. A plow must have come through, but when?

He worked his way to the top of the bank–hauled himself up. With the stem of his crutch, Early chiseled out a place where he could park himself and wait. To get down in the roadway, to hobble on to a ranch, might get himself run over by some fool who couldn't see beyond his radiator cap in this fog. Maybe when it lifts.

Early pulled the sled up. He jammed the runners in the snow so the sled set flat.

Nothing more to do. So Early crossed his arms. He felt a shiver and hugged himself for warmth.

His eyelids drooped, losing their battle with gravity to stay open. Early unwrapped the lantern. He shook the blanket open and covered himself with it. He laid back against the snow and gave it up.

*

A motor woke him. How long had he been asleep?

Early rubbed at his eyes. The fog had lifted some, enough that he could see down a torturously steep snowbank and across the roadway to a fence post in the open. Early listened for the motor. He turned his head, his ears scoping. The sound came from the right, a light motor, maybe a car's engine, coming his way.

A brown Chevy coupe broke out of the fog.

Early shouted.

He waved his blanket.

The car came on. It didn't slow.

Early grabbed up the baseball bat. He flung it hard, and it spun out over the roadway as the car passed beneath. The bat windmilled on to lodge itself in the snow in the ditch on the far side of the road.

Early twisted after the car, and as quickly he twisted back. He grabbed at his damaged leg, panting from the pain his turning had caused. "Dammit, dammit, dammit!"

The lantern sat on the sled—a sentinel. Early saw it, the oil lamp. He hauled it over, ratchetted up the wick, then dug a Lucifer out of his breast pocket. Early scratched the match across the metal of the lamp's base, to fire the match and light the wick, but the match broke, the sulphur end flying away.

The sound of a heavy motor cut through the fog, the motor laboring toward Early. How much time–

He fumbled for another match, got one out, and raked it across the lamp's metal. The match snapped as it flamed. The flame fell in Early's crotch, and he beat the burning match head away as lights bored through the fog.

He dug out a new match and glanced up as a caterpillar yellow road grader snorted out of the fog, pushing snow to the far side of the road as it came along.

Early, his hand shaking, scratched the match on the metal and scratched it again when the sulphur didn't ignite. A third scratch– hurried–and fire. Early put it to the wick. He swung the lamp out at arm's length, as if the lamp was a grenade, then hurled it over the roof of the grader's cab. The lamp sailed across the roadway. It smashed against the fencepost, sending up a sheet of kerosene hot with flame.

CHAPTER 24

Savior in striped overalls

Hoolie Garret clambered down from the cab of his road grader. He stared up the snowbank to Early, hollered at him, "What ta hell you doin' up there, Cactus?"

"Trying to get myself saved."

"By Got, everbody in da Lord's creation is out lookin' for ya. What happened?"

"Fell a bit. Broke a leg."

"Oh Jesus."

Garret, a small man in striped overalls, a mackinaw, and a misshapened cowboy hat, kicked steps into the snowbank up to where Early laid. Garret grinned at him. "Cactus, you don't know how many people you got worried."

"Nobody more'n me."

"Tell that to the Esteses and your friends down to the courthouse. If I hold onto ya, ya think you kin let yourself down the bank without killin' either of us?"

"I'm for giving it a go."

Early gripped Garret's work-gloved hand. He pulled against it and swung his legs off his ledge, horsed his rump over. He slid, slid away from the ledge and down the bank at such a speed that he yanked Garret off his snow steps, the two tumbling into a heap at the bottom.

The grader man, after some moments, sorted himself out of the mess. He gazed at Early groaning and clutching his leg. And he saw the splint. "Cactus, I know bad when I see it. We gotta getcha to a doctor. Come on."

The two clasped hands, and Garret hauled Early up, steadied him as he hop-stepped to the grader. There Garret pushed Early up the ladder and into a cab that stank of grease and cigarette smoke. Early banged his splint against the hand brake. He yowled and fell across the seat into a corner away from the controls. He crumpled on a tool box. Early, still ooching, clamped his hands to his leg. He shifted it to get it straight.

"Cactus, I'm sorry," the grader man said as hoved up the steps and into the cab, "I shoulda been more careful gettin' ya in here. Ya all right now?"

"Think I'll make it," Early said through clenched teeth.

Garret yanked the door. He secured the latch and settled himself on the seat, casting his gaze at the damaged goods he'd rescued. "Opened this road a couple days ago. Just doin' some cleanup work when I seen that blaze. You do that?"

Early gave a wave.

"You were right smart there, Cactus. I never woulda seen you up top there if you hadn't." Garret spun a wheel beside him. "I'm lifting my blade, then we're gonna haul ass. This rig can do thirty-five miles an hour, you know that?"

Early shook his head.

Garret ground the transmission into low gear. He got the big machine rolling and clutched it three times up into road gear, the big tires–out of round–giving Early and him a loping ride. The grader man held tight to the steering wheel with one hand. With the other, he jammed a cigarette in the corner of his mouth–chewed on the butt, didn't light it–as he focused all his energy out through the windshield.

Not Early. For him his world was here, inside the cab, in the thawing comfort of the toasted air that swirled out from the cab's heater. The heat, the rocking, the high hum of the heavy motor behind him lolled him to sleep.

CHAPTER 25

January 8–Late afternoon
The white ward

Early heard something. Voices?

Sounded like that, but hollow and metallic, as if they were coming through a heating pipe.

He forced open an eye only to have it assaulted by white. Early squinted. He shifted his field of vision and shifted it again, scanning for that tree or the wreck of a school building, anything familiar.

But everywhere bleached bed-sheet white, even covering him, yet he felt warm, not bone cold the way he expected, the way he had been. Early peered off to the side, and in the distance he saw shapes–forms–silhouetted by a light.

People?

Men?

One? No, two.

"Shame, isn't it?" came a voice from that direction. "He was a good man."

"He was that," came another. "Now if you'll just release the body, I'll have the undertaker pick it up, and we'll get things ready for the funeral."

"At your church?"

"Yes, Jimmy was one of ours for a long time."

Jimmy?

Me?

I'm dead?

Early pinched his thigh, pinched it hard and it hurt like a wasp's sting. He worked his way up onto an elbow, bellowing, "Hey. Hey!"

The two turned in Early's direction.

"We're not talking to you," one said. "We're talking about you."

"I'm not dead!"

The other came over. He put a hand on Early's forehead and cast his gaze heavenward. "Glory," he announced with a preacherly intonation, "it's a miracle. Doc, Jimmy–he's alive."

The first man, balding–laughing–waggled a finger at Early. "We had you going there, now admit it."

Early flopped back. "This better by God be a hospital."

"Manhattan Memorial."

"How long have I been here?"

Doc Grafton came over, his hands stuffed in his pockets, a loop of stethoscope tubing hanging from one. "Two days. We had to dope you up pretty bad so I could fillet your leg and lash those busted bones back together."

"Can I walk?"

"Not for a bit. Cactus, it's been like Union Station here, people in and out to see you. You owe the Bear big time."

"How's that?"

"When Garret hauled you in with that big damn grader of his, the old Bear, he comes dancing in a couple minutes later, looking for you. I don't know how he knew you were here."

The second man–the Bear–Hubert Arnold, preacher at the Worrisome Baptist Church, cleared his throat. He pointed up. "I got contacts."

"Anyway, he hasn't left you since. We had to drag a bed in for him."

Arnold sat on the side of Early's bed, and it sagged under the preacher's bulk.

Early reached for Arnold's hand. "Bear, you're some friend."

"Well, I figured if the good Lord could keep you alive out there as long as he did, least I could do is help look after you 'til you can sit up and take nourishment."

"Did I talk when I was out?"

"Now why would you ask that?"

"Did I?"

"Jimmy, the truth–I couldn't shut you up. You rambled on about the strangest things, like this Smith character. What a name you gave him–Legzeligs something and something."

"Halcyon Thanatos. He's real."

Arnold laughed. "If you want to believe that, you go right ahead."

"You don't?"

"Jimmy, Doc says anesthetics have odd effects on people as they work off, so what you were babbling about?" The Bear shook his head. "No."

Grafton took hold of Early's wrist. He put his fingertips on the radial artery. "How about you two shutting your yaps a minute."

Early watched the surgeon, watched him count and check his count against his watch. "Like your tie," Early said. "Real bright."

Grafton flipped the wide end of his necktie out from his buttoned suit coat. "Bear, you shouldn't look at this," he said and turned more fully to Early. "Ocean blue and red posies hand-painted on it. And see this, a hula girl? If you wiggle her just so–my wife's brother got it for me in Hawaii, so I have to wear it."

Grafton winked.

"All the white I've seen," Early said, "thought I'd go blind out there. And now you've got me in this white room."

"It's a hospital, Cactus."

"Never thought much about colors. Came to miss 'em, though, even Gladys' purple hair. Thought I'd never hear myself say that."

"Well, you're not going to get me to dye my hair, what little I've got left."

"How about maybe you paint your bald spot?"

"You leave my bald spot alone." Grafton glanced toward the door, then back. "Look, there are people in this place in a lot worse shape than you, so I'm going to go tend to them. I'll stop back."

Early caught Grafton's sleeve. He pulled him in. "I gotta pee," he whispered.

"I suppose you do. I'll tell a nurse to bring you a bed pan."

"Me pee with a nurse here? Get me to the flusher."

"Cactus, I can't have you up, not yet, not on that leg."

The Bear intervened. "Doc, you go about your business. I'll carry him. I was an orderly before I went to Bible school, so I know how to handle big boys like this one."

He threw back the cover and scooped Early up before he could object. "Get the door, Doc."

Early blanched. "We're going out in the hall?"

"A couple doors down, that's where the bathroom is. You in your backless hospital jammies with your fanny hanging out, you're going to get some whistles from the nurses."

*

The Bear sat on a shabby green chair, peeling an orange, the citrus aroma a sharp relief from the smell of hospital disinfectant that dominated the room. "Did you know Brownie over at the funeral home sent you that bowl of fruit?" he asked. He parked his feet up on Early's bed. "Yessir, Brownie sure was hoping to get you for a customer."

A woman bustled in wearing a storm coat and a hat with ostrich feathers on it. She came straight to Early and whopped him in the shoulder.

His mouth gaped open, and he gabbled for words.

"Don't you talk to me, James Early. I'm mad at you. The worry you caused me, not knowing whether you were alive or dead. And after four days I made my peace that you were dead, dead out there in some snow-covered pasture, and it would serve you right if they didn't find your wretched bones until July."

"Gladys–"

"Don't you Gladys me," Early's secretary said. She blew her nose into a pink handkerchief. "You ever go do this again and you can just go find yourself someone else to keep your department from going to H-E-double-toothpicks because you're always messing up the paperwork and you can never fill out your expense report on time. And schedules, you don't know what schedules are."

"Are you done?"

"No–yes–I don't know." Gladys Morton, a tear trickling from the corner of her eye, grabbed Early. She crushed him in a hug, smothered him in her more than ample bosom.

He struggled for air, the air scented with lilac perfume. When he broke free, he gasped and panted and asked, "What color is your hair today?"

"What difference is it to you? You don't care."

"I'd just like to know."

She took off her hat. "I tried something new. Hot cinnamon."

"It's more pumpkin," Early whispered.

"That's it. Make fun of me."

"I'm not making fun. Just observing. I like it. Kinda."

Morton fixed Early with a steely stare.

"You know the Bear?" he asked, gesturing at Arnold still peeling his orange.

Arnold rose. He wiped a hand on his trouser leg before he reached for Gladys Morton's hand. "Dear lady," he said with a warming smile, "I'm Reverend Hubert Arnold, salvager of lost souls."

"That pretty well describes our sheriff, now, doesn't it? I'm Gladys Morton."

"Department secretary, I gather."

"Thirty-two years."

"James has told me many splendid things about you."

"Really?" She turned to Early, and he put on his best Teddy Roosevelt grin.

John Silver Fox leaned through the doorway. "Room for more company?"

The Bear waved him in. "You just missed the show."

"What's that?"

"Missus Morton here, your department secretary, she was beating on Jimmy."

"She told me," Silver Fox said, "she was going to pound nobs on his head."

"She didn't hurt him too bad. I'll hold your coat if you want to take a poke at him."

Early pitched a chunk of orange peel at Arnold, got him in the ear. "I thought you were looking out for me."

"I do what I can," the Bear said. He brushed the side of his face clean.

Morton looked at Silver Fox, then at Early. "I suppose you two want to huddle about all the business you've missed."

"No. I'm sure John took care of everything."

"He certainly did, and he did it very well. Anyway, my husband's waiting on supper." She squeezed Early's hand, her eyes tearing up. She covered her quivering lip with her handkerchief and hurried away.

Silver Fox bumped the Bear's shoulder. "Is he being a good patient?"

"For as long as he's been awake. When he was sleeping, he raved like a lunatic."

"Yes, the quiet ones do that. My mother tells me I carry on when I sleep. I guess maybe I do." Silver Fox came over to Early. He held out a small bottle. "Special medicine. My father made it for you."

"Tell him I thank him." Early twisted at the cap, but Silver Fox stopped him.

"Maybe when no one's here. Very potent stuff. The inner bark stripped from a black gum tree and boiled, Wolf's bane, juice from skunk cabbage, and sheep's blood."

Early jacked up an eyebrow.

"Don't tell Doc," Silver Fox said. "He thinks we're primitives." He inclined his head toward the door. "Did you see him out there, where you were?"

"Out there?" Early asked. "In the snow, you mean? The preacher?"

"Yes."

Early sucked in a breath. He held it a moment, then he dipped his chin.

"I figured," Silver Fox said. "Sometime we should talk about that. On another matter, Judge Crooke is pressing me on the Garret murders. I've not found anything. What do you want me to do?"

Early took a glass from the bedside table. He sipped on the water. "I've got a few scraps, but I've been thinking maybe we should call them unsolved. Tell you, though, I would like to talk to Hoolie first. I was in a bad way when he found me, so we didn't get to say much."

"He's in town tonight. I'll get him. How long do you expect to be laid up here?"

The Bear handed a section of orange to Early. "Eat this," he said. To Silver Fox he said, "Doctor Grafton told me he wants to keep Jimmy here a week, then he'll be able to get around some. Six weeks before the cast comes off."

"I had guessed about that," Silver Fox said. "Well, Chief, I'll go find Hoolie for you." He stopped at the door, looked down the hall, and turned back. "You've got more company coming–Walter and Nadine, and they've got a package."

He left. Early heard an exchange of pleasantries beyond the doorway. A moment passed and an elderly rancher and his plump wife shuffled in, she carrying a bundle in her arms.

Walter Estes shook Early's hand. "Good to see you awake, Jimmy. We brought you a surprise."

Nadine Estes laid the blanket-wrapped parcel in the crook of Early's arm. She peeled back the front of the covering, exposing the face of a cherub whose gaze wandered here and there, to the light, to the big man–the Bear wiggling his fingers at her–and to Early's face. She blew bubbles and reached for him.

With a look of love, Early pulled her up more closely, and she latched onto his nose. "Missed you, Toot. How you doing?"

"Toot?" Nadine asked.

"Well, sometimes when she gets gas, she lets go with one."

"Jimmy, really."

*

Something–or someone–shook Early awake.

He looked up at Doc Grafton still with his hand on Early's foot. Early focused his eyes, then peered down at the child curled, sleeping beside him, his arm holding her away from the edge of the bed.

"Isn't she something?" Early asked.

"That she is. She's not supposed to be here, you do know that."

"Why?"

"Germs. She might infect somebody. That's why the hospital's got a policy against kids coming here, unless they're patients."

"I don't think much of that, Doc."

"Frankly, I don't either. How'd she get here, walk?"

"Walter and Nadine brought her."

"Sneaked her in, you mean." Grafton scratched at the sandpapery stubble on his chin. "They've gone home?"

"Uh-huh."

"Hoo boy. Cactus, here's what I'm willing to do–and I'm putting my job on the line here–the child can stay until I'm done with my rounds, then I'll take her home."

"Hey–"

"Don't hey me, the wife and I know how to take care of babies. We did a pretty good job with our own. In the morning, I'll take her back out to the Esteses' ranch. Now the night nurse–she's a stickler for the rules–she's going to get real mad about this, so if you hear some shouting out in the hall, that's what it's gonna be about. Where's the Bear?"

Early stared at the green chair, empty except for a newspaper that laid open across an arm. "I don't know. We were talking about Toot when I must have dozed off."

"Toot?"

"Barbie Sue."

"You do have a way with names." Grafton snugged the blanket over the baby's bare feet. She squirmed a bit, then resettled. "I never thought you'd be a dad, Cactus, but you're doing all right."

*

Early felt the side of his bed dip, and he woke, startled. In the weak light from the lamp on his bedside table, he saw a lone individual in an olive-drab field jacket and cap sitting next to his cast, two-thirds of the way down the bed. "Sonny?"

"It's good to see you're alive," the soldier said in a voice little more than a whisper. He pulled off his cap and stuffed it in his pocket. "Heard on K-man radio they'd found you and brought you here. Thought I'd better come." Sonny Estes gestured toward the child asleep in Early's arms. "Your little baby, huh?"

"Yeah."

"Saw her out at my folks' house. She's a cute little kid, sheriff. Ma and Pap really love her."

"They do that."

"I'm glad I could help you back there in the fall, bring her into the world for you. Kin I hold her?"

"She's sleeping."

"I won't wake her."

Estes lifted the child and her blanket from Early's arms. He cradled her. "Think some day I'll be a poppy?"

"If you don't go off to a war where they shoot at you, I expect you will. So how's your training coming?"

"They got me running tanks around the reservation's back forty, real monsters. Pretty amazing for someone who'd only driven his pap's truck."

"Where to after this?"

"The sarge says Germany. We ship out in a month. It's kinda tense there with the Russians on the other side of the Fulda Gap. They showed us on a map. We'll be the front line if all hell breaks loose."

"If that happens, you may not get to be a poppy."

"That's the risk, I guess. By the way, I found those boys yer looking for."

"Our car rustlers?"

"The very ones."

"You get in with them?"

"Uh-huh." Estes giggled. "They loved it when they found out I was in trouble with you, an' how I outfoxed you so many times."

"You told them that?"

"Every teeny, tiny little detail over a couple packs of beers. They've been watching that car lot, for one last chance to make a big steal."

"Pardon?"

"They ship out to Fort Hood, Monday, but there's always a police car parked on the ridge across the way. They figure you're watching the lot, too."

"What if I were to have that car driven off?" Early asked.

"That'd be helpful. They really want to go in there tomorrow night, about one. Everything's shut down in Ogden by then, so they can drive right through and onto the post with no one the wiser."

"Why are these bandits doing this?"

"You don't know?"

Early raked the tips of his fingers through a sideburn.

"It's this way," Estes said. Then he stopped. His nose wrinkled. "Sheriff, I think she just put a load in her diaper. I didn't know they could do that in their sleep. You want to change her?"

"Me? I can't get up to do that."

"Then I'll get a nurse."

"No, you don't. I'm already in trouble with them for having Toot in here. Over there in the drawer," Early waved a hand at a small bureau by a wash sink, "they tell me I got a shirt in there. Make a diaper of that."

"Sheriff, this is crazy."

"Crazy or not, you do it."

Estes handed the baby back to Early, and Early's nose wrinkled.

"I told you," Estes said. He rummaged in the drawer. He unearthed a blue chambray shirt and held it up.

Early nodded.

Estes laid it out on top of the bureau. He pressed the shirt flat and studied it while he massaged the back of his neck. Then he lifted one side of the shirt and folded it in, then the other side. Next he brought the tail up to the collar, making the whole shirt about the size of a diaper. Satisfied, he went to the sink. Estes turned on the hot water. He ran it a bit before he soaked a wash cloth under the spigot. He wrung the cloth out, set it aside, and came to Early.

"All right, baby," Estes said as he attacked the job of unpinning the putrid diaper. When he had it open, he lifted the child away, she half awake, her lower lip moving. "Don't she ever cry?" Estes asked.

"You're leaving me with this mess?"

"Well, I'm kinda busy here." He went to the sink, hefting the baby across his shoulder as he did. With the wet cloth, Estes wiped her bottom clean. A towel hung beside the sink, perfect for drying. "Don't suppose you've got any powder for her butt?"

"Wouldn't think so."

"We'll just have to get along without."

Estes laid the child on the well-folded shirt. He pulled the lower portion up between her legs, to her belly button. He next drew the arms up around her sides and across the folded-over shirt tail. Estes pinned it, then wrapped the arms around one more time and tied them. "You like yer poppy's shirt?" he asked, and the baby cooed at him.

Estes held her up, for Early to inspect. "Did right good for an Army grunt, wouldn't you say?"

"Give her to me."

"You gotta get rid of that loaded diaper first."

"How can I?"

"Right." Estes handed the baby off. He folded the dirty diaper in on itself while he gandered around the room. A wastebasket under the sink, Estes went for it.

"Whoa, not there," Early said. "The night nurse'll know what happened here, and I sure don't want that."

"Then where?"

"Outside, down the hall, I don't care."

Estes gave Early a questioning look, then he jogged from the room, holding the package with the tips of his fingers. Early, for his part, settled the baby back in her blanket. She latched onto his thumb and squeezed it.

"Yeah," Early said, "you'd think we were Keystone cops the way we do things around here."

Estes strolled back in, rubbing his hands as a conspirator might.

"Well?" Early asked.

"Put it in a drawer of a desk out there. They'll never know it was us."

Early looked to the ceiling, as if asking for forgiveness.

Estes sniffed the air. "Pretty rancid in here. What do we do about that?"

Early snapped his fingers. He waved them in the direction of the bureau. "They say they brought my shaving stuff, that it's in there with my clothes. See if my Old Spice is there."

Estes ripped open the drawer. He dug in, pawed his way through, separating socks from jeans and jeans from shaving soap. "Here it 'tis." He whipped out a bottle. Estes opened it and sprinkled some of the contents around the room, splashing some on Early and on himself.

Early coughed. He fanned at the air. "Smells like a barbershop now."

"It's better than what it was," Estes said as he returned the bottle to the drawer. "Oh jeez, what's on my shirt?"

Early tilted his head for a better look. "Baby poop?"

"Cripes." Estes went to the sink. He stripped out of his field jacket, then his shirt. He plunged the shirt under the hot water and scrubbed–held it up, examined it, sniffed it, then wrung the water out his shirt until there was no water to squeeze out.

"Not too bad," Estes said as he pulled his field jacket back on. "Shirt, it's kinda damp now. Guess I'll just stuff it in my pocket."

Early half grinned. "You were telling me why these guys are stealing Fat Willy's cars."

"It isn't all of them. It's one trooper in particular. The rest go just 'cause they think it's a thrill."

"Who's the one?" Early asked.

"Thomas Jay Pritchard, as buck-a-private as they come. His older brother, Ernie, when he was at the fort, he bought a car from Fat Willy. The engine blew up on him and he was killed."

"We didn't get any paper on that."

"You wouldn't. It happened over in Junction City. Anyway, Thomas Jay blames the car man for it. When he got posted here, he set out to get him."

"So it's not money, then, not steal a car and sell it."

"Never was."

"Revenge."

"Yup."

Early sucked on his teeth. "Fat Willy does sell junk. Sonny, what about this? I get that police car off the ridge, and I put a car that our bad boys can't resist in among Fat Willy's."

"Make it a Lincoln. They'll go for that."

"How about a Cadillac?"

"Better."

"A Cadillac hearse. I know where I can get one, a bit elderly. I can have it out there with no plates on it, just like the rest of Fat Willy's cars."

"A hearse, you're kiddin' here, right?"

"No."

"Come on, sheriff."

"I've got my reasons. That car, Sonny, that one, you have our bad boys steal that car."

"Thomas Jay's angry enough he just might go for it. And you're gonna catch them?"

"That's the idea."

"How?"

"I've not worked all that out just yet."

"All right, but tell me this, what if they get away–they have before–and they destroy the car?"

"I'll have some big-time explaining to do to a lot of folks."

Hoolie Garret, a stub of a cigarette in the corner of his mouth, poked his head into the room. "You wanted to see me, Cactus?"

Early waved the wiry little man in. To Estes, Early said, "Nice of you to come by. How about you come back real soon?"

Estes looked like he wanted to say something, but, after a moment, he pulled out his cap and slicked it over his hair. He left, giving a nod to Garret as he squeezed past him.

"Do I know that young fella?" Garret asked.

"Not likely. He's not from your part of the county."

Garret took a drag on his cigarette, and Early responded with a raised finger. "I'm not big on smoking," he said.

"Oh, sorry." Garret pinched out the flame. He shredded the stub into his hand, then looked for a place to deposit the debris. He settled for the smoker's solution–a cuff of his coveralls. That done, Garret sampled the air. "You been shaving?"

"It's the Old Spice, huh?"

"Seems you were a bit generous. That a baby there?"

"Yeah."

"Yours?"

"Uh-huh."

"Sleepin' I take it?"

"It's that time."

"She wake up much, squall for a bottle?"

"Not at night."

"You're pretty lucky, Cactus. Ours sure did." Garret took off his tired cowboy hat, revealing gray hair sticking out in odd directions. "Your deputy found me at the boarding house where I stay when I can't get home. Said you wanted to see me. You doin' all right?"

"Thanks to you. And I do want to thank you, Hoolie."

"Twasn't nothin' you wouldna done for me."

"Yeah, I guess we're both in the helping business. Like to sit some?"

"I'd just as soon stand."

Early took the measure of Garret. The way he stood by the bed, one leg was bowed. Too many years of riding horses, he thought.

"Hoolie, I've been thinking about your grandson and Marlene and your great grandbabies. I know who didn't kill them."

"You do?"

"It's wasn't the Kansas City gamblers, and it wasn't Al's neighbor, Gilly, although he had reason as did a handful of others Al cheated and gypped." Early surveyed Garret again. He wondered what was going through the old man's mind. He saw him chew on the inside of his lip, and he knew.

"Hoolie," he said, "let me tell you what I think happened. Al, he was boxed in. He'd gambled away his ranch. Others were after him. It was all going to come apart, and the shame, I think it became too much for him. Is this making sense?"

The old man shifted his weight. Garret concentrated his gaze, not on Early, but down, on the scuffed toes of his boots.

"The only thing left was to kill himself, Hoolie–his family first, though I don't understand that–but kill himself."

The old man–aging visibly as Early talked–snuffled up a tear.

"Hoolie, we didn't find Al's gun. You know that, and you know why we didn't find it. Virgie Brand saw a pickup truck with hay in the back in the yard of the Circle G that morning. Hoolie, it was you. You came by. You saw the grievous mess, and you took your grandson's revolver, to cover up that it was a murder-suicide."

Garret twisted the brim of the hat he clutched before him.

"Well?" Early asked.

Garret snuffled again. His hand shaking, he drew his coverall sleeve across the tip of his nose. "I couldn't let my Mazie know that our grandson did such a thing. It woulda killed her. You gonna tell her?"

"No. Hoolie, I don't know where you hid the gun, but you get it, and you take it over to Geary County, and you drop it down the deepest well you can find. Come spring, you and Mazie, you move to south Texas, and don't you come back–ever."

CHAPTER 26

January 9–Evening
The rustlers strike again

Early sat with his back against a pillow, reading the Capper's Weekly livestock market page. The blizzard had sent the price for fat cattle rocketing . . . if only Walter and me had something to sell–

A man who, by his size, could bring a top price if he were a steer, squeezed through the doorway and into the hospital room. He, in a storm coat, pulled off his fedora and swiped the sweat from his forehead.

Early peered over his paper. "Fat Willy."

"Sheriff."

"Unless you're bringing me a box of candy, I'd just as soon not see you."

"It's that damn Indian deputy of yours," the used car dealer said.

"Fat Willy, my deputy's got a name–John Silver Fox."

"That damn Indian John Silver Fox says I can't go back to my sales trailer tonight."

"It's Saturday night, do you ever?"

"No, but there's something going on here. What is it?"

"I'd ask you to sit, but I don't think that chair will hold you."

"Being nice don't win you no points. What's going on here?"

"Fat Willy, we're gonna catch your car rustlers tonight, and we don't want you in the way."

"I'll be in the way if I by damn want to be in the way. It's my office, my lot, and my cars."

"I could jail you."

"For what?"

"Interfering."

"You do and I'll yell so loud I'll have a judge springing me before you can count to eighteen and a half."

Early sighed. "Willy, you are a trial."

"You got that right. That's why I'm gonna run over you in the spring election."

"Take a number. You're not the only one fool enough to want this job."

"You don't think they'll elect me, do you?"

"Fat Willy, I don't know. My leg hurts, so please go away."

Silver Fox, in his heavy mackinaw and black hat, toted a duffle into the room. He stared at Fat Willy Johnson. "Are you here to complain?"

"I made my point." The car man waddled to the door. He pumped his fist at Early and pushed on out.

"He is a hard man to get along with," Silver Fox said. He opened the duffle and horsed it up on the bed. "For the record, Chief–if there were a record–I don't think what you want to do is a good thing."

"You're probably right. You bring the cards?"

Silver Fox fished a deck of playing cards out of the duffle. He tossed the box on the bedside table.

Early stared at it. "Authors?"

"It's this or Shoot the Moon."

"You went to Haskell over in Lawrence, didn't you?"

"A fine college for us red people."

"They made you read a lot, I'll bet."

"Uh-huh."

"You're gonna whump me, aren'tcha?"

A smile tugged at Silver Fox's mouth as he took the cards from the box.

*

Early woke with a snort. A half-dozen playing cards laid spilled across his lap. He rubbed his face, rubbed in wakefulness before he sailed a card at Silver Fox asleep in the green chair. The card clipped his cheekbone and he, too, woke. Silver Fox yawned. He stretched and wrung his wrists.

"What time is it?" he asked.

Early leaned toward the bedside table, the better to see his father's pocket watch. Early had never had one of his own. "Good Lord, it's after one. We gotta git."

"I'm still against this."

"The day you become sheriff, that's the day you become the big decider." Early shucked himself out of his hospital gown and waggled a hand at Silver Fox. The deputy brought a shirt out of the duffle and gave it over.

Early pushed his arms into the sleeves, then laid back while he buttoned the front. "You did get the hearse."

"Of course. It's by the back door."

"Shorts?"

Silver Fox brought out a pair of khaki boxers.

"You're gonna have to help me with those."

Silver Fox shook the shorts open. He slipped Early's cast through one leg hole, then his good leg through the other. Working together, with Early rouncing and wriggling, they hauled the top up around Early's waist.

"Socks now. And did you split the leg on my pants?"

"Done," Silver Fox said. He snugged Early's good foot into one sock, and the other he rolled down until it was a wad with a toe. This he fitted over Early's toes that stuck out of the foot end of his leg cast.

Out from the duffle came a pair of department tans. Silver Fox helped Early in, Early again rouncing as he had before.

The deputy brought out a boot. "Do you ever think of getting some foot powder? This boot is putrid."

Early gave Silver Fox the cold eye. He pulled his boot on and went back to buckling his belt. Early then swung his good leg off the bed and waved for Silver Fox to help him stand. "Think I could walk on this," he said as he tried his cast on the floor.

"You do and you'll bust up everything Doc's done. I've got a wheelchair in the hall." Silver Fox brought out Early's sheepskin coat. He helped him into it and, after that, handed him gloves.

Early pulled one on. "My gun?"

"In your coat pocket. You won't be able to handle it with a glove on."

"I could always bean someone with it."

"Don't you go beaning anybody. You let us do the work."

Silver Fox went out into the hall. He returned pushing a wheelchair, one of the chair's leg supports out straight. Silver Fox helped Early down onto the chair and lifted the cast up on the support. He gazed into Early's eyes. "This is it, Chief, your last chance to back out."

"Gimme my hat."

Silver Fox shrugged. He went to the duffle. There he pulled Early's cattleman's hat out and handed it on.

Early slapped it over his wild thatch, then motioned at the door.

Silver Fox, already behind the wheelchair, pushed–but stopped when a heavy-set nurse stepped into the doorway. She parked her knuckles on her hips and gave an all-business stare at Early. "All right, what's going on here?"

He turned to Silver Fox for help, but when none came forth, he hemmed. "It's this way," he said, "we thought we'd maybe get us some fresh air. John tells me it's a pretty night. Might even look up to see if Orion's out."

"My foot. Get back in that bed."

Early scratched at his mustache, then he brought out his forty-five. He leveled it at the nurse. "I'm not above shooting you to get my way. How about you go tend to somebody else?"

She shook a finger at Early. "I'll get you for this when you come back."

"I expect you will. Now step out of the doorway."

As she did, Silver Fox whisked Early and the chair past her and out into the hallway. He hustled for the back door where he wheeled the chair around and backed out, so the door wouldn't bang against Early's cast.

In the light from a lone bulb outside, mounted above the door, stood a black Cadillac hearse. Silver Fox opened the rear. He pulled the tailgate down and dragged a casket out. Silver Fox shoved the casket's top up. That done, he came back, his breath a white mist in the night air. He hefted Early out of the chair, as one might a sack of potatoes, and into the casket. "Chief," he said, "this has got to be the nuts."

"I'm in a leg cast, it's the only way. You got the blankets?"

"One and a buffalo robe from my family. I'm not going to let you freeze." Silver Fox flapped the coverings over Early. After he tucked the sides down, he slid the casket, top still propped open, into the back of the hearse. Silver Fox closed the rear of the vehicle, got in the front, and started the engine.

Early called out to him, "Drive like you're in a funeral procession. I don't want to get banged around back here."

Silver Fox eased the big car out onto a city street. "I won't get out of first gear," he said.

*

Silver Fox twisted around. He peered back over his arm across the seatback at the view out the rear window as he backed the hearse into an open slot in the line of Fat Willy Johnson's used cars.

He stopped and turned off the ignition.

"That twas a right comfortable ride, Big John," Early said from the back. "If this is the way it is going to the cemetery, come my time, I won't mind it much. Speaking of time, how much we got left?"

"Ten minutes, fifteen at the most if you've got this right."

"Trust me, John, I got this right. Where you gonna be?"

"In the woods about twenty yards off."

"Got a walkie for me?"

"I'll bring it back to you."

Silver Fox took two walkie-talkies and a flare pistol from the seat beside him. He got out and gazed around at the stillness of the scene, the dozen cars, the humpback trailer, and the snow, all of it eerie in the pallid light of the quarter moon. He went to the rear of the hearse and handed a walkie into Early reclining in the casket.

"Oh, one thing more," Early said. "Throw some snow on the hood of the car. I want that hood cold. You didn't run the heater, did you?"

"I didn't run the heater. Are you ready for me to shut you in?"

"Go ahead."

Silver Fox lowered the cover on the casket, and Early heard him close up the rear of the hearse.

Sure is dark in here, he thought. Enough pillows, though, I could go to sleep. Better not.

He sucked in a deep breath.

Was that a mistake? How much air have I got in here anyway? Jiggers, it's stuffy. And dang hot under this buffalo robe.

Early's walkie hummed. A click came next and Silver Fox's voice.

"Roll call. Dandy and Hank?"

"We're at the side of the road, around Sunset, ready to chase the bad guys up to Trooper Plemmons."

"Trooper?"

"Top of Ogden hill. Cactus here?"

Early brought up his walkie. He squeezed the transmit button. "I'm here."

"You keep in your box. John? A Studebaker four-door just passed by."

"Coming our way?"

"Dead right."

"Got your night scope on him?"

"Yessiree Bobby-oh. Brake lights came on."

"One more thing." Again it was Silver Fox's voice. "If this goes wrong, I shoot off a flare and you all come lights and sirens."

"Car's turning in."

Early's walkie went silent. Outside he heard car doors open and close, then boots crunching through the snow.

"How about that one?" a voice asked.

"There's a stove-bolt six," another voice said. "That's a real scat car."

"Look at the beast over here." Sonny Estes's voice.

"A hearse?"

Early held his breath. He listened hard. Steps in the snow came closer and stopped.

"See in there? Looks like a coffin. We could have some fun with that."

"Yeah, make us a target of it on the tank firing range. Boom. Blow it ta hell."

"All right, the Whisperer and me, we'll hot-wire this one. You follow us."

Early exhaled. Footsteps moved away, and the doors of the hearse opened.

"Got your lighter?" That voice came from inside the hearse.

Early heard the scratch of a friction wheel on flint.

"Good. Here are the wires. I touch them together like so." The hearse's starter whirred up. The engine fired.

Early raised the lid of his coffin. He sat up, his Army forty-five in his ungloved hand. "Morning, boys," he said.

The driver glanced up at the mirror. He cursed and tromped the accelerator to the floor.

The hearse shot forward. It threw Early back and slammed the lid down on him.

The car whanged down into the ditch, bouncing Early as he struggled with the lid. It banged down on him a second time, and his gun went off, deafening him as the hearse powered on up the other side of the ditch. The big car hit something. It rolled, and the roll threw the casket and Early out the back and the driver out his door.

The casket hammered down. It broke, spilling out Early and the buffalo robe and blanket in a great tangle in the snow.

A door banged open behind Early. He twisted around as Fat Willy Johnson came galloping his way, a pump shotgun in his hands.

"Steal my goddamn car, will you?" Johnson bellowed, huffing hard as he pounded on. "I'll blow your goddamn head off."

He slid to a stop by the driver on his back in the snow, took aim. The young soldier whipped his hand up over his face.

"Fat Willy, don't do it," Early hollered.

A flare burst overhead, flooding the night sky with a phosphorescent brilliance.

Johnson, startled, looked up. A crack—like a firecracker—and he fell in a heap.

The driver, clutching a revolver, came up. He twisted toward Early and banged off three shots.

Early rapid-fired his pistol. He emptied the magazine and more, the hammer clicking on the metal frame.

Silver Fox ran in, with his own gun out. He came down on his knees next to Early, pressed Early's forty-five out of the way. The stench of cordite filled the air. "What happened?"

"Fat Willy," Early said, his voice harsh, his hand trembling. "Fat Willy. The driver shot him. I didn't know he had a gun."

"You shoot the driver?"

"Had to."

"The other car, did you see it?"

"No. Gone I guess."

Sirens sounded in the distance, coming this way. Silver Fox pushed himself up. He trotted over to the driver still visible in the dwindling light of the flare that swung and weaved like a leaf on its fall toward the earth. Silver Fox kicked the gun from the driver's hand. He felt for a pulse in the man's neck, the snow around him darkening from oozing blood. "Dead," he called back.

"Fat Willy?"

Silver Fox tried for the same artery on the car man's neck. He found it. "Dead, too."

"Second soldier, you see him?"

"No."

"Maybe in the car?"

Silver Fox went down into the ditch, to the hearse on its roof, one wheel still turning. He aimed his Everready through a broken window. "Found him."

"Alive?"

"Can't tell."

Silver Fox hunkered down. He reached in. His hat fell away as he extended his hand as far as he could. Silver Fox felt something like an arm. He worked his fingertips down to the wrist and pressed on it for a pulse.

The strain of the reach caused Silver Fox to grimace. A couple moments passed by, then he extricated himself. Silver Fox found his hat. He reshaped it and saw blood on the side of the crown. Silver Fox stared at the palm of his hand–more blood. He grubbed out his bandana for a bandage.

"What's going on?" Early called out.

Silver Fox wrapped his palm. "I must have put my hand in some glass."

"You all right?"

"I'll live."

"Think I took a bullet in my cast," Early said.

"Doc's not going to like that."

"Won't be the only thing he doesn't like tonight. The fella in the car?"

"Yeah?"

"He dead?"

"He's got a pulse. He's alive."

"Good," Early said. "He's one of us. That's Sonny Estes."

ABOUT THE AUTHOR

Jerry Peterson got his start as a writer when, as a kid of twelve, his parents gave him a toy printing press for Christmas. That winter, the stories he wrote he set in rubber type which he inked and printed on paper that came with the rotary press.

He eventually joined the world of corporate communications and public relations, writing and editing membership publications for state Farm Bureaus in Wisconsin, Michigan and Kansas. In 1979, Peterson became a real journalist–a reporter and columnist for the Douglas County News-Press in Castle Rock, Colorado. He went on to report for and edit weekly, semi-weekly, and daily newspapers in West Virginia, Virginia, and Tennessee.

Peterson left journalism to become a graduate student at the University of Tennessee. There he collected stories that he put into short stories and novels set in the Great Smoky Mountains. At UT, he studied creative writing under novelists Wilma Dykeman and Allen Wier. Years later, he participated in writing workshops led by novelists Lee Smith and Robert Morgan, mystery writers Jeremiah Healy and Anne Perry, and thriller writer David Morrell.

Peterson is a member of *Tuesdays with Story*, a writers group in Madison, Wisconsin; the Knoxville, Tennessee, Writers Guild; and the Mystery Writers of America.

The Great Manhattan Mystery Conclave fostered the creation of James Early, Peterson's Kansas sheriff. Early appears in two short stories the conclave published in its 2005 anthology, *Manhattan Mysteries*. Five Star published the first James Early mystery, *Early's Fall*, in 2009.

37120407R00187

Made in the USA
Middletown, DE
20 November 2016